Alone

A Novel

By
Barbara De Smedt

www.DarkInkBooks.com

www.AMInkPublishing.com

An Estimated 12 to 16 percent of women,
and 4 to 7 percent of men,
will be stalked in their lifetime.

*Source: PyschologyToday.com

Prologue

He's lying on the ground. A shadow falls over him.

"Hey, are you okay?"

His head hurts; his fingers feel a bump on his left temple.

"I saw what happened. They did it on purpose."

He squints his eyes, his arm on his head, and tries to see who is talking to him.

A girl—he doesn't know her—presses a bottle of water into his hand. It feels deliciously cool.

"I've brought ice, too, for your head," she says, gently moving his arm and holding the ice on the bump.

He breathes in sharply, the pain shooting into his teeth.

"Are you okay?" she asks again.

He swallows. She smells nice.

"I'm Julie. What's your name?"

He looks at her from under his white eyelashes. He feels his head getting red and hot, drops of ice water rolling past his temples into the grass.

"Oscar," he replies.

Oscar & Julie

Oscar
1992

From his open window, he sees Julie cycling along the path to the house. She's wearing shorts; her knees are dirty and scratched. Her ponytail has come undone, and tangled strands frame her sweaty face. The doorbell rings.

"Hello, Mrs. Plessers. Is Oscar home?" he hears her saying. Her voice is so sweet, so fresh.

"Yeah, why?" his mother replies.

"Can he come and play soccer?"

"Play soccer? With you little kids?"

In his mind, he sees his mother staggering and holding onto the doorframe, considering how much wine she'd already consumed before lunch.

"He doesn't have time for that."

"But... we're short of one player," Julie protests. If she's offended by the words 'little kids,' she doesn't show it. She's eleven, which makes her one year younger than Oscar.

"I said he doesn't have time," Oscar's mother snarls. "Now get lost!"

The door closes. Julie shrugs her shoulders and jumps back on her bike.

Oscar's house is remote and it's rare for anyone other than the postman to take the path. From his bedroom window, he watches the little figure cycling away, struggling to avoid the potholes.

Julie.

His Julie.

He feels his heart beating in his throat. She came for *him*. She came to get him, Oscar, to play soccer with her.

Since the day she helped him, when some bullies had pushed him to the ground, he's been in love with her. They go to the same school, although she's a year lower. Every day he goes to school looking forward to seeing her, although they never talk to each other. And now, for the very first time, she came to see him. It must be a sign—a very good one.

His skinny legs tremble slightly. When he regains control of his limbs, he tiptoes down the stairs, quietly opens the front door, and then runs along the path to the soccer field.

***

The match is over. The kids are all covered in sweat so they decide to cool down in the pond behind the pitch. T-shirts and shorts are peeled off and carelessly thrown on the grass. In their swimsuits the children jump into the green water, screaming loudly, causing the ducks to panic and look elsewhere.

A few feet away, Oscar observes the scene from behind a tree. He digs up the tin in which he keeps his things: his binoculars, a packet of chewing gum, a lighter, and a few cigars he stole from his mother. He doesn't smoke, but he likes to hold the cigars.

Oscar rolls one between his fingers and smells it with satisfaction. The smoky smell gives him a tickle in his stomach. He's tall for his twelve years, with long arms and legs. His nails have black edges, his white hair is long and unwashed, and his clothes are too small. The only pastimes his mother allows him are fishing and reading, because they're free.

The sound of wild splashing in the pond makes him look up.

"First one out wins!" shouts Tobias, the bike mechanic's red-haired son, who takes off like a rocket. With an indignant scream, Julie starts the pursuit. The others shout encouragement from the bank.

"Come on, Julie!"

"Go, Tobias!"

Out of breath, they reach the bank at the same time. Julie drops to the grass. "Cheater, if we had started at the same time, I would've won for sure!" she shouts, aggrieved.

"You just can't stand losing," Tobias gasps, but they both laugh and warm up on the grass and in the sunlight that shines through the trees.

Oscar wished he were Tobias and lying next to her. Then he would study the blonde hairs on her arms and make jokes to see her smile. He knows he's different. He knows the kids think he's strange, like a dog without a tail. The boys call him worm boy, because of the bait he collects to go fishing. Or whitey. It doesn't matter, as long as Julie sees him. He rests his lanky body against a tree and stretches his legs out in front of him, careful not to make a sound.

Julie wrings out her hair, the drops falling onto the t-shirt she has put on over her bikini. She says something to Tobias and he laughs, but Oscar can't hear it. He scratches a scab on his knee until it bleeds, and then scratches some more.

It doesn't matter; his time will come. He's already planned everything. He's going to be a doctor. As soon as he has his diploma and starts working in the hospital, he'll look for Julie again. This isn't some childish infatuation; it goes much deeper than that. He *needs* her, and she needs *him*.

In his favorite fantasy, he sees Julie again after a few years and she doesn't immediately recognize him because he looks so different. "Oscar!" she'll exclaim. "You've changed so much! You look amazing!" And then he'll take her out to dinner to "catch up." She'll be impressed by him and by his doctor's title (he'll have business cards printed with his name and title; he'll give her one so she'll have his number) and so it will begin, and after a year of dating, he'll ask her to marry him and they'll buy a beautiful house together, close to the city, but still in the countryside, and… and… and…

Twilight is falling; the children are gone; Julie is gone. Oscar gets up stiffly, carefully buries the tin, and slowly trudges home again.

Julie

February 2005

I press my palms to my eyes. It feels like they've been scooped out of their sockets, pumped up by a bike pump, and then stuffed back into my face.

"What...?" Slowly, the memory of last night resurfaces from the mush of thoughts my brain is producing. I remember going with Eloise to Billy's, my usual pub, same as every weekend. Tom, my ex, wasn't there and I remember being disappointed. Eloise and I got to talking to a couple of guys and sat at a table together. They were buying. We had one shot after another.

Groaning, I turn on my side to get my phone and look at the time. With great difficulty I open my eyes. Ten o'clock already. It's Sunday, so I don't have to go anywhere, even though I have a mountain of work to do at the university. I turn over on my back again and bump my leg against something hairy.

Oh God.

Immediately I'm wide awake and sit straight up in bed.

Which is not *my* bed.

Where am I? Whose room is this? The body next to me moves, and a heavy arm falls over me. It belongs to one of the guys from yesterday. Dean? Dan? Donny? I can't remember.

I push the arm away and hoist myself out of bed. My clothes are scattered around the room, which is so small that I can find everything in a blink. I have to get out of here, and I have to pee, so I quickly pull my dress over my head and grab the rest of my things. I can't find my coat.

To spare both the guy in the bed and myself an awkward conversation, I open the bedroom door as quietly as possible. I'll quickly go to the bathroom, find my coat, and then get out.

Oh no.

This is not a house...

This is not a flat...

This is a student dorm with a shared bathroom.

I swear as I stumble down the long corridor and search for the bathroom. In the meantime, I fervently resolve never to drink another drop of alcohol again. I pull open one of the stalls and sink down in relief.

Would Eloise know that I'm here? I'm angry with myself. Hadn't I promised to drink less? February is always a difficult month for me. But still.

My inner swearing is interrupted when I hear the bathroom door open. In the stall next to me, someone lets out a long, drawn-out fart and I can't believe that I've ended up in this situation *again*. Unbelievable.

I quickly put on the rest of my clothes and grab my bag. I run out of the bathroom and into the stairwell, following the exit signs. Moments later, I'm back on the street. It's cold without my coat and I breathe in the clean air. Now that I see where I am, my heartbeat slows to a regular pace. I'm near Billy's, in the student district. Apparently, in my festive mood last night, I didn't bring my bike, so I walk the few minutes to the café with my arms folded around me. I'm acutely aware of the rat's nest on my head and the smudged walk-of-shame mascara under my eyes.

This has to stop, Julie. This really has to stop.

Oscar
1993

He feels as if he's being stabbed in the stomach when he thinks of the letter from social services that he found this morning. His mother was still sleeping it off. He'd had all the time in the world to open it and read it: it was over.

He knew this would happen. He had been called to the social worker's office a couple of times at school, and last week social services had paid them a visit. He'd done his best to tidy up the house. He'd really done his best. He'd collected the empty bottles that were strewn about the house and hid them in the garden shed. He'd washed the dishes that had been there for weeks. He'd washed himself, put on clean clothes, made coffee, and bought biscuits.

Unfortunately, they were already on the doorstep at nine o'clock in the morning and he couldn't get his mother out of bed.

It was hopeless.

The two social workers had looked at him pityingly when they found her upstairs in bed.

He hates them. He hates the juvenile court. And he hates his mother. Because where he's going, he won't be able to see Julie again.

Julie
March 2005

No, this isn't how it was supposed to go, I think as I hang over Eloise's toilet bowl. How is it possible that I've let myself go again? I was going to recite a funny poem for Eloise's twenty-fourth birthday. One that emphasizes her many love conquests and the broken hearts she leaves behind wherever she goes.

Eloise is my best friend—we've known each other for years—but we don't have much in common, especially not our circle of friends. I'd been a bit nervous beforehand, which is why I'd downed those three rum and Cokes: to take the edge off my nervousness.

Oh dear, had I really done it?

Yes, I had.

In a drunken state, I'd tapped my ring against my glass to catch everyone's attention. Thirty of Eloise's hipster friends, many of them customers of her clothing shop and, therefore, all perfectly dressed, were standing around with drinks in their hands. I was a little out of place in my denim dress. When I'd arrived at the party, I was wearing beautiful shoes with high heels, but these were lying abandoned in a corner somewhere by now, so I was standing barefoot, with unpainted toenails, looking at the group in front of me. I'm not a shy person, really, but a living room full of strangers can turn your throat dry as a bone.

I promptly forgot what the poem was about and couldn't remember where I'd put the piece of paper on which it was written, so I started singing a clumsy "Happy Birthday to You" and then, very embarrassingly, got the giggles.

Fortunately, this proved to be contagious, as Eloise laughed out loud, followed by the rest of the crowd.

Only then did I see Tom, my ex, coming towards me. I hadn't seen him come in at all and hadn't spoken to him since we'd broken up two months ago. He put a fourth rum and Coke in my hand.

"You've earned it," he said in that typical half-shy yet so sexy way of his. And now here I am, hanging over the white porcelain of the toilet bowl in Eloise's turquoise bathroom, wondering whether or not to take him back to my flat.

Tom is handsome, without a doubt. His dark brown hair is a tad too long and curls at the ends. If you look closely, you can see that it's not completely brown but has a hint of red. It shows in his stubble if he leaves it. He has a sweet face filled with freckles and laughter lines around his soft brown eyes. And his teeth! I've never seen such perfect white teeth in my life.

With one hand he holds my hair out of my face, while the other gently strokes my back.

"Shall I take you home?" he murmurs, as if he can read my thoughts. And so it happens that a little later, against my better judgment, I let myself sink into the passenger seat of his car. He puts my bike in the boot and his presence feels as familiar as ever. When he gets into the car, I deeply inhale his warm scent.

He looks at me, concerned. "Are you okay?"

"Yeah, just a little bit tipsy," I lie.

"If you're going to throw up again, tell me in time," he replies dryly, but his eyes are smiling. I stick out my tongue.

"I didn't expect you to come to Eloise's party," I say. Tom is no party animal; if he hadn't been a music teacher in high school, he would be a downright recluse—in a house with a well and solar panels, where he happily grows vegetables and plays music with the only audience being the birds and squirrels.

"I wasn't going to." He looks straight ahead, but when I turn my head to look out, I feel his eyes following me. As I stare out the window, my stomach makes disturbing noises and I keep my hand ready on the door handle. Just like my body, my head is rumbling. If he had no intention of coming to the party, then why was he there? For me? Or just for Eloise? I can't deny that I'm glad to see his familiar face, but his behavior towards me is confusing to say the least. Contradictory, even, when I think of our last conversation in which he told me that he would rather not see me again.

Tom quickly pulls into a parking space right in front of my flat and helps me out. He lifts my bike out and walks me to the front door.

"Are you coming in?" I ask.

He shrugs. "I don't know if that's a good idea."

Even more confusing behavior. What does he really want?

"Jesus, Tom, I'm not asking you to get married! Fine. I'll see you around then. Thanks for driving me home," I snarl. But when I push open the hall door, I stop abruptly and turn around.

"What is it?" he asks.

"Quiet," I say, peering into the dark street. I glance past a few parked cars; the horses in the pasture across the street are in their stalls. Everything else seems deserted. I strain my ears and hear the reassuring thunder of a train in the distance. I must have imagined it, but I have the feeling that we were not alone.

"It's nothing. I thought I heard something," I say.

"Is your stalker back?" asks Tom, his tone suddenly concerned.

Last year, I started receiving strange phone calls; it was during the time when I was with Tom. The caller was anonymous and didn't say a word when I answered. When I stopped answering, the calls stopped too. There are strange people in this world. I still don't know who it was. Someone who was bored, probably.

"No, no. Are you coming in or not?" I ask, irritated.

He rolls his eyes, puts my bike inside, and then looks like he wants to step out again but changes his mind.

"I didn't want to break up, you know," he says, looking straight at me.

I swallow. I know that I'm the reason for our break-up. I'm the one who doesn't want a serious relationship with him, who isn't prepared to make concessions—like moving in together—which makes him think that I don't love him as much as he loves me. Or even that I don't love him at all, which isn't true; I just don't want to live with him. I want to do my own thing. Decide for myself how to decorate my flat. Play loud music whenever I want and dance in my living room. Eat pizza out of the box. And work. Work on becoming a vet, with my own practice. Yes, I want Tom in my life, but only when it's convenient for me. For Tom, that's not enough and he put a stop to "us."

I feel a little sting in my stomach. Is it regret? Or just the fear of being alone? I look from the dark stairwell to his face. He looks hurt. I hate to see him like this.

"Just come in, I don't like it when you go home like this," I say.

"If you're sure," he replies, his gaze lowered. I want to take him in my arms, run my hands through his hair.

"Sure, come on. Then you can make me tea and massage my feet."

He laughs and shakes his head. "Oh, Julie, what are you doing to me?" The dark clouds have moved away from his face.

Indeed, what am I doing to him? He would do anything for me, as long as I showed him I cared, like a stray dog you chase away that keeps coming back to you, always happy to see you. Grateful for every tiny little crumb of attention.

I plop down on the L-shaped sofa in my living room and kick off my shoes with a sigh of relief. "You know the way," I say with my eyes closed.

Tom chuckles and walks into the kitchen to make some tea. His presence wraps itself around me like a blanket of comfort and I fall into a wonderful dreamless sleep.

Oscar

1994-1995

Oscar became a regular customer in foster care. After each placement, he went home again like a boomerang. There, things would go well for a while...until he was placed again. In spite of everything, he managed to keep up with his schoolwork and not fail, even if it was at a snail's pace.

The foster families couldn't make sense of him. They described him as a quiet boy who locked himself up in his room. In his file, it said that most people found him a bit scary, which meant he couldn't stay anywhere for long—that is until Oscar turned fourteen and ended up with Kirsten and Robert De Ridder, the first family that treated him with affection. His food was much better than at home, he could study undisturbed, and his grades soared. His room was clean, his sheets were washed, and he had a wardrobe full of new clothes.

His foster parents didn't ask much of him; they were just happy he was there. Why, he didn't know. They'd had a son once, but that was a long time ago. There were photos of him on the sideboard in the living room, showing him no older than about fifteen. Kirsten lit a candle by them every night. Oscar never asked what had happened to the boy and they never told him. For him it was fine, as they left him alone and he kept quiet; it was a good deal. Besides, Kirsten and Robert's bookcase was much more interesting than his mother's, as it turned out. To make things even better, every Sunday they went to the big library in the city together where he was allowed to choose five books. It was the highlight of his week.

At Christmas, his mother came to visit for the first time; she looked different, better. She had a new boyfriend and was trying to stop drinking, his foster parents told him. He'd heard that before. The memory of his mother's last boyfriend was still fresh in his mind, with a crooked nose as a constant reminder. He breathed a sigh of relief when she left. The green jumper she had brought him as a present disappeared, unworn, into the back of his wardrobe.

His foster parents also gave him a present on Christmas morning.

"Close your eyes," Kirsten said as Robert walked into the kitchen. A moment later, Oscar heard him come in again and put something down beside him.

"You can open your eyes now," said Robert.

Curious, Oscar peered through his white eyelashes at the thing sitting on the ground beside him. It was a large box, he suspected. He couldn't see it well because a towel was hanging over it. He looked questioningly at his foster parents.

"Go on, take off the towel."

Carefully, he pulled the piece of cloth away to reveal a cage.

"Oh," Oscar uttered timidly when he saw what was inside. It was a rabbit with hair as white as his own.

"It's a dwarf rabbit." Kirsten smiled. "He's yours. You can take him out."

Oscar sat motionless, watching the little animal scurry nervously around in its cage.

His foster dad patted him on the shoulder. "I think our Oscar is a bit overwhelmed. Shall I take him out?"

Oscar nodded, and Robert gently placed the soft furry ball into Oscar's hands. Oscar pressed the warm rabbit against his chest and felt its heart beating fast. His fingers melted into the rabbit's white fur; tears pricked behind his eyes and found their way out. They dripped down from his cheeks to his hands, and he felt the little animal getting wet. A pet. His alone. Gently, he wiped the wet fur dry with the towel, and, in his mind, he solemnly promised he would love his new friend unconditionally.

Into its soft ears, he murmured, "Don't be afraid, little rabbit. This is a good home. Nothing will happen to you here. I'll protect you."

When she thought Oscar wasn't looking, Kirsten gave Robert a telling look.

***

Winter came to an end and passed into spring. Oscar still lived with Kirsten and Robert, together with his new best friend. He'd named him Nivens, after the white rabbit from *Alice in Wonderland*.

More often now, he got this warm feeling deep inside. A feeling he remembered from when his grandpa was alive and they would go fishing or do a puzzle together at night or play cards while drinking chocolate milk. The time before his mother changed.

Could it be happiness?

There was only one problem: he didn't see Julie anymore. The village was too far away. He wasn't allowed to go out on his bike and his foster mom kept a close eye on him. She brought him to school by car every day and picked him up again at the end of the afternoon, so there wasn't much room to escape. In hindsight, if he had known then that he would be staying with Kirsten and Robert for so long, he would've tried to slip away.

When he wasn't doing his homework or burying his nose in a book while Nivens was scurrying around, he was lying on his bed, thinking about Julie. He knew, of course, that she was a teenager, fourteen by then. He closed his eyes and tried to picture her face, the dimple in her cheek, her eyes that always seemed to smile. With her, he had never seen the disgust that the people of his village felt towards him and his mother, especially the children. The more he thought of her, the more he became convinced that she, too, had deeper feelings for him.

Then, unable to control it, the image in his mind's eye jumped to that of his mother's face. To the look she gave him when she'd been drinking. How the light in her eyes would go out and she'd look at him as if he were made of glass and she could see through him. Those were the moments he avoided her as much as possible. He shook his head to make the image disappear and to relieve the pressure on his chest, but didn't succeed.

The last time she'd visited Kirsten and Robert, she had really looked at him, into his eyes. That had been very strange. It had made him uncomfortable, so he'd looked away.

"My boy," she had said, "my handsome boy, how I've missed you."

Later, he thought about it; he didn't understand why she'd acted so differently, as if she wanted him back. But he wanted to believe it. Because if she got better, he could go home, and going home meant seeing Julie again.

***

Summer came. It was the last day of school and the long holiday lay ahead of him. When his foster mom picked him up that afternoon in her white Fiesta, she was wearing dark sunglasses. She didn't look at him when he got in. Her hands clasped the steering wheel, the knuckles white. Her grey hair was in a tight bun at the back of her head.

"Are you putting your seatbelt on?" she said, and her voice cracked a little.

Silently, he clicked the buckle, his hands resting on his lap. He had grown tremendously in recent months and his knees were sticking up. His white hair was neatly cut and not long like before. As the car started to move, he stared outside with his icy blue eyes. She didn't have to say it; he understood it just as well. A thick knot wrapped itself around his stomach.

His time with Kirsten and Robert was over.

Julie
Easter Holidays 2005

I wake up in my own bed and turn over again with no idea how I got from the sofa to the bedroom last night. I feel for the spot next to me, but it's cold and unoccupied. Did Tom go home? He had appeared so suddenly at the party, it must have been some trick of Eloise's to get us back together. She'd like nothing better.

I roll out of bed and walk to the bathroom. The sight of the toilet brings back the memory of my embarrassment in Eloise's bathroom and I have to swallow a sour belch. In the shower, I punish myself by letting the cold-water spray down on my sensitive skin. It feels like ten thousand sharp needles and I can barely suppress a scream. I quickly turn on the hot water tap, but then a new wave of nausea hits. I reach the toilet just in time. *This must be the worst hangover I've ever had*, I think as the last bits of bile leave my body and I hang over the toilet like a wet rag. *Again.*

I live in a duplex flat, and after my shower I walk somewhat refreshed down the spiral staircase. The small hall leads to a bright living room with an adjoining white open kitchen. It's not large, but it's cozy with a balcony that offers a wonderful wide view over the fields. The view reminds me of the village where I grew up, which is the reason I bought this flat. It's far from the hustle and bustle of the city and yet close to everything, with my bike as my best friend.

Tom is making toast in his boxer shorts. So, he slept over after all. On the sofa, probably. He doesn't hear me come in, so I seize the moment to run my gaze over his sinewy body: his long neck, with strong shoulders below it, and beautiful arms, tanned to the edge of his imaginary t-shirt. Narrow hips, not a shred of fat. Long legs.

Again, I feel that strange stab in my stomach. My studies are my life. In a few years' time, when I have my own successful practice, I might have time for a family. Or at least for a husband; we'll see if there will be children. But Tom sees it differently: he wants to plan our future, live together, preferably as soon as possible. As if our love can be measured by the number of hours we spend at the same table. Or in the same bed.

I step towards him and put my head against his back, wrap my arms around him from behind, and deeply inhale his scent. His body reacts with surprise for a moment, but then relaxes under my touch. He squeezes my hands briefly and then takes two mugs from the sink: tea for him and coffee for me.

"I put extra sugar in it for you. I figured you could use some today," he chuckles as he pulls out of my embrace. He puts the steaming cups on the table, together with a plate of toast, and we sit down opposite each other. With any other man, I'd be wondering now if we'd had sex last night, but not with Tom. He would never do that—not in the state I was in last night. I almost regret it.

Gratefully, I take a bite of my toast. "This is cozy."

"Yes, we should do it more often," he replies with a lopsided grin.

"Funny. *You* broke up with *me*, remember?"

"I certainly do remember. And I remember why as well."

I sigh. I don't want to argue.

"Sorry," he says. "That came out spontaneously."

I nod and put my hands around the warm mug of coffee. I like it when Tom is with me, and I must admit that I've missed him. It's one thing to be home alone and know there's someone who cares about you and is there when you need them, but it's another to really be all alone. *Always*. Especially for an extrovert like myself.

"I was just thinking," Tom begins, "I know you don't want to live together and I can understand that in a way, but it's really hard for me not to be with you." He brushes his hair away from his face and I see the muscles in his upper arm bulge.

I swallow and take a sip of my sweet coffee.

"So I thought, maybe, I can rent the flat above you. It's empty, right?"

I look at him in surprise. "What about your own flat?"

Tom, like Eloise, lives in the city, close to everything, whereas I live a long way out in a newly built neighborhood surrounded by fields.

"I'll rent it out or sell it. It doesn't matter. But then we could see each other more often and you could still have your own place."

This is so typical of Tom. I reject him, break his heart, drive him to the point of breaking up with me, and what does he do? Takes my needs into account. I quickly dive back into my mug to cover my face. With a sip of hot coffee, I melt away the lump of ice that's in my throat.

"It's rented," I say.

"What?"

"The flat upstairs. It's been rented. Only recently. The new tenants haven't moved in yet, but it's not vacant anymore." I'm not lying, as it *has* just been rented out—the owner came to tell me—and I don't know whether to be disappointed or not.

"Oh."

"Yeah. Too bad."

"Would you have thought it was a good idea otherwise?"

I shrug semi-nonchalantly. "Maybe."

Tom raises his eyebrows.

"I don't know, Tom. I really don't want to live together, but I have to admit that I've missed you the past few weeks. So yes, *maybe*. But it's rented, so there's no point in fantasizing about it, is there?"

"No, there isn't," he says, but the disappointment can be read on his face. "How's your thesis coming along?"

"Good, but I have a lot of work. I'd planned to work through some this afternoon." I don't mean to push him away, but I really have a lot to do. I'm in my last year of veterinary medicine. He nods.

An hour later, I walk him out. I watch him cross the street and I wait for him to get into his car so I can wave goodbye, but he's just standing there, as if petrified.

"What is it?" I call across the street.

He looks at me in bewilderment and mumbles something, but I can't understand it. Worried, I run across the street in my slippers. His expression has changed from bewilderment to anger.

"Look!" he shouts. "Who would do something like this?"

There are long scratches all over his blue VW Golf. Dozens of them. A vandal must have had a go at it. It's an act of pure senseless aggression and I feel the hairs on my arms rise one by one.

Oscar

1995

The juvenile court ordered Oscar to return home, to the place he hated. When his grandpa was still alive, everything was different. His mother didn't drink so much and she went to work every day. Oscar and Grandpa were like two peas in a pod. When Grandpa talked about the war, Oscar would hang on his every word. Grandpa had lived through two world wars and could talk for hours about the battle of Dunkirk, which he'd survived. His family had been killed in a bombing raid; he had lost his mom, dad, brothers, and sisters overnight. That's why he had dug an air-raid shelter as soon as he built his own house.

"If they ever try that again, we'll be prepared, Oscar," he'd said. "No one will be able to hurt us. There's enough food for a whole year." That was no lie. Once in a while, when Grandpa went on his monthly inspection, he would take Oscar with him to the shelter. It was exciting and *top secret*. He had to promise not to talk about it with anyone—absolutely no one. Not ever.

"Because if they know your hiding place, you're dead," Grandpa had cautioned.

The shelter had a large living area with two bunk beds, a table, and four chairs. A small kitchenette was equipped with a cooker, and there was also a separate toilet and even a small bathroom. The storeroom was filled to the brim with drinking water (in case the tap water became polluted) and tins of beans in tomato sauce, bolognaise sauce, soup, sardines, and goulash. Next to it was a whole supply of oatmeal, rice, and pasta—more than anyone could ever eat in a lifetime. It was all very impressive to Oscar and it was his favorite place.

After Grandpa died, Mom had inherited the house and the two of them stayed there. Oscar didn't know who his father was. It was always Grandpa, Mom, and Oscar. And then Mom and Oscar and sometimes a new friend of Mom's. She always drank the most when she had a fight with her boyfriend or when they broke up. She would stay in bed for days. Oscar soon learned to set his own alarm clock, make his own sandwiches, and cycle to school on his own.

One day, when Oscar was about eleven, his mother had received a letter from work; they didn't want her to come back. Mom had roared loudly when she read the letter and smashed her glass of red wine against the wall of the living room. There is still a brownish stain there today in the shape of a dog's head. She had also screamed at Oscar, who fled to his room and crawled under the covers with his hands over his ears.

From that day on, she stayed in bed even more often. The bottles piled up. Oscar became afraid of his mother and stayed away from her as much as possible. Sometimes she would run around the house all night, shouting so loudly and for so long that he couldn't sleep and nodded off at school. The house fell into disrepair, the garden became wild, and the path to the garden shed with the shelter underneath became impassable because of the many thorny bushes that were given free play. It seemed as if the shelter had never been there. But the thorny bushes couldn't overpower Oscar's memories and make them disappear. They couldn't make him forget how it had once been.

And yet that was what the juvenile judge had asked of him. According to her, Mom had learned from her mistakes and was going to do her best, so Oscar had to leave Kirsten and Robert and go home.

At first, things went pretty well. Mom's new boyfriend was called Bruno, a big, quiet man with a fierce beard and a Harley-Davidson. He had a dog, a fluffy mongrel who responded to the name Jeff and who followed him everywhere. Mom, indeed, didn't drink anymore, there was food in the house again, and Bruno worked in the garden until it looked presentable. The overgrown path to the garden house became passable once more. Together with Oscar, Bruno painted the garden shed green, just as it had been before. Then Bruno started making a doghouse for Jeff so he could stay outside when they weren't home.

As soon as Oscar thought that no one was looking, he went searching for the trapdoor in the floor of the garden shed: the entrance to the air-raid shelter. To do this, you had to stick your finger into one of the old rotten floorboards and pull, and four of the boards would come up at the same time, forming a hatch through a hidden hinge. You couldn't see it with the naked eye.

The hinge, of course, was completely rusted and it took Oscar a lot of effort to get it to move, but eventually it did, and with a few drops of lubricant, he made sure that next time he would have less trouble getting it open.

Carefully, he descended the concrete stairs. It smelled musty and damp in the shelter. He reached for the light switch with his hand. Miraculously, the ceiling lamp lit up the whole room. Oscar held his breath, overwhelmed by the memories of his grandpa. This place stirred up so many feelings that he stopped to take everything in. The grey walls, the rusty beds, the cold floor. Although the shelter looked anything but cozy, it felt so familiar that it made him happy. Excitedly, he walked further into the room, cobwebs hitting his face as an idea formed: he would clean up the shelter and make it his hiding place. A place for him alone where no one could find him.

Oscar started walking briskly through the shelter. First, he went to find the source of the putrid smell he hadn't noticed earlier. He opened the door to the storeroom and inspected the pantry. Dead flour beetles were everywhere; they had feasted on the oats and rice, he suspected. Time to get rid of it all. He looked at the tins and saw that they were, of course, all expired. Then he lugged the mattresses outside and lay them in the sun behind the garden shed so Mom and Bruno wouldn't see them. Not that they cared.

It became a project to get through the endless summer holidays. In the days that followed, he smuggled cans of detergent into the shelter and scrubbed it clean from top to bottom, as if his life depended on it. As soon as the place was livable again, he dragged in the mattresses and some blankets, on which he laid Nivens. The rabbit kept him company during the hard work. Oscar chatted aloud to the animal, telling him what he was doing and why. It was a new beginning for him, he explained to Nivens. Now he, too, had a burrow, just like rabbits have. A place where he, as well as Nivens, was safe, just as Grandpa had promised.

Julie

Easter Holidays 2005

It's beautiful spring weather, the kind of day that makes you want to cycle with your arms spread wide and feel the wind in your hair while singing "Bohemian Rhapsody." I've arranged to meet Eloise at Billy's.

The café has been around longer than I have; it's a legend. Old black and white photographs from the glory days of the bar hang on the dark-painted walls—from the days when people still went out, as Fred always says. The old café owner has been close to bankruptcy several times, but he refuses to give up.

"If they want to close down Billy's, they'll have to carry me out. I'd rather hang myself," he growls through his beard to anyone who will listen. The weathered floor is scratched from the countless times chairs have been pushed across it. It looks like an old astronomical map. The smell of tobacco has penetrated the furniture and the walls. An old Tigra advertisement hanging behind the massive bar is the silent witness to the many deeply philosophical conversations that have taken place there over the years. A rusty fan dangles from the ceiling.

"Hey, ZZ Top, bring us another round here!" A group of youngsters has been quite noisy for some time. On the terrace is a sign that says "no service."

Right, it's the Easter holidays. The thought that Tom is off work immediately flashes through my head. I could call him and ask him to do something together. Maybe he could stay the night? But I know that's not fair to him. I have to stop this; he's too nice a guy. He deserves better.

"Hi, Fred. Can I have a Perrier with lots of ice, please?" No more alcohol for me. Lesson learned.

"Hello, beautiful. Coming right up. First I'm going to set those losers straight."

I take a seat on a wooden barstool and watch as Fred, almost five foot six, comes out from behind the bar. With a shrill whistle, he wakes Boris, his bull terrier, from his nap. With the dog wagging at his side, he slaps the bill on the group's table.

"Time to go somewhere else, fellas," he says. "This is a bar for big boys. I think there's some room at the karaoke bar across the road." He stands there with his arms folded across his chest. Although Boris sits next to him like a sack of potatoes, the huge teeth peeking out from his snout have the desired effect. One of the boys wants to get up immediately but is pulled down again by his mate.

"We don't want to go to the karaoke place. We want to stay here and we want beer. Now!" says the guy who had demanded a round before.

The terrace is packed and the surrounding conversations fall silent. Nobody wants to miss an outburst from Fred. They're not disappointed; with a loud bang he slams his fist on the rickety table.

"Pay up and get out," he threatens. "This fellow hasn't had his supper yet."

Boris growls on cue.

The boys pull their mate by his sleeve. "Come on, Dries, it's not worth it." The young man grumbles and gives in. They throw some cash on the table and walk away, some a bit shakier on their feet than others.

I can hardly contain my laughter. Fred is a soft-boiled egg, and he has never hurt anyone in his life, but he's damn good at pretending. I got to know this place at the start of my studies. It was the faculty's student bar then and it seemed like a good idea to throw myself into student life right away. Meanwhile, after the umpteenth brawl, the student union found a new home, but I stayed. Billy's became my refuge when my flat became too lonely, when memories of my mom took my breath away. I met Tom here a year ago. He's now the regular pianist on Friday nights.

My phone rings: anonymous number. I frown, but answer anyway. "This is Julie speaking."

No answer. I only hear a soft noise in the distance. Waves, or trees rustling in the wind. A chill runs through my body and I quickly end the call. Damn, I thought I had put this behind me. Those annoying phone calls had been a real plague last year. I was so relieved to be rid of them. Just like then, I still don't understand why anyone would want to bother me with this. It's such annoying behavior, so childish. I had planned to change my number if it happened again, but that's such a hassle.

I sigh deeply and take a sip of my Perrier when Eloise pops up next to me.

"Hey, have you been here long?"

My dad used to call us Yin and Yang when we were in high school. Eloise, with her African roots, is as dark as I'm pale. Today she's dressed in a super-feminine yellow frock; a cloud of J'Adore perfume blows in with her. I feel more cheerful at once.

"No, I only just sat down."

Eloise signals to Fred, who pours her a glass of white wine.

"Cheers," she says. "How's the hangover?"

I grin and take a sip of my water. "That was yesterday, wasn't it?"

Eloise looks at me inquiringly. "Okay. What about the other thing that happened yesterday? Did he stay the night?"

See, that's typical Eloise. She will always interfere in my love life or lack thereof. I care about her very much, but today I really don't feel like it.

"Yes, he slept over, and no, nothing happened."

Eloise sighs theatrically. "I'll never understand it. You two were made for each other."

"That's what *you* think," I say, irritated. "We're old and wise enough to make our own decisions."

"Yes, I know," she soothes, "but it's just such a shame: you two are a perfect match, yin and yang. It's only because *he* wants to live together and you don't that you've split up. Such a shame!" She makes wild arm gestures, spilling some white wine over the rim of her glass. "I'm just wondering if you made the right choice by rejecting him, that's all," she carries on. "I mean, aren't you getting too old to wake up in a different bed every weekend?"

"Excuse me? As if you're such an example for making good choices. What was the name of your last hookup again?" I spit back venomously.

That shuts her up and for a moment we sit at the bar in silence, staring at our glasses. After high school, I went to study veterinary medicine, which surprised no one, and Eloise decided to go to the Fashion Academy, which did surprise *everyone*. No one had ever seen her hold a drawing pencil, only ultra-thin Cartier cigarettes. But she succeeded and graduated last year. Unfortunately, she couldn't find work as a designer, so she took a job at the clothes shop where she had worked as a student to pay for her studies. A "boutique," as she calls it. It seems to go well for her because since then she has become the manager of the "boutique." It's only when it comes to love that she sometimes lets things slide, and Daniel, her latest fling, is a good example of that: handsome, rich, successful and married. Not that I'm much better; my longest relationship lasted nine months and that was with Tom. I'm starting to feel a little guilty about my remarks.

"Sorry, sweetheart, I didn't mean it like that. I'm just not feeling well today; that hangover from yesterday still has me in its clutches, it seems. Besides, I just got another strange phone call."

"You're kidding? From the same weirdo as a few months ago?"

"Well, I don't know because he or she doesn't say anything when I pick up," I sigh.

She puts a hand on my knee. "Girl, maybe you should go to the police. And you do look a bit drained. Are you okay?"

"Yes, I'm fine, but I'm not going to stay out too late."

"Would you rather go home? We'll catch up another time," she says, lighting a cigarette.

"Are you crazy?" I protest, blowing away the smoke. "Besides, you have to tell me all about your new boyfriend Daniel."

"Okay, to your health," says Eloise and we clink our glasses together.

***

Later that evening, I let the bathtub run. I haven't lied to Eloise: I really don't feel too good these days. I can't keep my eyes open for long at night and more often than not I fall asleep in front of the TV. I suspect I'm suffering from a virus and pour a dash of eucalyptus oil into the bathwater. With a groan, I sink into it and it doesn't take long before I fall asleep.

In my dream, I'm sitting on the beach with my parents; the wind is playing through my white-blonde hair. My toddler fingers are rooting through the sand, looking for "jumpy bugs," which is what I called the sand lice back then. Mom has an orange bandana in her dark curls and she smells of sun cream. Dad is reading the newspaper under a parasol a little further on. Suddenly, someone shouts something. Loud and ugly. I can't understand it well, but it's not friendly. Mom looks up, startled. I look around to find the source of the ugly noise, but see nothing special. Dad reads on undisturbed, engrossed in his newspaper.

The shouting sounds louder. Someone is angry. Very angry.

"Whore!" I hear. "Bitch!"

Again I look around me, but now the beach is deserted. There is no one left. Where are Mummy and Daddy? I look around in panic, throwing my head from side to side, my hair swaying in the wind.

I'm completely alone.

***

I wake up with a pounding heart; my forehead damp with sweat, the rest of my body has become ice cold from the cooled bath water. It's not often that I dream about my parents, and certainly not about my mom. With a strange feeling in my stomach and a heartbeat that is accelerated, I sit up straight. The sun has set and the flat is quiet as a mouse. Then I hear it again.

"Dirty whore! I hate you!"

In an instant I'm standing upright in the bathtub, dripping, my senses wide awake and attuned to every sound.

What was that? Where did that come from?

My heart is beating like crazy; I feel naked and vulnerable and automatically I wrap my arms around my body in protection.

What kind of madman could be shouting like that? It really sounded like it was nearby. Could someone be standing in the street?

I put my wet feet on the bathmat, wrap a towel around myself, and sneak on tiptoes to the bedroom, the window of which faces the street. I peep out through the curtains. There is nothing to see on the street, just a few parked cars and a cyclist riding past in the twilight.

There are a lot of houses being built in my neighborhood and only a few are inhabited, so it's very quiet. The meadows on the other side are peaceful.

I didn't dream it, did I?

No, I heard it clearly: it was a man's voice and it sounded like an enormous rage. A couple with two teenagers has just moved into the house next door. Was that man maybe shouting at his wife? Imagine that.

I sit on the bed with my towel wrapped around me and prick up my ears, alert to the sound of breaking crockery or other signs of domestic violence, ready to call the police. But it remains quiet. How strange. Could it have been a passerby after all? The person on the bike perhaps? Or was it meant for me, just like those phone calls?

I don't scare easily, but sometimes it's scary to live alone. Especially when things happen that you can't immediately explain or when your instincts tell you something is wrong. I want nothing more than to call Tom, but even I realize that would be really selfish.

That night, I fall asleep feeling very confused.

Oscar

1995

Julie went to a different secondary school, so their paths didn't automatically cross; for that he had to lie in wait. He couldn't do that in front of her house; that would be too conspicuous, so every day he would wait in the little cobbled street next to the village bakery. He knew she had to pass there on her bike.

The first time he saw her cycling, his heart almost stopped. She hadn't seen him, as she was busy talking to Tobias next to her. It was a bleak September day and her cheeks were flushed by the wind, yet her coat hung open and she pedaled at her leisure, as if it were summer. Her clear voice drifted towards him in the alley: "You are... because... he said..." he heard her say. And then she was gone again. It seemed as if he were floating, racing to school like an accomplished cyclist, where he entered the schoolyard just in time.

It went on like that for a few weeks. Oscar was okay with it. He was left in peace at home. He could even have gone to the soccer field to hang out with the other kids without his mom and Bruno noticing, but he didn't want to. He was used to being alone and preferred to go to his den. The musty smell had slowly made way for his own. He had managed to get the stove working and could now make coffee. He focused on his homework and his books, which he dragged in piles to the shelter. As long as he kept focused on his plan to become a doctor, everything would be all right. He spent hours there, with Nivens to keep him company. For the time being, he was content with the daily glimpse he caught of Julie. His time would come.

One morning in October, he had taken up position next to the bakery, but this time things were different. Julie and Tobias didn't cycle past but stopped exactly where he was hiding. He dove into the alleyway, but they hadn't seen him. Busily gesticulating, they entered the shop. This was his chance to be close to her. It wouldn't get any better.

Oscar parked his bike against the wall, ran a hand through his white hair, which had already grown back over his ears, and entered the bakery after them. It smelt of freshly baked bread and croissants and there was a line of people in front of the counter. Julie and Tobias joined the line and Oscar stood behind them. He towered over them. It was hot in the bakery and he felt a bead of sweat forming on his forehead, which he wiped away with his sleeve.

He was so close. He opened his nostrils, hoping to catch a whiff of her scent, but all he could smell was the sweet perfume of filled biscuits and cinnamon. If he wanted to, he could touch her now. He could slip a lock of her hair between his fingers and she wouldn't notice. He forced his arms tightly beside his body to resist the urge and closed his eyes. She was busy talking to Tobias again and this time Oscar could follow the conversation word for word. It was about an assignment Julie had to write because she'd been talking in class.

"I wasn't the only one, you know," she said indignantly. "Two currant buns and a filled biscuit, please," she ordered.

"And for me a croissant and a chocolate roll," Tobias added. The baker put the biscuits in paper bags and they paid. Oscar opened his eyes and waited anxiously for Julie to turn around. The two unzipped their rucksacks, put their loot inside and swung them back on their backs. With a wave, they turned and marched towards the exit, passing Oscar without even noticing him. A gust of wind blew in when the door opened and it chilled his neck.

Ding-dong.

The door chimed and off they went. He looked after them in bewilderment.

"What can I get you, son?" the lady asked, but Oscar stood there petrified, his arms stiff beside him. Not a word came to his mind; his mouth was as dry as a desert.

"Eh," he said. "Eh." He hadn't thought this through; he didn't want anything from the bakery at all. Though the delicious smells made his mouth water, he had no money with him. He wasn't given pocket money, and a job was hard to find in this hole. With a jolt, he turned, bolted out the door, and fled into the protective darkness of the alley where he stood with his back pressed against the wall, his heart pounding in his throat.

What a failure. She hadn't even seen him standing there. Who did he think he was? Stupid idiot. He banged his head against the wall. What did he expect? That she would have a chat with him? That they would become friends? How did he get it into his head that she would ever look back at him? He was a loser and didn't deserve her. Not as he was now. She deserved better. He had to work even harder at school and make sure she couldn't ignore him. Maybe he should go to the gym? But how could he afford that? In despair, he began to undo his bike lock.

"Hey, Oscar, what's up?"

Startled, he dropped the lock on the ground. His knees felt like soft blubber and he sought support against the wall. Julie looked at him inquiringly, sitting on her bike with one foot on the ground and one on the pedal.

"You feeling okay?" she continued with a hint of concern in her voice.

"Yes, I'm fine," he rasped back. This wasn't how he had imagined reuniting with her. Confused, he picked up his lock from the ground and hung it on his handlebars. She remembers my name, he thought. She recognized me after all. Lights flashed before his eyes and he had to blink to get a good look at her.

"If you're sure... then I'll go. I'm already late," Julie said apologetically.

He nodded in reply because he no longer trusted his voice.

"Welcome back, by the way," she called out as she quickly kicked off.

Deep inside, Oscar felt a heat spreading from his stomach to his chest and then to his face. His cheeks were glowing.

"Julie," he whispered. She hadn't forgotten him. Of course not—not Julie. How could he ever have doubted her?

Julie

April 2005

I was so convinced that I had my life under control; I was following my "big plan" rigorously, leaving nothing to chance. Or so I thought. And now I'm sitting here in a grimy toilet cubicle, with my trousers around my ankles and my heart in my throat.

An hour ago, on my way to the university, I bought a pregnancy test to reassure myself. Of course I'm not pregnant, I tell myself. I don't have a boyfriend. Duh.

The symptoms are there, if you know what you're looking for. At first I thought I had the stomach flu when I kept vomiting for days after Eloise's party. Then the smell of my daily cup of coffee made me gag and it dawned on me that it had been a while since I'd had my period. Not that I keep track.

Unfortunately, I don't have a container of any kind to pee in, so I try to aim the jet at the tester wand, which I can't do without getting my hand wet. Irritated, I slide the dripping wet stick back into the holder, wrap it in a generous amount of toilet paper, stuff it into my bag, and wash my hands.

The leaflet says to "wait for two minutes."

I set the alarm on my phone and walk to my next class. Lately, I rarely spend a day at the university because I'm mainly busy with my internship and thesis. This is one of the last times I'll enter the auditorium, I realize. This should make me happy, but in these circumstances, it doesn't. I sink down on my chair and hear my alarm go off but switch it off without looking. This isn't the right moment. What if the test is positive? I decide to wait until lunchtime, but that, too, passes without me daring to look.

For the rest of the day, the little bundle at the bottom of my bag screams for attention like a whining child (pun intended), but I refuse to give in. Only when I'm back home, where no one can disturb me or see my reaction, do I feel brave enough. I kick off my shoes and walk barefoot to the living room, where I sit down at the table. My handbag feels like it's filled with rocks. I pull the heavy thing onto my lap and pop out the test, hidden at the very bottom. Slowly, I start to unwind the thick bundle, each sheet of paper bringing me closer to a truth I don't want to know.

The plastic thing now lies upside down in front of me on the table; its secret remains safely hidden from me for the time being. I realize this could be a turning point in my life, but at the same time I immediately put it into perspective. That's what I'm good at: being rational, focusing on the plan, not allowing any distractions, and certainly not allowing any uncontrolled emotions to get in the way. Whatever the outcome, I'll solve it. Right? I turn it over; two thick stripes give me a big, positive smile.

"Damn you, Julie! What were you thinking?" I shout out loud. It's strange how a piece of plastic can change everything. How the same result can make one woman overjoyed and bring another to the brink of a panic attack. I throw the test in the trash can and curse my carelessness. With my medical background, I should have known better. How often had I taken my pill too late? Not often, but it has happened. This is my own stupid fault.

How far along would I be? When was my last period? I open the calendar on my laptop and try to figure it out. I think it was at least two months ago. Maybe longer.

The thoughts fly through my head as if in a race. It can't be that Dean or Donny from a few weeks ago, can it? No. No. I had safe sex; the proof was there on the floor in that student dorm, I remember. But you never know… a condom can tear. Oh, God. Oh, God. Please let it be Tom's…though if it is, then I'll probably have passed the twelve-week mark, which is the legal limit for abortion in Belgium.

The panic that I was able to suppress a moment ago is now creeping further into my throat. I'm not going to have a baby, no way. Not now. And not with Tom. Babies are cute to look at, but that's it. Unlike a baby elephant, a human baby can't walk within an hour of being born. It takes at least a year, and much longer for a child to be able to talk. I do a quick calculation and arrive at six years of wiping mouths and assisting toilet visits before the child would go to school and at least learn to read and write. And even then, it would be completely dependent on its parents, on me, until it was of age and could stand on its own two feet. I continue to calculate and already have reached an astonishing minimum of eighteen years that I would have to devote to a child, while I have not even begun living my own life. And all this on the assumption that I would give birth to a healthy child, but with the amount of alcohol I've been guzzling over the past few weeks, the chances of that are already slim.

No.

I take the wet ends of the hair I've been unconsciously chewing on out of my mouth and shake my head decisively; this isn't going to happen. Countless women have preceded me in making this decision; I'm going to have the pregnancy terminated. It's not a baby yet, only a crumb.

I hope.

With trembling legs, I walk to the kitchen and open the fridge to pour myself a glass of wine. That usually helps me to relax. Only when I put the glass to my lips I realize this might not be a good idea. Even if I have the abortion, right now I'm still pregnant. I empty the glass into the sink and open all the kitchen cupboards until I find an unopened jar of peanut butter. It's probably left from when Tom used to sleep over because I never buy the stuff myself. Without thinking, I open the jar, take a spoon from the drawer, and start eating on autopilot while staring out the window.

Twilight is falling and the sky turns pink above the horse pasture. A car drives by slowly and parks a little further on. Someone steps out of it, but I can't see who it is. A man, judging by his build. The stranger shuts his car and crosses the street towards my flat. For a moment, I think it's my new upstairs neighbor, but he stops two houses down, takes a key out of his pocket, and enters. Another new resident. Could it be the "screamer"? No, too far.

I sigh. The bottom of the peanut butter jar is in sight and I know I can no longer put off what is inevitable, so I grab my cell and call Tom. We haven't spoken since the morning after Eloise's party.

"Hey." He sounds like he's trying his best not to be too excited to hear from me, which irritates me.

"Hey," I reply. "Are you at home?"

"Yes, just got in. Why?"

"Would you be able to come over?"

"To your place? Yeah… Sure. Is everything okay?"

"I don't know yet, but I think so. I hope so."

"Julie? What's going on?" He sounds worried, but I resist the urge to explain more on the phone.

"Just come over, please. I'll explain then," I say, and I hang up.

Oscar

New Year's Eve 1995

A thick carpet of snow covers the streets and roofs of the village, contrasting sharply with the dark sky. Today is the last day of the year, a day that symbolizes good intentions, making plans, looking to the future.

Not for Oscar.

From his bedroom window, with Nivens on his lap, he watches the swirling flakes. It's too cold in his shelter now; Grandpa had installed heating, but it's been disconnected. Downstairs, he hears his mom ranting and raving. She and Bruno argue more these days.

The idea was to have a pleasant evening together, but despite her promises, his mother had started drinking wine early. She had been drunk during the aperitif and Bruno had threatened to leave. Nobody paid any attention to the chicken that was in the oven, or to Oscar, who snuck upstairs.

He fidgets with his hands through Nivens' fur and decides to go outside, away from the shouting. In the village, as every year, there is a fair and soon there will be fireworks. Normally, he would never go there, but the walls are closing in on him and he needs some fresh air.

He puts Nivens in his cage, throws a towel over it, and rushes down the stairs. There's no point in being quiet now anyway. Downstairs, he grabs his coat and hat from the coat rack and a moment later he's outside, breathing out white clouds.

The path to the house has turned into a treacherous carpet of snow. It's impossible to cycle through, so he starts walking towards the village. It's dark, but Oscar knows the road like the back of his hand and the moon lights up the path.

He loves stepping over the crunching snow in the darkness, with no other sound than his own shoes. He has always loved snow. The white flakes that look so fragile and yet have so much power. They can ground planes, close schools, bring a country to its knees. He smiles and sticks out his tongue to catch a flake. Pure air fills his lungs and makes his body tingle. His toes get wet from the snow seeping through his thin shoe soles, but he doesn't care. It's as if the village's festive atmosphere is contained in the oxygen molecules he breathes. A feeling of happy anticipation fills him.

The market square buzzes with the chatter of the villagers warming up at the gin stall, mixed with Christmas music blaring through the speakers. The smell of cotton candy and waffles makes his mouth water.

Oscar walks into the square with his head tucked down between his shoulders and finds himself right next to a stall for catching ducks. Across the square, he hears screams coming from the bumper cars; to his right, some dads are having a friendly game at the shooting range.

With his hat pulled deeply over his ears, he tries to get closer to the bumper cars, where Julie must be hanging out. He's not even halfway when a shrill voice shouts, "Hey, whitey, watch out! We can't see you walking in the snow!" followed by hysterical laughter.

His shoulders are hunched and he continues on his way, but there they are, blocking his way: Kevin, Arthur, and Oliver—the village boys. They're in their last year of secondary school and stand high above him, despite the fact that Oscar is tall for his almost sixteen years.

Kevin gives him a shove. "Where are you going, whitey? You're not afraid of us, are you?" he snarls.

Oscar wobbles a little on his legs and takes a step backwards, his nose still pointed at the ground.

"Hey, I asked you something," says Kevin. "Or is it true that albinos are deaf?"

The other two laugh loudly.

"Hello!" Kevin shouts in Oscar's ear. "Can you hear me?"

Oscar cringes; there is nothing wrong with his hearing.

"Or maybe you're not a real albino?" Kevin says to his face as he tears off Oscar's hat and throws it on the ground.

The two others are almost rolling on the floor with laughter.

"Yes, you are," Arthur laughs. "As white as a ghost!"

"Leave him alone!" someone shouts in the distance.

Oscar continues to look down rigidly. His white hair hangs down in front of his face, the snow clinging to his eyelashes.

"He hasn't done anything to you, so leave him alone!" she repeats, coming closer. First he sees her feet. She's wearing moon boots, red ones. Like two rescue beacons, they stand before him in the snow.

"Stay out of it, Julie," Kevin growls.

Oscar can smell the gin on his breath. In his mind, he tries to push Julie away; this is not a good idea.

She puts her arms to her side. "Why are you harassing him? Go and bother someone else, Kevin, or I'll call Van Rooy!"

Mr. Van Rooy is the police commissioner and a good friend of Julie's dad. Meanwhile, her high-pitched voice has attracted the attention of a number of villagers and the three teenagers start to look around uneasily.

"Tsss, a piece of white trash like you isn't worth it," says Kevin and he spits a white slimy squirt on Oscar's hat, which is still on the ground. "Come on, guys, let's go. I'm buying." With their lanky steps, they walk away towards the bar.

Julie is wearing a Santa hat and is holding a half-eaten packet of *oliebollen* between her red mittens. She looks like a miniature Christmas woman.

"*Oliebol?*" She offers Oscar the packet.

He looks at her and searches in her eyes for the pity he expects there, but finds only a sincere questioning look. His light eyes stare at her, not knowing what to do.

"Would you like a fritter, Oscar?" asks Julie again, a little more impatiently. She holds out the bag to him and saliva fills his mouth. Hesitantly, he stretches out his hand and reaches into the bag. His fingers recoil from the heat; feeling as if tiny needles are pricking them, he resists the pain, grabs a greasy ball from the bag, and brings it to his mouth.

"Watch out! Hot!" warns Julie just in time. His mouth is already open and the ball is hanging in front of his face, but instead of giving in to the urge to eat it straight away, he blows on it. A cloud of white icing sugar lands on Julie's red mittens. She laughs and blows a cloud of sugar back at him, some landing on his nose. She takes something out of her coat, pretends to wipe his nose, and then pushes a cotton handkerchief into his hands.

"Here, take this." She smiles.

Oscar stiffens. The situation confuses him. He has no idea how to react so he doesn't. With his eyes fixed on the ground, he accepts the handkerchief, wipes his nose, and then takes a bite of the fritter. It's delicious. He tastes the fatty sweetness and becomes light-headed because of the sugar rush. With every bite, his insides heat up and he wants more, but at the same time, he realizes he's out without a penny and can't expect Julie to buy him food. He eats his loot extra slowly. When Julie offers him a second one, he refuses.

"Thank you, but I'm not hungry," he lies in a soft voice. For a moment, he sees a frown slide across her face, but that may be his imagination because seconds later she's looking at him with a smile.

"Are you coming to the bumper cars?"

"Um, I want to watch?" he replies hesitantly. But he doesn't want to. He wants to be alone with Julie and not hang around with the rest of the group. They're standing next to the bumper cars, staring at them, and he feels uneasy.

"Julie! It's our turn! Come on!" shouts Tobias.

"I'm coming!" Julie shouts back. "Come on, Oscar."

She turns around and runs to the stall where the rest are waiting for her. When she looks back to see where Oscar is, he's already gone.

It's all right, those few minutes were well worth his trip to the village. He knows exactly when he's welcome and when it's time to leave. With Julie's handkerchief still clutched in his hand, he resumes his journey home. Although the temperature has dropped a few degrees below zero and he no longer has a hat, the cold doesn't bother him. The walk does him good, and half an hour later, with a blissful smile on his face, he steps onto the path to his house as the first bangs resound and fireworks paint colorful mandalas on the night sky above.

Julie
April 2005

From the balcony, I see Tom drive up and I watch him for a moment. He parks his VW Golf in front of the building and gets out, his lanky body bending over to lock the car. I know he doesn't like parking his car here since a vandal scratched it, but I don't have a garage, only a bike shed. In the streetlight, his face looks almost feminine; his hair hangs down in front of his eyes and he runs his fingers through it. Then he sees me and raises his hand.

A little later we stand face to face. He looks the same as two weeks ago and yet everything is different. For me, at least. I look at him with different eyes, as if I'm seeing him for the first time. I study his questioning face, his inquisitive eyes. He gives me a peck on the cheek and his stubble sends a shiver down my body.

"Come in, sit down," I say. "What are you drinking?" He wants a Coke. I have one myself and sit next to him on the sofa, my legs tucked up under me. I want to say something to break the ice, but I don't know how or what, so I cough and drink from my can without looking at him. Here I am: Julie the extroverted conversationalist. The can shakes in my hands.

"Julie, are you okay? What's the matter? You're freaking me out." His eyes force mine to look at his. "Are you ill? You look so pale."

"No, sorry, I'm fine, really. I have to tell you something and I don't quite know how to say it," I laugh sheepishly. I take a deep breath and avert my eyes again. I just have to say it; get it over and done with, like waxing my legs. There's no point in procrastinating.

Here I go.

"I'm pregnant."

The words leave my mouth and I leave my body. Or at least it seems that way during the silence that falls. The seconds tick by. Why doesn't he say anything? He keeps staring at my face, as if he expects me to say more. Like I'm an oracle.

Then he says, "Ha!" and then nothing.

My eyelid begins to twitch and an itch moves up from my stomach. He keeps staring at me and I feel like a magician having to show off her next trick, one that is even cleverer than the last. The longer I look at Tom's bewildered face, the harder it starts to bubble. I suppress the urge to say "Tadaaa!" but it takes so much effort that I lose the battle. To my shame, I start to roar with laughter.

"Yes, ha! You can say that again! Ha!" I laugh.

Tom is watching me with his mouth open. I must look like a complete idiot, with tears rolling down my bright red cheeks as I gasp for breath. I try not to look at him, but my gaze is drawn to him again and again, so I keep on laughing.

"I'll get you a glass of water," he says, and gets up. With that, he puts an end to my embarrassing performance.

"Sorry," I hiccup. "When I'm nervous, I start laughing."

"I know," he says dryly. He hands me the glass of water. I sip it until my breathing calms down. "Are you okay?"

"I'm fine."

"Good. So. Pregnant." With a concentrated face, he begins to arrange the coasters lying on my coffee table, making a neat pile of them. "Do you know how far along you are?"

I tell him what I know, which isn't much: about my first suspicions, the test in the university bathroom, my excessive drinking. I say nothing about Dean, Dan, or Donny. He just nods and keeps silent.

"I think it's best to terminate the pregnancy. I'll call the doctor tomorrow morning," I say, concluding my story. I hardly dare look him in the eye and am shocked at myself. I'm not like that at all. I'm never that insecure. It seems as if we've suddenly turned the tables.

Perhaps he draws strength from my stammering, because I've never seen *him* so confident when he says, "You don't need to have an abortion, Julie. We can do this together. You and me."

I start to protest, but with a wave of his hand he silences me.

"Let me finish," he says firmly. He then outlines a scenario for me in which I hand in my thesis as planned. "You can get your degree perfectly well before giving birth," he says. (If we did the math right, I was probably ten to twelve weeks pregnant and the baby would be born around October or November, well after I graduate). "After the baby is born, you can stay at home for a year and during that time I can support us financially." He says it with such enthusiasm, such conviction. "You'll only lose one year, Julie. After that, the baby can go to daycare and you can start your career. I can take over most of the care and I have all the school holidays off anyway. What do you think?"

What do I think? I think I don't want a Tom in my house, let alone a Tom and a baby. I want to start my career, my life. *My* life. After all those years of hard work and sacrifice. After all the sadness. That's what I think.

"But, Tom, we've split up!" I shout in frustration.

"So what? We'll just get back together then, won't we? I want you in my life anyway, Julie." His confidence only increases. I wish I felt the same about him as he feels about me; it would make everything easier.

"Um, I don't think it's that simple. You have to know each other well before you know whether you want to spend the rest of your life with someone. I already didn't want to live with you, let alone have a child with you!"

"Do you feel like you don't know me, then?" he continues unperturbed, as if I haven't just rejected him outright. Again.

"Yes... No... At least, not really." No, of course I don't know Tom. Besides, he's not the man I ever expected to marry. I would know that man better than I know myself, and I would recognize him from the first moment. In my fantasy, my husband has a medical profession, just like me. Maybe he's a doctor or a surgeon. Together, we would be a successful couple with a beautiful house and a flourishing career. We would only have children later in life. Planned. Not like this head-over-heels story of Tom and me.

I feel like I'm losing it. I'm so far outside my comfort zone that the world looks unrecognizable. Tom totally confuses me. You can't get to know someone intimately in a few months. And even then, it's far too early to start having children, isn't it?

"Come on, then, what else do you want to know?" he asks as he opens a second can of Coke. His eyes smile and I feel a tingling in my stomach. Pregnancy hormones, probably. He looks good in his old leather jacket and I'm going crazy from the contradictory feelings, as if my head and my body want different things. My head wants me to kick him out and call the doctor tomorrow. My body wants my head to shut up and to cuddle up close to him, to disappear into his warm arms. I know I shouldn't be doing this, but I play along with his game of questions, even if it's just to distract my mind.

"What's your favorite food?"

"Pizza."

"Your favorite band?"

"No band. Jeff Buckley. But you already knew that."

"Favorite color?"

"Blue. Ask me a serious question."

"What do your parents do?" The moment I ask, I realize how shameful it is that I don't know.

"They have a furniture shop."

I raise my eyebrows in surprise. It's understandable that he never entered the family business. "Tell me about your brother and sister?"

"They're both much older than me. I was a late addition."

"Are you close with them?"

He shrugs. "It's okay, but we're not that close. They both work in the family business. Nobody minded that I didn't want to. I've always been allowed to go my own way, which is fine by me."

I don't quite believe that he thinks it's all "fine," but I'm slowly getting into the swing of things and want to find out more about him, this mysterious man by whom I'm impregnated, however brief the pregnancy may be.

"What are you most afraid of?"

"I can't stand blood."

"Really?" In spite of everything, I laugh a little. As a would-be veterinarian, I've seen my share of blood over the years and it doesn't bother me much.

"Really."

"Okay... What would you do if you won the lottery?"

He has to think about that for a moment. He puts his can of Coke on the table, sinks down on the sofa, and presses his hands against his eyes. His t-shirt creeps up a little and I swallow.

"I would buy a van that I would have converted into a camper, or maybe I would do it myself, with a double bed in the back and a big storage space for a Vespa and some bikes. Then I would travel around with it for at least a year. If I came back, I would still be teaching music, but for free. Maybe I'd set up a special school where underprivileged children could be taught."

"And what if you had a baby? Then you wouldn't be able to do all that."

He removes his hands from his eyes. "Why not? I told you I'd put a double bed in the back of the camper, big enough for you and a baby." He grins.

The conversation is going in the wrong direction, so I take control again. "What's the worst thing you've ever experienced?" I pull my legs up into a cross-legged position, fix my gaze on his eyes, and try to look as serious as possible.

"The worst..." he repeats. "That's easy: losing Grandpa."

"Oh?"

"Yeah, when I was sixteen. This jacket was his, by the way." His long fingers stroke the leather and his expression becomes sad. His grandpa must have been important to him. Maybe because his parents worked so hard? Could he have been raised by him? He says nothing more. Why do I always have to resist the urge to touch him? I'm not in love with him anymore, am I?

"It must have been difficult for you," I say. I know, unfortunately, how it feels to lose someone you love so dearly. It never wears off. I swallow a lump and unconsciously reach for the necklace around my neck.

"Very difficult. Still is, by the way."

He looks so sad. I can't help it. I lean against him and lay my head on his shoulder. He smells of shower gel and grass.

"Did I make you sad?"

He smiles. "I don't play games, Julie. I never have. What you see is what you get. When I was little and my parents had a fight, I couldn't sleep. I came to their bedside at night, crying, begging them not to divorce, which, of course, they never intended to do—that would be bad for business." He turns his face towards me and kisses me on the crown, which makes my body tingle.

Why doesn't my head want this when my body so clearly does? Why am I so scared? His proposal makes sense, as it's indeed possible to have the child. I'm not a sixteen-year-old girl anymore, but an almost twenty-four-year-old woman, and he's twenty-seven, so of course, it's possible. Or is that a naive thought?

We don't make a decision that evening and he doesn't stay for the night. I wave him off from my balcony and watch as he walks around his car to check it for new scratches. As if he would really be that unlucky. I can't deny that, although my decision seemed so clearly right to me earlier, I am now in doubt again.

Oscar
1996

When Oscar gets home from school that evening, he immediately knows that something's wrong. There's no Jeff cheerfully barking and jumping out to meet him, and no Bruno's Harley in the driveway. He opens the front door and hangs his coat on the rack. He's met by a sour smell. After one look in the living room, he knows exactly what's going on. He shuffles up the stairs to his room and takes Nivens in his arms. Together they go to the garden shed, where he opens the hatch and hides in the darkness. It's freezing cold.

Please, don't let him be gone. Do not let him be gone.

He sits down on the mattress and rocks his body back and forth. If Bruno's gone, no one can stop his mother from drinking. He'll be sent away again. The juvenile court had warned him that next time he would be placed permanently. Permanently! That means he may not see Julie again for years, if ever at all. Now that everything is going so well. She waves at him every day from her bike and stops now and then to have a chat, while Tobias stands sullenly waiting. He has told her about Nivens and the books he reads. He suspects that Tobias is jealous and that gives him an unfamiliar feeling. Pride, maybe. Quite different from what is racing through his body right now. Pure panic wells up in his stomach and pushes the air out of his lungs. Tears prickle behind his eyelids.

Stupid bitch! He hates his mother. She ruins everything for him; as long as she's alive he will never be happy. She's a cancer. But what can he do? He's a sixteen-year-old boy. A tall slouch with white hair growing over his ears who is exceptionally good at math and who has read all the great classics. But what use is that to him? He has no money and now no hope. There is no one he can turn to. He has only Nivens.

***

He hides the wine bottles in the garden shed and avoids his mother as much as possible. It doesn't stop her; she just gets in the car and goes out to get new booze. He hopes that during one of those drunken shopping trips, she will drive into a tree. Then he would finally be free.

Things start disappearing from the house. Oscar suspects his mother is selling stuff for money, so he hides all his valuables in his ice-cold shelter. However, he forgets that his fishing tackle is in the garage and thus loses his main way of finding food, with the kitchen cupboards being empty.

He stays in his den wrapped in blankets for hours, together with Nivens. He goes to bed without eating. In the morning, he drags his body to school, his stomach grumbling so loudly that he disrupts the classes.

During the break, he sees a boy throwing away a half-eaten sandwich. He waits until the bell rings and everyone is inside. Then he tries to reach the paper bag with his long arm. He manages to pinch it between two fingers and hoists it out of the bin.

"What are you doing there, young man?"

Oscar is startled and drops his loot. "Eh, I, eh," he stammers.

It's a teacher he doesn't know, a new one teaching the lower classes. The man looks at him inquisitively, studying his thin face, his hollow eyes, his too-short trousers. "Haven't you got any food with you?"

There you have it again, that pitying look.

"I do, sir, but I accidentally threw my fork in the dustbin with my garbage," he improvises.

"Your fork, you say?"

"Yes, sir. But I don't think I can reach it. I'll just go back to my class."

"One moment. What's your name, friend?"

"Oscar, sir."

"Oscar who?"

"Oscar Plessers."

"Fine, Oscar Plessers. Go wash your hands and get back to class. And stay out of the bins from now on, understand?"

Oscar nods and runs off. His empty stomach contracts like a squeezed lemon.

***

That evening, after school, he tiptoes through the house. As usual, his mother is sleeping it off on the sofa in the living room. His stomach still rattles. He hopes she got some groceries today. He walks to the kitchen and quietly opens the pantry; apart from a pack of flour and some pasta, there's nothing in it. He tucks a pack of spaghetti under his jumper and sneaks out of the kitchen to fetch Nivens from his room. He knows exactly which steps creak and which don't, so he makes very little noise going up them. Oscar has put Nivens' cage in front of his bedroom window so the animal can look out while he's away.

"Hello, little fellow," he says endearingly to the white fuzzy ball. The rabbit shuffles happily back and forth in its cage now that his owner is back. Oscar lifts him up, cuddles him in his arms, and feels Nivens' heart racing like a miniature sewing machine.

With the prospect of eating a plate of hot pasta soon, he walks down the stairs again. Too late. He feels the pack slip from under his arm; he can't stop it without dropping Nivens. He tries to catch it with his foot but fails and has to watch the pasta tumble down the stairs.

"Oscar? Oscar!"

There you have it: she's awake.

"Oscar! Is that you? Get your ass over here!"

He cringes and takes a firm hold of Nivens as he walks down the stairs to confront his mother. She looks terrible. Her hair stands in all directions and an odor of sweat and alcohol surrounds her like a stinking fog.

"Remember, you have to drop off the empty bottles at the store," she spits in his face. He sees that her hands are trembling.

"I can't. I have homework to do," he mumbles, his gaze fixed on a stain on her dressing gown just above the right pocket.

"Can't, can't? Who do you think you are? The king?" She laughs, cackling at her own joke and then stops abruptly. "Take. That. Bin. Away. Now," she hisses at him, waving her hand in his face. "And get me a bottle of vodka with the refund."

"No, Mom, I'm not buying you any more drinks," Oscar replies, taking a step backwards. But she's faster than him, perhaps because he's paralyzed by fear and hunger. Before he knows it, she's snatched Nivens from his hands.

"Mom! No!"

"Go and don't come back without my vodka, understand?" she rants, clutching the rabbit in both her hands.

Tears run down Oscar's cheeks as he rushes into the hall, puts the glass bottles in the bin, and races on his bike to the local shop. He's never cycled so fast. Sweat gushes down his temples and back and his hair sticks to his skull. Barely half an hour later, he's back with a bottle of cheap vodka in a paper bag. His mother is lying on the sofa as if nothing has happened.

"Where is Nivens?" he exclaims, his eyes wide open as his gaze scans the room.

"Nivens? Who is Nivens?" mutters his mother. She holds out her hand to accept the bag.

"Nivens! My rabbit! What have you done to him?"

She doesn't reply, but her trembling hand remains outstretched towards him. Confused, he hands her the bag and she immediately unscrews the cap from the bottle. "Must be around here somewhere, don't know. He can't be far." And she plops her skinny body back down on the sofa.

***

Hours later, Oscar is sitting on his bed, crying. He has looked everywhere, but the rabbit's nowhere to be found. As it gets colder outside, he feels the emptiness growing inside him.

"Fucking rabbit!" he roars as raging tears roll down his cheeks. "Stupid animal! Traitor!"

How can Nivens do this to him? He's his only friend. He jumps from his bed and slams Nivens' cage hard against the ground. Immediately afterwards, he regrets his action. Did Nivens slip out through the screen door in the kitchen? Or did his mother deliberately take him outside and let him go?

He lies down on the bed and stares at the ceiling with his almost transparent eyes. Before Nivens was here, he had no one to talk to, just like now, yet it feels worse now. He was just as alone then, so why does it feel so different? Why does his stomach hurt so much?

***

Not only that night, but also in the days that followed, when the villagers saw him wandering everywhere looking for Nivens, the emptiness kept growing. He refused to go to school and didn't give up his search, even though it was freezing and he knew he would never see his friend alive again.

It was only when social services came to the door a week later that he had to abandon his mission. This time, Oscar hadn't been able to intercept the letter and the two social workers couldn't hide their disgust. The house had never looked so bad, Oscar was skinnier than ever, and his mother was babbling gibberish. He knew it was only a matter of days before the order would come to place him out of the house.

When they had gone, he went to his room. Nivens' cage was still on the floor. Downstairs, he heard his drunken mother stumble, followed by the slamming of the front door. She started the car and drove off to stock up. He sat down at his desk and stared out the window. He waited for the anger that would soon overwhelm him, or the sadness that would drown him, but nothing came. The only thing Oscar felt was an infinite emptiness.

Oscar

1996, February 14th

Smoke. Suffocating smoke.

It fills the room in black waves.

It's everywhere. In his eyes, in his mouth.

He coughs, his eyes burn. A moment ago, he could still see the door to his bedroom, but not anymore.

He shouldn't have gone upstairs again; the fire consumes everything so quickly. Too quickly.

He searches his way by touch.

There.

Quick.

Down the stairs, into the dark hall.

The front door beckons. If he goes out now, he's saved.

But he can't resist the urge; has to see with his own eyes. His lungs are burning, his ears are ringing, his eyes are dry.

Hot. It's so hot.

He has to be quick. He pulls open the living room door.

Yells.

His hand!

Flames screeching through the door, roaring past him.

Pain!

That smell. He's nauseous. He wants to bend over but can't stay here. He has to leave. His legs can no longer carry him, but he has to go. Has to.

One last look at her, on the sofa. He doesn't see her, only flames and black smoke. She must be there. For sure. He has to leave now.

He has to.

The floor is burning, the ceiling is burning, his pajamas are burning. A few more feet; come on, Oscar, a few more feet.

He throws his body out onto the wet grass, his loot clutched in his hands. Rolls as far as he can.

Pain.

Pain everywhere.

Sirens.

And then nothing.

Julie

April 2005

"It's your decision, but I say go for it. You'll have a mega cute baby and I'll have another great excuse to go shopping." Eloise follows her words with a burst of laughter. It's typical of her to ignore all the obstacles and to continue to see the fun in everything.

I cycled straight to her after my doctor's visit, needing to talk to someone about it. The doctor has taken a blood sample and I can call tomorrow morning to hear the results, and then I'll know how far the pregnancy has progressed. And what options I have.

It's maddening, and my mind is ping-ponging from left to right. One minute I'm fantasizing about Tom pushing a pram through the park, walking next to him with a happy grin on my face. Then I dismiss all the "we're keeping the baby" options and never want to see him again.

"No, seriously, you have to think it through, of course. But tell me honestly, don't you believe this is a trick of the universe to get you guys back together?"

"Oh, stop it!" I shout. "Is it your purpose in life to get Tom and me back together? I'm sure there are nobler and more achievable missions than that."

We're in Eloise's living room. Her flat is the coziest place I know, full of cushions and candles. She grew up in a family of seven siblings and never had a bedroom of her own. This is her sanctuary, her refuge. This is what she's worked so hard for.

I've never had to do a side hustle in my life. If I needed money, I just asked Dad. For Eloise, it was very different.

Barbara De Smedt

Every weekend she was cleaning, washing up, or serving somewhere.

I sink into the protective softness of her beige sofa and lay my legs on the ottoman. I'm exhausted. The living room smells of fresh mint tea she just made for me. It's cooling off on the coffee table with a bowl of almond biscuits next to it.

"Admit that you're in love with him."

"No, I won't. I'll only admit that I have more feelings for him now that he no longer lives with me than when he did." Because that's the truth. When I saw Tom every day, he used to get on my nerves, but now I sometimes feel the same itch I felt at the beginning of our relationship.

"Would you prefer a LAT relationship?"

"No, I'd rather not *have* a relationship," I sigh. But it feels like I'm pretending and Eloise sees through me immediately.

"Come on, Julie, you have feelings for him. That's fine. Why do you act like that's a weakness?"

"Because it is. I don't have time for a relationship."

"That's ridiculous and you know it. In a few months' time, you'll graduate and finally be free of your time-consuming study. There's plenty of time."

She's right. It's hard to fool Eloise: she knows me better than anyone. There's more to it than just lack of time.

"All right, then. It's going to end badly anyway," I admit.

"Go on."

"I really tried. And you know it. I can see he's a great guy, and a talented one, too. With a gorgeous body."

"Yes?"

"But good things never last forever." I sigh. I don't know how to explain it to her. That I can't stand it when things start to feel too good between us, and that I'll start an argument whenever that happens. That Tom never responds to my fits and just waits for me to calm down, in silence. That I've pushed away every guy I've started a relationship with in the last few years.

"Why do you say that?"

"It's true, isn't it? Where else do you think the expression comes from?"

"Hm. Could it be that you just don't want it to go well?" says Eloise as she carefully studies her nails, green this week.

"Why wouldn't I want that?"

"Because then you would get too attached to him."

"Okay, Miss Psychologist, and that would be a problem because…?"

"Because of your mom's death, you're afraid to commit to people. If you let him come closer, he might hurt you and you don't want that. You don't want to get hurt, you don't want to be abandoned, so you try to avoid it by scaring him off yourself."

I swallow. Not that I haven't thought of it before, but when you hear the truth coming from someone else's mouth, it sounds louder, like a tune that you only hear in your own head first and then suddenly it roars through the speakers on a festival stage.

I never went to therapy after Mom died. Dad and I focused on picking up what little thread remained of our lives after the most important person had been torn out. Our sudden move to the city had devastated me. I missed my school, my friends, my village, but it had helped me to forget and start again. Like Dad, I was very good at tucking away what had happened in a place somewhere deep inside me. Locked away. Few people knew what had happened to my mom and I never talked about it. I didn't want to keep opening that wound. I often think about her though, and I only take off the necklace she gave me when I turned ten when I really have to. It's a gold pendant with a four-leaf clover—a bit childish, but I don't care. It's one of the few tangible things I have of her. Lost in thought, I play with the pendant until Eloise brings me back to the present.

"What are you thinking of?"

"My mom," I reply with a thick throat.

Eloise slides my mint tea towards me and takes a sip of hers. We didn't know each other yet when Mom died. I never talk about her to Eloise either. She only knows that she was hit by a car when I was a teenager and that I've been left alone with Dad ever since. She understands instinctively that I don't want to talk about the subject, so we sit there drinking in silence for a while.

"Maybe you have a point," I say finally. "You may be right about my relationship with Tom. Maybe I should give him a chance. But that doesn't mean I should have a baby with him, too."

Eloise sighs and puts her hand on my knee. "You know, Julie, you don't have to decide anything today. Tomorrow you'll know more, but think carefully about what you'll do with the baby. It's rather final."

"I can't put it back in, if that's what you mean," I grumble.

She chuckles, puts a biscuit in her mouth, and chews it.

I grin at my own remark and see that she tries to avoid my gaze. I feel a giggle coming on. Then she looks at my face and we both burst out laughing, biscuit crumbs flying around.

It feels so liberating to have a good laugh. For a moment, I have no more worries on my mind. No graduation stress, no baby stress, no Tom stress.

Then my phone rings.

I read "Anonymous" on the screen, and with every ring on my phone, the alarm bells in my head ring even louder.

Oscar

1997, One Year After the Fire

Like a stray cat, he licked his wounds. Battered and scarred forever, but still there. Weeds never die.

After the fire, everything had gone wrong. No, that wasn't true. It had already gone wrong *during* the fire. He shouldn't have gone back upstairs.

His injuries were so severe that he'd been in the hospital for months. His mother hadn't survived. He hadn't gone to her funeral, still being in a coma at the time. Not that he would have gone otherwise. Her funeral card was on the cabinet next to his bed; one of the nurses had put it there. He didn't dare throw it away immediately.

There were no visitors. Every time the door opened, he hoped to see Julie, but she never came. He couldn't wrap his head around that. Didn't the whole village know what had happened? Why didn't she visit him? The police were the only company he had. In the beginning, when he woke up, they were at his bedside every day. Again and again he had to tell them what had happened. That he woke up to the sound of breaking glass. That the smoke immediately caught him when he opened the door. That he walked downstairs and only then realized that the house was on fire and that soon enough everything would go up in flames. That the living room was already ablaze and there was nothing he could do for his mother, who had fallen asleep on the sofa, probably with a burning cigar between her fingers. That he almost hadn't made it out of the burning house.

They had believed it. What was there not to believe? His mother was known for her addiction. She'd probably drunk herself into a coma. Social services had recently visited the house and had ordered the juvenile court to place Oscar permanently out of his home.

It seemed like a done deal, and yet the police wanted to hear the story again and again. The inspectors always came in pairs, a man and a woman. He wasn't afraid of the man; he was an idiot, that much was obvious. But that woman... in her eyes he could read something that tickled under his skin. Not once did he see pity in them, although he looked quite pitiful with his bandaged limbs.

According to the doctors, he'd been very lucky; when he opened the front door, the fire had raced out, chasing the oxygen-rich air. In the process, it had hit the left side of his body hard. It didn't feel like luck. For the rest of his life, he would be disfigured in his left arm and leg, but his face had remained quasi-unharmed, with only superficial burns.

It shouldn't have gone like that. That had never been his intention. But he couldn't turn it back now.

The days were long and light, so bright that they hurt his eyes and skin, but the nights were even longer and his dreams dark and cold. He cried out in pain and frustration as the numerous hospital noises kept him awake. He cried every time he bent over on the toilet.

The nurses avoided his gaze and rarely chatted with "the white one." His singed hair had slowly grown back, as had his eyebrows, but his cold eyes remained without lashes and stayed empty for a long time, as if someone had forgotten to switch on the light. Oscar closed off from everyone and threw himself into his studies, as before, because despite the fact that Julie wasn't coming, his plan to impress her later with a doctor's degree was more alive than ever.

Julie
April 2005
13 Weeks Pregnant

It's too late.

One day you think you have a choice, the next it turns out the choice has been made for you without you ever being consulted about it. The cards were dealt and I was left holding the bag.

Strange things are happening to my otherwise rational mind. For example, when I just heard from the doctor that I was past the twelve-week mark and couldn't legally have an abortion in this country, I first felt relief because now I knew for sure that Tom was the father. Yes, that's right, not panic, but relief. A weight was lifted from my shoulders. After that came a feeling of resignation, like a mental shrug.

Where has my fighting spirit gone? Where is the anger, the feeling of powerlessness?

Am I relieved that *I* don't have to make the decision now? Or have I fooled myself this entire time and I actually do *want* the baby? It turns out there are different versions of Julie Meskens, not just the Julie who makes rational decisions and has a compartment for everything. Another Julie has taken over now, a Julie with different compartments. Someone who wants to be a mom and who has no problem turning her life upside down.

With an appointment for the baby's first ultrasound in my diary, I cycle home, wondering how I'm going to break the news to Dad. If I'm having such a hard time with this, it will be a disaster for him. I swallow a rising feeling of guilt and try to stay positive. He's going to be a grandpa. Maybe this is just what he needs to be happy again?

I'm faced with a fait accompli. My doctor also gave me a leaflet about adoption, which I accepted with a heavy heart. Is that an option?

The thoughts tumble over each other in my head as the spring sun warms my face. I love cycling in spring; normally it gives me a powerful feeling of freedom, as if I can handle anything, but this time I feel anything but strong. I need to think.

Oscar

1997

When he'd recovered sufficiently, he was placed in the system again, this time in a children's home, as there was no foster family available. He had his own room and adapted quietly, to the point that he had as good as melted into the white-painted walls of the house and nobody knew exactly when he was there or not. Being invisible was one of Oscar's talents.

As soon as he returned to his normal school routine, he started planning his trip. He had to see Julie and there was only one way to accomplish that: he had to take the bus to the village. And so he does.

***

That day, he leaves his schoolbooks in his room. His rucksack contains only the bare necessities, some food, and a flashlight. Like every day, he's dropped off at the school gate with the others. As soon as they enter the old building, Oscar slips away to the bathroom and hides in a cubicle. There he sits until he hears the school bell, followed by the rumbling of rows of teenagers rushing to their classrooms.

He waits, biting his nails, until it's quiet again. In the cubicle, all sorts of obscenities are written. He tries not to look at them. It smells of bleach and cabbage. Carefully, he comes out of his hiding place. There's no one there. He listens at the door that leads to the hallway, but there's no sound there, either. He jerks the door open and dashes down the corridor to the exit without looking back. He trusts that no one will see him and that he won't bump into a latecomer.

He's lucky. He runs as fast as his bad leg will let him until he's rounded the street corner. With his hands on his knees, he gasps for breath. Now he mustn't draw attention; he has to stay calm. He can already smell his freedom, if only for a moment. Out of breath, he arrives at the bus stop where he sits down on the bench, relieved.

He did it.

With a broad grin, he waits for the bus.

The drive to the village takes half an hour, time he uses to fantasize about the reunion with Julie. He'll wait for her at the school gate and approach her nonchalantly. It's been over a year since he last saw her. He imagines her coming down the stairs, her rucksack slung carelessly over her shoulder, her blonde hair in a high ponytail. She must be about sixteen. Would she have changed much? Oscar's heart beats in his throat and he swallows, his tongue feeling like sandpaper. He takes a sip of water from his bottle, wipes his mouth with the back of his good hand. Would she recognize him?

Most girls don't look at him. That's the downside of being invisible. He's become quite good at hiding his disfigurement. Only the limp will never really go away, according to the doctor. His joints were too badly burned.

He runs his good hand through his hair and looks outside where the landscape slowly changes. Vast meadows take over from the grey concrete. It should calm him down, but the closer he gets to the village, the tighter his fingers clench his knees. With every mile the bus travels, he gets closer to his old life, the life he hated so much. Still, he wants to see with his own eyes what his old house looks like now. What remains of it after the fire.

Just in time, he pushes the bell and the bus comes to a halt at the stop in the center of the village. He strolls past his old school and past the sports pitch where Julie and her friends used to play soccer. Nothing seems to have changed.

He's not alone on the street, so he keeps his face to the ground. Across the street, a woman he doesn't recognize is pushing a pram; a man is cutting the grass on the sports field with a small tractor.

He walks steadily until he reaches the country road that leads to his house. The road has always been in a bad state, but the potholes seem to have gotten even deeper. The plantain trees on either side do their best to make the place look less shabby, but to no avail. His shoes sink deep into the mud and with sucking noises they protest against this bad plan. He should have brought rubber boots with him.

Then the house looms up before him... or at least what's left of it. A gaping hole where the door used to be is framed by blackened bricks, all the windows are gone, and the roof consists only of a few broken beams sticking out in all directions like broken bones, with sheets of yellowish insulation material in between. It looks like pus.

He swallows.

This is the house that Grandpa once built with his own hands. Next to it is the burnt-out wreck of his mother's car. Tears sting behind his eyes and his stomach does something strange, but he pulls himself together. What's done is done; he can't change any of it. He carefully walks past the house to the garden at the back. The path to the garden shed is overgrown now that nobody has looked after it for over a year.

Since his mother's death, the house has been his, but he won't receive the title deeds until he's an adult. He's just turned seventeen. The thorns tear at his trousers but his gaze remains focused on the garden shed. It looks just like the last time he was here, although the green paint is already peeling off. Being here feels strange.

He exhales heavily, puts down his rucksack, and tries to push open the wooden door. No movement. He takes a step back and tries again, this time with his entire body, but the result is nothing more than some creaking and a sore arm. In the end, he tries running. With his strange limp he takes a few long strides and then throws the right side of his body against the door.

Success. He's inside.

He staggers for a moment; his eyes have to get used to the darkness. Inside the wooden construction, he discovers a lawnmower, a shovel, a whole bunch of rakes of different sizes, and a lot of trash. The boxes of empty bottles he'd hidden are still there. At the memory, his mouth contracts in a grim line. It doesn't look like anyone has been here since the fire.

He takes a few steps and knocks a cobweb out of his face. It smells like rotting leaves here. His hand hurts and he feels a cramp coming on, but he wants to be absolutely sure that the shelter is intact. He squats down against the back wall of the shed and shines his flashlight across the floor. He used to hide the entrance to his secret place by putting a bag of potting soil and some old flowerpots on the hatch. Everything is still in place. With his good arm, he drags the bag away, cursing as the black soil spills out through a crack. One by one, he drags the pots and then shines his flashlight over the cleared piece of wooden floor. He gets down on his knees and runs his hand over the boards until he feels the hole.

Got it.

He hooks his finger in it and pulls the hatch open until it can go no further. The metal flap is exposed now. He pulls the handle and, as he expected, this one opens easily. You can only lock it from the inside, he remembers.

He descends the stairs and reaches for the light switch with his hand, but the room remains dark so he switches on the torch again. Nothing has changed, it seems. He exhales with relief. He hadn't even noticed that he'd been holding his breath all this time.

Oscar stands in the middle of the shelter and looks around satisfied; this is his real home. Then he sits down on his mattress and, aided by the flashlight, leafs through the books he had left here. His old anatomy book is there, as well as the homework for science that he'd been working on during the week of the fire. He stretches out on the mattress and puts his good arm under his head.

Because he grows so fast, he's constantly hurting in his joints and in the places where his skin has been burnt. Not only is his body growing too fast, but his mind is, too. Oscar is no longer a child or even a teenager, if he ever was one. Slowly, the tension caused by his trip drains from his body and Oscar feels a rare sense of calm. Until now, he hadn't even noticed how tired he was. His transparent eyelashes fall down and his facial expression softens. He looks almost normal, like a carefree boy on an afternoon nap.

In his dream, he returns to the time before the fire, in his old room, before Nivens disappeared. He takes the soft rabbit in his arms and cradles him like a child.

"I'll protect you," he says. "Don't worry, you're safe with me." Then his surroundings change and he finds himself fishing at the edge of the pond on a beautiful spring day. His float sinks. He's caught something. Quickly, he reels in his line; he's caught a big fish. Excited, he focuses his gaze on the spot in the water's surface where his catch will emerge.

There! Yes! That's a big one.

Happy, he hauls in the line and pulls the fish to one side. Only then does he notice that this fish has no scales, but fur. A white coat. Oscar screams.

"Nivens!"

Desperately, he tries to get the rabbit off the hook. He lays it down on the mossy ground and checks for a heartbeat or any other sign of life but can't find one. Weeping, he lifts his friend up and holds him against his body, slumping against a tree.

"I'm sorry, Nivens, I'm so sorry," he repeats, over and over. As the sun sets, he digs a small grave. Gently, he lays Nivens in it. "Goodbye, friend. Be well." He turns to throw a handful of black earth on the white fur, but instead of the rabbit there is only a white piece of cloth in the grave. It's Julie's handkerchief...the one she gave him on New Year's Eve.

***

Oscar wakes up with a start and looks around confused. It takes him a few seconds to understand where he is and why. Damn, what a time to fall asleep. He checks his watch; it's already noon. He has to hurry or he'll miss Julie.

Quickly, he runs up the stairs of the shelter and closes the shutters. As fast as he can, he drags the torn sack of potting soil and the flowerpots back on top. On his way out, he snatches up his rucksack, which he left next to the door of the garden shed. He should be more careful. He turns his back on his old home and walks along the muddy path back to the village.

The image of Nivens on the fishhook stays with him. Just like the one of Julie's handkerchief, which had held her scent for so long. He should never have kept it.

Julie

15 Weeks Pregnant

I drive past a cute little shop selling baby clothes. The window is painted with white clouds and there's a teddy bear with a large four-leaf clover on its belly that reminds me of my mom.

Without thinking, I lock my bike and walk into the shop. There's a cream-colored carpet on the floor, and my shoes sink into it a little. I make myself small as I look around, nervously. The shop seems empty and my muscles relax. I sniff the air: a bit sweet, mixed with fresh wood. New furniture. I hadn't noticed the shop before; I suspect it has only opened recently.

I run my hands over a pale-yellow terrycloth sleeping bag that feels so soft my fingers only touch air. My imagination runs wild. I see Tom standing at the window of my flat with our baby in his arms. The baby is holding out his hand to me, crowing with laughter.

Suddenly, I get an irrepressible urge to go home and clear out the second bedroom in my flat. I could paint the walls yellow and put in white furniture.

My hands slip to my belly. Since I found out I was pregnant, it's suddenly starting to grow, as if it was waiting for me. For my permission.

Am I really going to do this?

Adoption seems so hard: carrying a child for nine months and then giving it up... My lip trembles at the thought. If I go through with the pregnancy now, and it looks like I will, I think I'll have no choice but to come to terms with my reality: I'm pregnant, and in six months' time I'll give birth to a fresh little baby. I just haven't decided whether I'll be able to cope on my own or whether I want Tom by my side. The conversation with Eloise keeps running through my head. Is it really my fear of losing Tom that keeps me pushing him away? If so, that would mean I really care for him; otherwise, I wouldn't be afraid of losing him. Would I?

"Can I help you?" Through my reverie, I didn't hear that a young woman appeared from a room at the back of the shop. She looks at me kindly.

"No, thank you," I stammer. I still have the sleeping bag in my hands and quickly put it back. "I'm just looking around a bit."

"No problem, those are nice," she says kindly. "If you're looking for something in particular, just say so." She bends over a box of feeding bottles to be unpacked.

I feel awkward, so I pretend to be interested in the prams. Why am I being so weird about this? If having a child is what's going to happen, then I'd better start acting like it now, right? Planning is one of my strengths, so why not use it? I'm at the source, and this woman doesn't know me and wants to help.

I turn around again and ask, "What would you say one absolutely needs to take care of a newborn?"

Surprised, she looks up from her work, her eyes sliding to my belly. "Is it for you?"

I nod and feel strangely proud.

"Congratulations! How far along are you?"

"Fifteen weeks," I reply with red cheeks.

***

Half an hour later, I'm back at my bike with a stack of glossy brochures that I stuff into my saddlebag. It may be a small step, but compiling a list of necessities gives me the feeling of getting a grip. I even feel happy, elated, with no sign of fear or doubt. I survived my mom's death when I was fifteen, and I'll survive this, too.

I get on my bike and want to ride off, but I can't. It's as if someone is holding the bike back with an invisible hand. Surprised, I get off again and put it up against the façade of a neighboring house to inspect it.

Damn, I have a flat tire. No, strike that. I have *two* flat tires. How is that even possible? I look around to see if there's any glass where I may have ridden through, but there's nothing. It must have happened earlier on the road without me noticing. That could well be it, with all my daydreaming.

With a deep sigh, I start pushing the bike; I can't fix it here and I don't want to leave it. That means walking. It's a disappointment, but I won't let it ruin my good mood. It's not yet dusk and I only live a few miles away. If I keep walking, I'll be home in an hour.

Oscar
1997

Opposite the secondary school is a small park where the kids sometimes hang out to secretly smoke. There, hidden behind a tree, Oscar stakes out the entrance. He feels a tingling in his stomach, like walking out of a shop without paying. He still doesn't know what to say to her. He mainly wants to know why she didn't come to visit him in the hospital.

When the school bell rings, he watches the first pupils stroll out of the gate. When he doesn't see her, doubt begins to cloud his mind. Perhaps she stays at school for lunch? He narrows his eyes to make sure he doesn't miss her.

A man walks by with a dog and the animal walks right up to Oscar, sniffing the ground with its nose. The man stops, looks at him strangely, and then walks on, the dog reluctantly following. All the while, Oscar keeps his eyes on the school, but after a few minutes, hardly any children come out anymore. After another five minutes, he knows he has waited in vain. He'll have to come back at four and that means he'll be late for his own bus.

Frustrated, he kicks a branch with his good leg, consequently almost knocking himself off-balance. Damn. Now what? He could go back to his shelter. Or he could go to the pond, maybe he'll manage to wash the potting soil off his trousers? No, stupid idea. Then he'll get green stains instead of brown ones. He could walk past Julie's house. He might as well wait for her there instead of at the school.

Yes, that's a much better plan. At her house, it's much quieter and they won't be disturbed.

He starts walking in a more cheerful mood. Julie's house is only a few blocks away; it's a small terraced building of red brick with a gabled roof. In the driveway is a bike shed where Julie used to park her bike with the wicker basket. Now, of course, it's at school.

As he approaches the house, he notices it looks different. He can't put his finger on it right away, but his white eyebrows furrow unconsciously. He can't sit and wait in front of the house, so he walks past it to take a closer look. There's a kid's bike in the driveway. That's weird. And one of the bikes has a toddler seat. That's even weirder. Maybe Julie's got a little brother or sister? He saunters out of the street and turns left so he can walk around the block and look at the house a second time. With a dark foreboding, he turns the corner. In the distance, he sees the red letterbox in front of the house again. Has it always been red? He doesn't remember.

There's a sudden movement at the house and Oscar comes to a halt. He quickly looks around, but there's no one on the road. He crosses the street, pretending to look for something in his rucksack, while peering at the house from under his eyelashes. Someone is coming out. No, some*thing* is coming out. A pram bounces gently off the threshold, followed by a young woman carrying a toddler.

She has a short black haircut and is young. Not Julie's mom, that's for sure. As she comes closer, Oscar quickly grabs a handkerchief from his rucksack and pretends to blow his nose noisily. When she's disappeared around the corner, he steps towards the house, glances over his shoulder to make sure no one can see him, and then stops in front of the letterbox.

The nameplate says "Vandeloo-Teniers." Not "Meskens," as it should say.

Black dots appear before his eyes. He blinks frantically but they keep coming. He has to sit down. He drops down next to the letterbox and tries to think, but his brain seems to be without power. Nothing comes at all.

Someone starts talking to him, but he can't see who it is; the black dots obscure his vision.

"You look a bit pale. Is everything all right?" It's a woman's voice, she's come out of the house next door and sounds worried. "Wait a minute, sit tight," she says when he doesn't reply, walking back to her front door.

She returns with an ice-cold can of cola, which she pushes into his hand.

"Here, drink. It will do you good."

He obeys and puts the can to his mouth, letting the sugar and caffeine do their work.

"Better, huh?" the woman says, and he nods meekly. He can't think, let alone talk.

"You've just missed Katrine. I think she's gone to the supermarket with the children."

Katrine? Who is she talking about? The black dots slowly fade away and Oscar tries to fit the pieces of the puzzle together. Julie doesn't live here anymore, he realizes.

"No," he replies hoarsely. "I actually came for Julie. Has she moved?" He still doesn't look at the woman.

"Julie? Oh, the Meskens family, you mean?"

Oscar nods.

"They moved last year, which was quite a drama. That poor woman. They were such sweet people. He was sometimes rather surly. At least, that's how he came across to me. She was so sweet; eccentric though, with those long skirts. Nice girl, too, that Julie. A tomboy. I think they moved to the city, but they didn't leave an address, so I don't know for sure..."

The woman prattles on while Oscar gets up and drains the can. He's heard only one thing: Julie has moved away.

Away from him. He crumples the can with his good hand and gives it back to the woman.

"Thanks for the Coke," he says in a low voice, his face turned towards the pavement.

"You're welcome, you're welcome. Are you sure you don't want to come in?" she asks, but he's already moving on. He throws his rucksack over his shoulder, his hands clenched in his pockets. He has to leave this place as soon as possible. There's no reason to stay any longer in this godforsaken village. Not one.

Julie's gone. She's moved away, without so much as a word of farewell. She has abandoned him.

Julie

17 Weeks Pregnant

"Look, see that slit here? And there? That's not from glass. Your tires were punctured."

"Punctured? What do you mean, with a knife or something?"

Tom puts down the tire and looks at me with furrowed brows. "Where did you say this happened?"

"In front of the new children's shop on the Vaartstraat. My bike was parked against the façade, and when I tried to leave, the tires were flat. I hadn't been in there for more than half an hour."

"And you didn't see anyone?"

"No, but I wasn't paying attention. I was inside."

"What were you doing there anyway?"

"Nothing. Just looking. And talking."

"About?"

"Is that important now? I mean, shouldn't we go to the police? This is vandalism!"

"I think so. And I also think you should tell them about the phone calls. Have you had any more?"

I shrug. "A few. Would there be a connection?"

"I don't know, but I think you should tell them. If you want, we can go together so you don't have to ride on this piece of shit." He's referring to the rusty spare bike I've been using ever since.

"Okay," I say and grab my handbag.

***

An hour and a half later, we're back home. The woman who spoke to us at the police station was very friendly, although she immediately told us not to have high expectations. The phone calls were not a threat in itself, so the police couldn't do much about them. They would, however, investigate further both the punctured tires and the scratches on Tom's car.

"Funny that nobody else in the street has reported vandalism, eh?" remarks Tom.

We're in my living room again. Since I told him I wanted to keep the baby, we've talked on the phone every day. We still haven't decided how to proceed, but knowing he's here for me is enough for now. As scared as I am of sharing my life with Tom, I'm even more scared of raising the baby alone…which isn't an option for him anyway: he wants to be a father.

"Yes, that is indeed strange," I reply. I stretch my legs and play with the pendant around my neck. "But as the policeman said, there's little chance that my bike and your car were damaged by the same person. We were just unlucky."

He grunts in agreement, but I don't think he's entirely reassured. His eyes follow my hand.

"Is there any meaning behind this necklace of yours?"

Now that I'm pregnant, I've been seeing Mom's face more frequently. I miss her so much. All those important moments I spent alone: my first kiss, my first boyfriend, my first heartbreak. They weren't things I could talk about with my dad. Although I know he loves me, he's not much of a talker.

When I turned eighteen, I bought this flat from my mom's estate. I submerged myself in my studies and followed The Great Plan step by step. Ever since I was little, I wanted to become a veterinarian. In summer, I could spend hours rescuing beetles and other unfortunate creatures floundering helplessly in the paddling pool in our garden. With a branch or a leaf, I would bring the victims to dry land and stay with them until their wings had dried enough to continue their journey. Together with Dad, I built nesting boxes that we hung on the trees. In spring, he would lift me up high and I would peek through the roof of the boxes to see the little baby chicks.

My mom was my biggest fan.

"She was so proud of you, her clever daughter," my dad told me more than once. And now I wouldn't only graduate without her, but also have my first child.

"It was my mom's," I say.

"Oh, sorry."

"That's okay."

"It must be hard for you to go through this without your mom being here," he says.

Oh, sweet Tom... I feel my eyes getting moist and put my head on his shoulder.

"Tom?"

"Yes?"

"Will you move in with me?"

Oscar
1997

Oscar notices only too late that Rutger is waiting for him in the bathroom. He pushes Oscar into a cubicle, closes the door, and holds him down, his face pressed against the wall.

"I know you want it, freak. You like it, don't you? Say it! Say it!" hisses the older and stronger boy, clasping Oscar's neck with one arm and pulling down his trousers with the other.

Oscar wants to scream, but all the air seems to be squeezed out of his lungs and he feels tears running down his cheeks.

"Say it!" grunts Rutger again, in his ear. He stinks of greasy hair, sweat, and rotten teeth.

While he's suppressing the pain, Oscar answers, "Yes, Rutger, I like it." What else could he do?

It didn't stop with that one time. From the moment Oscar had come to live in the foster home, he'd attracted Rutger's attention. No matter how hard he tried not to be noticed, he always found him. At night, he was afraid to go to sleep and lay there with his ears pricked up, listening for someone coming to his bed. He had blue circles under his eyes and fell asleep increasingly often in class. His grades plummeted. If any of his teachers had asked him at the time if he was okay, he would have talked. If anyone in the home had taken him aside or wondered why he washed his hands all the time, he would have told them. But nobody asked. Oscar was alone in the world and his hell only became more bearable the day Rutger left the home, when he became of age.

Oscar often had nightmares. He dreamed about the fire, about his mother, and about Rutger. Sometimes he dreamed about Julie. He had resigned to the fact he'd never been able to count on his mother; she'd had her punishment anyway. He would take care of Rutger, too. But that Julie had betrayed him made his blood boil. First, she'd made him think she saw him, that he meant something to her, and then she had coldly abandoned him the moment he felt most alone. What kind of person does something like that? Of all people, she was the last person he would have expected this from, which is why he hated her the most. Not only had she not come to see him in the hospital, she had also moved. Disappeared. Gone. Without a single word.

Even during the day, he thought of her. Every day his hatred grew like an ink stain spreading on blotting paper. He began to have fantasies about her in which he was the one in charge. He imagined how he would take revenge on her. Sometimes he would threaten her with a knife, sometimes his arms would hold her down in the village pond, sometimes his hands would wrap around her throat. In all scenarios, he was the one in control, and the climax was the moment he saw the look in her eyes change from incomprehension to recognition and then fear.

***

Oscar failed to recover at school. His teachers always caught him drawing or just staring out the window during class. He spent his breaks in the bathroom, constantly washing his hands until they were red and rough and the scars were glaring.

He was forced to repeat his year and change schools, but his supervisors had no idea what to do with him. They were relieved when he suggested he wanted to become a nurse. That was the closest thing to his dream of becoming a doctor. A life with Julie was now the last thing on his mind.

He had a much better plan.

Julie

20 Weeks Pregnant

"No, Tom! No! Put me down!" I scream, right into his ear. We look like a couple in a romantic movie.

"Hey, whoa! Calm down, I'm not deaf," he says in a feigned calm voice as he carries me through the door to my own flat. I'm quite muscular, with a reasonable belly by now, so I'm a lot heavier than I look. He's not a tough guy, so he stumbles into the living room. He carefully sets me down on the wooden floor, which looks like gold in the sunlight coming in through the sliding windows of the balcony.

We spent the whole day driving back and forth from Tom's flat to mine. Starting next week, his place will be rented out completely furnished, so we only had to move his most important things: boxes of CDs, records, and books about music. And a small suitcase with some clothes.

His most precious possession runs like a white fury from one corner of the room to the other, completely mad with excitement about her new home: Dolly, Tom's super-cute cat. The scene makes me daydream. I can just imagine how our child will play and crawl around here.

Our daughter.

Last week, we went to the gynecologist together for the first time and had an ultrasound. It's a girl. It was indescribable to see her move around in my belly; it makes it all so much more real.

"Hey, daydreamer, what's on your mind? I asked if you want to go out for dinner to celebrate us moving in together. Or are you too tired?"

I snap out of my thoughts, notice that my stomach is rumbling, and rub my belly. "Hm, hungry but tired indeed. Maybe we can order pizza?"

"Pizza it is," says Tom, giving me a peck on the cheek as he opens the patio doors and pulls his phone out of his pocket. The cool evening air finds its way through the flat. I look at him, endeared, as he orders two pizzas, one margherita and one Hawaiian, with sweeping hand gestures, and he insists twice that the courier must press the bottom bell. Dear Tom. Dear quiet, responsible, hard-working, and insanely talented Tom. I could've done a lot worse.

After the phone call, he stays on the balcony for a while to keep an eye on his car. That's something he can't let go of yet.

***

When the doorbell rings, Dolly has flopped down on my lap. The poor animal is exhausted from her eventful day. Just like me.

Tom runs down the stairs and returns a moment later with two steaming pizza boxes and a shiny bag with white and yellow stripes.

"Hey, what have you got there?" I say in surprise.

"I don't know, it was placed at the front door."

"That wasn't there before, was it? Who's it for?"

He puts the pizzas in the kitchen and then dangles the bag in front of me, which has "Julie" written on it. Curious, I take it from him and peek inside. It contains a beautifully wrapped gift and I recognize the logo.

"It's from that new children's shop where I want to open our baby registry," I say, happily surprised. The package feels soft; the rustling has piqued Dolly's interest and she wants to stick her nose in.

"No way," says Tom, plucking her off my lap.

I pry open the wrapping paper and gasp when I see what's inside.

"Oh! It's that sleeping bag that I liked so much!"

I see that Tom doesn't understand so I give him the short version of my visit to the shop.

"Who is it from?" he asks.

"If I have to guess, I'll go for Eloise," I say. I hold the bag upside down and a card falls out. I read what it says and laugh. "You're good at pretending, too! How did you know about that sleeping bag?"

"What do you mean?"

"All right, you can stop now. Come here," I say endearingly. How sweet of him to surprise me like that.

Tom takes the card from my hands and reads what it says aloud: *For our baby.* He frowns and looks at me strangely. "Julie, this isn't from me."

"What do you mean it's not from you?" He seems to mean it.

"No, I don't know anything about it. Sorry."

Now it's my turn to frown.

"So then, who is it from?"

Oscar
1998

Finally, Oscar turned eighteen, which meant he could live on his own. He received a small allowance, which seemed generous to him, since he'd never owned any money in his life. The first thing Oscar did was change his name, not only because it was part of his plan, but it was also symbolic for him. The Oscar before the fire no longer existed. He would reinvent himself and, like a phoenix, rise again from the ashes. His life lay before him, not behind him. There lay only pain and sorrow, feelings he never wanted to feel again. Others had determined what happened to him for long enough, and that time was now gone. He took the reins of his life in his hands.

***

With the form in front of him, he sits at the desk of his rented room. It's in the middle of the busy city center, close to the nursing home where he can work as a caretaker after his internship.

It's simple work. He washes the elderly, brings food around, and changes the sheets. His colleagues have quickly realized that Oscar is no talker, but indeed a hard worker. Besides, here nobody bats an eye when he washes his hands so frequently; everyone does it.

Oscar prefers to take care of the demented elderly who can't talk anymore, that way he doesn't have to say anything. With the others, he just pretends to answer; most of them have such bad hearing that they don't understand a word and just nod their heads.

His heart is in his throat when his pen moves across the paper and he writes down his new name: Floris De Wachter. Six more months and Oscar Plessers will be a ghost of the past. Patience is all he needs. He puts the completed form in an envelope and puts it in his sports bag.

Like every morning, Oscar goes to the gym. He'd already started doing this at the foster home to make his body stronger. For his job, it's important that he builds up enough strength in his arms to be able to lift the elderly.

After showering, he gets dressed and stands in front of the man-sized mirror. Slowly, his physique is changing and he sees that he's getting bigger and stronger by the day. He rolls his biceps and watches with satisfaction as the edge of his t-shirt tightens around his upper arms. The thin fabric defines his pecks, and his jeans hang low on his hips. When he pulls his t-shirt up a bit, his abs are revealed. White hairs trace from his navel to his crotch. Then he brings his face closer to the mirror and studies his eyelashes, his eyebrows, his pale skin. He's too recognizable; he needs more than a new name to be reinvented.

He throws his bag over his shoulder and steps into the cool morning, his shift not starting until late afternoon. More than enough time to do some research at the nearby library where he can access the Internet.

Once inside, he drops his gym bag on the floor and starts up the computer. It's quiet in the large room. Nobody's interested in him or in what he's doing. Two minutes later, he's already found what he was looking for.

Now all he has to do is buy the necessary things at the chemist's and then phase one of his plan will be as good as done.

Julie
26 Weeks and 2 Days Pregnant

Dolly squirms around my legs while I admire the small bedroom that I used as storage before. It's the summer holidays and Tom is busy painting. The room has turned a pale yellow, and on the wall where the cot will be, he's painted a smiling frog with a sunflower in his hand. Because yes, the man can draw, too.

The better I get to know Tom, the more convinced I am that I've made the right decision, although sometimes the fear of what's to come squeezes my throat. Then I get grumpy and sarcastic and try to get Tom to admit that it was all a big mistake. That he doesn't love me and doesn't want a baby, especially not with me. He never gives in and stays by my side like a stubborn donkey. The harder I try to push him away, the tighter his grip becomes. At other times, I spit in his face that he'll never be able to support us with his teacher's salary, although I know very well that he can. Then, I scream that he's only staying with me to fill the emptiness he feels, to finally be part of a family. Something he's never known. Not once does he allow himself to be swayed, never does he yell back. He waits patiently for the fit to pass and then takes me in his arms while my tears wash the frustration from my body. As soon as I can breathe normally again, I tell him I'm sorry, I didn't mean it like that. I don't have to tell him that; I read in his eyes that he knows, but I do it anyway.

Apart from my own fears, there are so many other uncertainties. Tom's parents have reacted quite neutrally to the news of the pregnancy and have asked if we need anything to decorate the nursery. From their furniture shop, of course. According to Tom, it's their way of congratulating us. His older brother and sister have no children. Their reaction is slightly warmer than that of their parents. They don't seem to mind that he takes credit for the first grandchild. Tom's relatives all seem to be hard workers. People of few words who mean well. None of them condemn the pregnancy, but none of them are jumping for joy either. Tom's fine with it, so I am too.

My dad's reaction on the other hand... He couldn't believe that I let this happen. That I didn't consider other options, such as crossing the border to the Netherlands to have an abortion. That I'm risking my future for a man I barely know. I had hoped he would change his mind once he met Tom, but the opposite turned out to be true.

I suggested going for a meal at Cleo's, a restaurant I had frequented with Dad on the few occasions we did see each other. It was a catastrophe; no matter how hard I tried to keep the conversation going, Dad wouldn't budge. To him, Tom was the enemy, and nothing and nobody could make him change his mind. Even their shared love of folk music didn't soften him up. I didn't want to make a scene in the restaurant, although he deserved it. I love my dad, but that night a part of me hated him. Of course, I understand where his anger comes from. He's angry with himself; he thinks he's failed Mom because my life isn't going according to plan. His plan, which a few months ago was also my plan.

After half an hour of icy silence, Tom and I left the restaurant and I haven't heard from Dad since.

It doesn't leave me cold. Dad is the only family I have. His parents are no longer alive and Mom's relatives have been living in Greece for years. It tears me apart, as if I have to choose between my own dad and the father of my child. That's not a fair choice.

"Wait until the baby's born," Tom reassures me. "Then he'll come around. You'll see."

I just hope he's right. If Mom were still here, she would talk some sense into him. I swallow the rising grief and put the baby rompers I bought with Eloise in the top drawer of the wooden dresser—a gift from the Van de Velde furniture shop, of course.

The mystery of the anonymous parcel remains unsolved. After Tom had convinced me that he really didn't buy it, we thought of Eloise, but she didn't know anything either. Besides, it said *for our baby*, which only added to the mystery. I called the shop and asked if they could tell me who had bought the sleeping bag, but the woman only remembered being called by a man. She was busy with a customer when I called, so I didn't want to bother her any further.

"Could it be an attempt by my dad to make up for something?" I had suggested to Tom.

"But what about that note?"

"Maybe the shop made a mistake? Since the order was made by telephone?"

We left it at that.

***

I'm lying on my bed to get some rest. It's Friday afternoon and Tom's at an exhibition in town. Tonight he's performing at Billy's and, if I want to accompany him, I really need to take a nap. Relaxed, I stretch my body out on top of the cool sheets. My belly is enormous; I'm entering the third trimester and can't imagine that I'll get any bigger. I turn onto my side and put a pillow between my legs, hoping to find a comfortable position. I tuck my fears and doubts under the sheets and slowly let the soft hum of the ventilator lull me to sleep.

And right then, it starts again. Since that one time a few months ago, the day after Eloise's party, I hadn't heard it again. Until now, on this hot afternoon, when the words storm back into my consciousness, filled with rage.

"Dirty whore! I hate you!" I hear.

My heart is hammering in my chest.

It sounds close by and from someone who means every syllable passionately.

Oscar

1999

Oscar's metamorphosis was complete. Everyone now knew him as Floris De Wachter, the tall, quiet man with the pale skin. He shaved his head and dyed his eyelashes and eyebrows. He had no friends, nor did he need any. He had graduated as a nurse and filled his days with work and sports until he felt ready for his next step.

***

He finds a spot in the library where no one can look at his screen and logs in. His heart is hammering in his throat. What if he can't find her? What if she's moved to another country? He realizes that he's been putting off this moment out of fear, not out of his desire for perfection.

His fingers tremble and leave clammy marks on the keyboard. He begins to type. Seeing her name in black letters on the white background of the screen increases his excitement: Julie Meskens.

The cursor flashes expectantly. He takes a deep breath and presses enter. Immediately, he sees several results. He lets his eyes flash across the screen at lightning speed and lands on a link to the website of the local university. Faculty of Veterinary Medicine. He smiles.

Of course.

He can't believe it. She's so close. So close. Only a few miles from the chair he's sitting on. Finally, after all these years of preparation, he's moving on to phase two. He will see her again.

He takes a week's leave from the retirement home where he works and goes to the university every day. It will only be a matter of time before he sees her.

The hours he spends there, he's tossed to and fro between past and present. Again and again he sees himself on that cold February day in front of Julie's old house, sinking to his knees, all hope lost, with only a can of Coke to keep him upright. Those days are over. No one will ever hurt him like that again. Not his mother, not Rutger, and certainly not Julie.

After two days, his patience is rewarded and he sees her leave the building and walk towards the bike shed. For a moment he forgets to breathe. It's a warm day and she's wearing a short denim dress and sneakers. She slips her shoulder bag into the basket on her handlebars and squats down to undo her lock. He stands so close to her that his whole body tingles with the built-up tension. Again, his feelings swing to and fro like a pendulum, the attraction so great that he almost steps towards her to greet her. But then, suddenly, the urge to drag her off her bike takes over, so overwhelmingly that he can barely contain himself. That she looks so beautiful and carefree makes him want to beat her up even more, to scream in her face what she's done to him. She has left him. She abandoned him in the hospital. He wants her to know what a bitch she is and that he will make her life a living hell.

Just like his life has been. And still is.

How can she stand there fiddling with her bike as if nothing had happened? How could she leave him hanging when he lost everything?

His plan almost falls apart; his growing hatred takes over from his common sense. Fortunately, she rides off before he can do anything stupid. He urges himself to calm down and starts his car. There's no point in ruining everything with an impulsive action; he's come too far for that. So he follows her.

***

He follows her everywhere, as often as his work schedule permits. Soon he gets to know her friends, of whom Eloise turns out to be a regular. He also follows her to Billy's, but never enters the café. It's crucial that she doesn't see him, although she would never recognize him.

Slowly, phase three of his plan begins to take shape and he gains insight into what he needs to make it work. He decides that a job in a retirement home can't offer him enough opportunities; he needs to work in a hospital. So, he enrolls in a part-time nursing course. This temporarily gives him less time and freedom, but Oscar knows that he has to think not in the short term but in the long term.

He has time. And patience.

In summer, he sees her sitting on her balcony, her bare feet on the table and a glass of wine beside her. In winter, he sees her slip on her bike on her way home and hears her cursing when she falls down.

He won't be rushed; his body no longer reacts when he sees her. She's become a mere project, a prey. Like a fox lying patiently in front of a rabbit hole, Oscar waits for the perfect moment. He knows that, one day, his patience will be rewarded.

Julie

26 Weeks and 2 Days Pregnant

How I love to watch Tom when he plays the piano. When he does, it's like he radiates a light that comes from somewhere in his soul.

Billy's is packed tonight and I feel as proud as a peacock with my big belly. I can't wait to hold my daughter in my arms. Will she be as musically gifted as her dad? And sensitive? Or will she be a rational doer, like me?

Eloise is outside smoking and I'm alone at a table. After his session, Tom comes up to me with two glasses of Coke that are tinkling with ice cubes.

"Hello, beautiful," he says, kissing me full on the mouth. I feel even prouder. When he came back from the exhibition earlier, I didn't want to tell him about the shouting right away. I thought it might make him nervous being so close to a live session. I realize that I can't put it off any longer now and tell him what I heard this afternoon.

"And you have no idea where it came from?" he asks, worried.

"No, it must have come from one of the neighbors because there was no one on the street."

"Do you think it came from the new upstairs neighbor?"

"I don't know. The first time I heard it was a while ago when you weren't even living with me. I think the flat above was still empty then."

"Have you actually seen these people yet?"

"The upstairs neighbors? Once, maybe, in the hall downstairs. You?"

"I've seen a man come out, but no one else," says Tom, frowning.

"Hm, there's only one name on the bell. I think it's a guy living alone, so he wasn't yelling at his wife. Maybe he was on the phone?"

"Yes, possibly. Must be a real nice guy. He wasn't shouting at you, was he? I find it strange that it never happens when I'm home."

Of course, I'd thought of that, too. It did seem to be directed at me, strange as that sounds, but the idea of a complete stranger shouting at me, a pregnant woman, from another flat is absurd, isn't it? Although, our new upstairs neighbor could just as well be a madman shouting at a chimera. Anything is possible.

"Maybe we should invite that guy over," I suggest. "Because of you moving in and the baby, we haven't been very social."

"Good idea. And then we'll invite Eloise, too. Who knows, he might be a desirable bachelor," he laughs.

"What's that? I heard my name. What are you talking about?" Eloise calls from the terrace, her glass of wine in one hand and a Cartier cigarette in the other.

"Nothing," I say. "Just that you look beautiful tonight."

Tom and I look at each other conspiratorially and she rolls her eyes.

"Tsss, couples."

Oscar

2005

4 Months Before The Day

Oscar graduated as a nurse and found a job in the hospital near the university. In his spare time, he researched different types of anesthetics he could easily obtain and fantasized about his moment of glory.

Since he'd seen Julie stagger out of Billy's several times, each time in the arms of another guy, he was even more disgusted with her. He'd been so wrong about her. Unbelievable. The waiting was getting harder every day, but the right moment hadn't yet presented itself. He'd already taken enough risks by following her. That hadn't always gone unnoticed, and she was smart enough to take a taxi home if she had one too many.

When he found out that she had a boyfriend, he had gone crazy. It wasn't the first time he had seen her with a man, but those guys were always gone as quick as they had come. This one, though, kept showing up at her door with his ugly Golf. She hopped through life as if she had nothing to worry about. It made him furious. The whore.

***

That afternoon, after all this time, his luck finally turned. He was driving past her flat at a walking pace when he saw a sign that read FOR RENT hanging in the window of the flat above hers. His body began to radiate from head to toe. The time had come. This was the opportunity he had been looking for.

All these years, he hadn't spent a penny too much so that he would have money for when it was needed. His gym membership and his car were the only luxuries he had allowed himself. Now the time had come to use his savings to pay the flat deposit.

The estate agent was delighted with the new tenant: a quiet young man who worked in a hospital and immediately paid the deposit and first month's rent. He didn't even murmur about the pitiful state the previous tenant had left the flat in.

"So, just sign here, please." He slid the contract under Oscar's nose.

Gracefully, Oscar signed on the dotted line with "Floris De Wachter."

"Welcome, Mr. De Wachter, and good luck with your new home." The man grinned at him, his hand outstretched. And that was that.

Oscar made sure that Julie was never at home when he was working in the flat. He didn't want to lose his chance. Only a few days after he'd moved in did he meet her in the hall on his way out.

***

She's so close he can smell her, a sweet scent of freshly laundered clothes and a hint of deodorant. She nods at him absently and says hello.

He answers something unintelligible, keeping his gaze down and his big body pressed against the wall.

She turns around, sweeps her sleek hair over her shoulder, and carries her shopping up the stairs.

He doesn't want to, but he looks anyway. At her legs, her ankles, her tiny feet with the painted toes encased in gold-colored sandals. She's wearing a black dress. He wants to grab her ankle, drag her down the stairs, and shout in her face what she can't see: him, Oscar.

But not yet. No. Not yet. He isn't ready yet.

He turns around and steps outside. He has to prepare. He has much work to do.

Julie

29 Weeks and 2 Days Pregnant
2 Days Before The Day

Something's wrong. I feel it the minute he comes in.

"Hey, how did it go?" I ask. He had a piano lesson at a student's home.

He shrugs and kicks off his shoes. His brown eyes tell me he's hurt.

"Is everything okay?" I try again.

"I don't know. Better just leave me alone a bit. I'm going to take a shower," he says. I look at him, perplexed. I was just chopping tomatoes for the salad and, for want of another plan, I continue doing so. My anticipation of a pleasant evening with Tom is slightly dampened. He's gone so often, giving piano lessons, that I'm alone more than I expected. Not that I mind having my flat to myself a bit, but I don't really have much to do since I graduated and I decline Eloise's invitations to go out. Too tired.

I finish dinner and am about to drag the table out to the balcony when he comes back in, freshly showered and a little more cheerful.

"I'll do that. You can't carry heavy loads," he says, putting the table and chairs on the balcony. I kiss him on the cheek and check the oven where rosemary potatoes are roasting. Then I tie my hair into a high ponytail with an elastic band I wear around my wrist. It's another balmy summer evening and it's sticky hot in the duplex flat, so we like to eat outside where we can enjoy the beautiful view. I mix some more dressing through the salad and put the wooden bowl on the laid table.

"Dinner is served!" Playing house is my new favorite game.

"Let me serve you, mademoiselle," says Tom, playing along.

I smile as he fills my plate, but he can't fool me with his nonchalant attitude. Tom's an open book. Something's clearly off, but if he's decided not to talk about it, I don't want to force him.

"Have you seen Dolly?" he asks lightheartedly. That clever cat has discovered she can jump from the bathroom window onto the roof behind it, and since then she's been out and about every day. She usually comes back in the evening, but she's not here yet.

"She'll be here soon; hunger works like a magnet on her," I say.

He nods, but his thoughts are clearly elsewhere. What's bothering him? I decide to distract him and change course.

"You know, we should start talking about names for the baby. It's coming closer now."

Tom's face brightens immediately. "Yes, I was thinking about that just now. The pupil I was teaching this afternoon is called Thirza. That's a cool name, isn't it?"

I don't know what to say. Thirza? What kind of name is that? "Oh. Um. That's special, Thirza," I stammer.

"You don't like it," he says, a little disappointed.

"I don't think it's ugly either," I admit. "But I was thinking more along the lines of Emma or Mila or something..." I continue hesitantly. When I say the names out loud, I realize they're not very original, but they don't have to be, do they? I like simple names.

"Um..." says Tom.

"Zoë?" I try.

"Well..."

"Eline? Emily? Tess?"

He smiles and puts his hands up in the air. "Okay, okay, I think we have a little difference of opinion. Not that they aren't beautiful names, but you clearly like modern names and I don't. For me, a name has to mean something, or convey a certain power."

"Like Tom?" I say teasingly.

"No. Maybe that's why."

I nod. Another one of our many differences, and probably not the last. I'm a morning person; Tom's a night owl. I drink coffee; he drinks tea. I like sweet; he likes salty. I like a drink now and then; he avoids alcohol altogether. While I blurt out everything that pops into my head, he only opens his mouth when he thinks what he has to say is worthwhile, which rarely happens. My arguments are loud; his are quiet. And I could go on like this for a while. On the other hand, our characters do complement each other. His kind personality softens my sharp edges when necessary, and that's okay. We share the conviction not to eat animals and have the same political preferences, fortunately. And we frequent the same pub, of course.

Suddenly, a name pops into my head. A strong name, powerful. Classic, yet modern. A name that is very meaningful, for me that is. I take a sip of water, put my cutlery neatly on my plate, and wipe my mouth with a napkin. For a moment, I hesitate; this is quite an exciting moment. I'm going to expose myself a little. I let out a small cough.

"Tom, what do you think of Hannah?"

He looks at me questioningly. "Hannah..." he repeats, letting the name roll through his mouth, tasting it. I can see from his face that he's pleasantly surprised and I feel my neck muscles relax.

"How did you come up with that? I like it," he says.

"It was my mom's name," I reply, swallowing a lump.

He takes my hands in his across the table. "You talk so little about her. What was she like? Do you look like her?" he asks warmly.

"No, I'm my dad all over, but I think I got most of my character from her." My mom was a beautiful woman, tall and athletic, with dark curly hair and eyes the color of dark chocolate. When the accident happened, she was in her early forties, far too young. There wasn't a trace of silver in her hair. Like me, my mom loved nature and walked everywhere barefoot. She was the antithesis of my dad, but perhaps that was precisely what attracted them to each other. Whereas Mom cycled through life carefree and singing, Dad was constantly afraid of what was to come.

"You're living now, Jean-Pierre," Mom would say. "Not in the past, not in the future. Try to enjoy it." She never said it as a judgment, but rather as loving advice. She was my example, my sounding board, my everything.

"You miss her," Tom says, noticing I've fallen silent, not my usual behavior.

"Yes, increasingly more. I miss her now and will miss her even more when the baby comes."

He squeezes my hands. "I know I'm not much of a talker and you find that hard sometimes, but know that I'm here for you, whatever happens. For you and for the baby. I think Hannah is a perfect name."

I blink away the haze before my eyes and smile. "So we have a name?"

"We have a name," he laughs. He leans over the table and kisses me. Dusk is falling and mosquitoes are finding their way to our warm bodies, so we light a citronella candle to enjoy the outdoors as long as possible.

"Dolly!" I call a little later, rattling a box of cat food. "Dolly! Come on!"

"She'll come. Just leave the bathroom window ajar," says Tom. "It's a cat. They usually land on their feet."

"Just like us," I say.

"Just like us," he agrees, but I can see from his eyes that he's still a bit off his game. Why won't he confide in me?

Oscar

2005

9 Weeks Before The Day

When Oscar received the title deeds to the house after his eighteenth birthday, he had great plans for it, but both his studies and his work took up all his time. To his frustration, he had to keep putting off the repair work—until a year ago, when he could finally start.

First, he made the house windproof. He boarded up the door and the windows and repaired the roof. That was the hardest job. Then he started on the air-raid shelter. His excitement grew as the room took shape. Every spare moment he had, he labored. He did everything on his own, so the work progressed slowly, but he didn't mind. He adjusted the metal hatch, removed the lock on the inside, and replaced it with a sturdy bolt on the outside.

Just a few more weeks. Julie still had no idea who her new upstairs neighbor was. She didn't suspect anything. He didn't feel the need to follow her anymore now that he lived right above her. On the contrary: he tried to avoid seeing her as much as possible. To his relief, she hadn't yet come up to welcome him… which proved once more how egocentric she was.

***

That morning, for the first time in ages, he feels the need to see her again. He rises early and sneaks out of the building into his parked car. There, he waits for her to come out. Inside the car, it's chilly from the cool night. There's glistening dew on the grass of the pasture, but the sun's out, too, and he feels its warmth glowing on his skin through the car window.

Then the front door opens, and out she comes. She's wearing one of her many floppy dresses, a jean jacket over her shoulders. He watches her unhook her bike and frowns.

What the...?

He stares at her in disbelief as she gets on her bike and rides away.

This can't be true.

A lump is clearly visible under her dress. Julie is pregnant. Pregnant!

As soon as she reaches the end of the street, Oscar jumps out of his car and runs upstairs. He paces back and forth in his flat with his hands on his shaven head. He's out of his mind with rage; his plan can't move forward like this. He could never hurt a baby.

Frustrated, he starts scrubbing his hands, again and again until they start to bleed. He feels so powerless that he wants to scream.

"Whore!" he shouts. "Bitch!" Tears prickle behind his eyes.

Now what? Distraught, he runs downstairs again. He starts his car and drives to his old house. There he starts demolishing the burnt kitchen with a sledgehammer. In his mind's eye, he lets the hammer hit Tom's head and sees the blood squirting around.

"You bastard! Julie is mine, only mine!" Harder and harder he splinters the wood, until he can do no more.

Sweaty and exhausted, he lowers the hammer. He'll get that guy. He grins at the memory of Tom's face, that time when he stepped out unsuspectingly and confidently crossed the street, until he saw what his car looked like: full of scratches.

What Oscar will do with Julie, now that she's pregnant, he doesn't know yet, but he's confident that he'll figure out a new plan if he's patient, and that calms him down.

Julie

29 Weeks and 3 Days Pregnant
1 Day Before The Day

"Whore?" I say in surprise. "On your car?"

Tom nods. "On my windshield, written with a marker. It came off easily. I didn't want to bring it up right away yesterday, and then we had such a good time when we talked about the baby names."

So that was why he seemed so distracted yesterday. When he'd left for one of his piano lessons, he'd found his car vandalized again; no scratches this time, but the word "whore" written on it. It gives me the creeps.

He's just got home from yet another private lesson and I've been phoning nurseries all afternoon. Even though it would be more than a year before Hannah would go to the nursery, I have to put her on the waiting list today.

"I wish you'd told me right away," I say, worried. "Especially after the shouting I heard. You took a picture for the police, didn't you?"

"Yes, but you heard what they said about the scratches and your punctured tires, so I don't see the point in reporting it again right now. It was erasable ink. Really, Julie, don't worry. The tires of your bike were punctured in the city center and this happened here. The events aren't linked. Don't you agree?"

I don't know what to think. We walk up the stairs.

"Jesus, isn't that stench gone yet? It's getting worse." I wrinkle my nose as I walk into the bedroom.

"What stench? I don't smell a thing," Tom replies in surprise.

"Come on, I know pregnant women have an extremely good sense of smell, but you're not going to tell me you can't smell this. It started yesterday." I sniff the air and try to follow the trail. "I think it's coming from the bathroom," I continue. "Yes, that's definitely where it's coming from." With a disdainful face, I point in the direction of the scent. Tom meekly follows my finger and investigates.

"It could be the drain's clogged," he says a little later. "I'll unclog it and we'll keep the door closed for now so the smell doesn't spread, all right?"

"And how am I supposed to shower now? I'm sweating like a pig!"

"With extra-scented shower gel, as always." Tom laughs and slaps my butt.

I roll my eyes and peel off my maxi dress, my favorite garment during pregnancy. The fabric sticks to my body and I yearn for a refreshing shower and clean clothes. With only my panties and bra on, I stand in the middle of the bedroom. I breathe a sigh of relief when I take off the latter as well.

"Oh my, I feel so sticky. And these breasts are really no gift in these temperatures," I say, looking down at my unrecognizable bosom. "Goodbye, perky breasts. Hello, white udders," I sigh semi-disappointedly.

Tom smiles and walks towards me. "Come, come, white udders, a little respect for the ladies, eh," he says, placing his hands tenderly on my soft veined breasts. "A wonder of nature, that's what they are," he whispers in my ear, kissing me on the neck.

"No way! You promised to cook tonight. I get to relax and just enjoy."

"Mm, I want you to enjoy it," he growls. His grip tightens as he strokes the curve of my big belly.

"Tom Van de Velde!" I shout, suppressing a laugh.

"Present!" he replies, grinning.

"Eloise will be here in an hour. Let me through, I'm going to take a shower."

"At your service, General!" With a slight bow, he steps aside. Smiling from ear to ear, I step into the bathroom, yearning for the coolness of the shower water. Yes, we're doing just fine; physically we always find each other. So much so that I wonder if our new neighbor's ears have not already turned red.

Oscar

2005
5 Weeks Before The Day

Oscar's new plan was of a touching simplicity. He would get what he deserved and Julie would get what she deserved. If Julie hadn't abandoned him, he would have graduated and become a doctor and she could now be pregnant by him.

With a grin on his face, he drives to a supermarket he's never been to, in a village he's never been to, far away from his flat. He wanders the aisles that seem unforgivingly cold in the white fluorescent light. His left leg is always a little slower than the other, but most people don't even notice it because the difference is so minor, thanks to the pain he's had to endure in the gym for all these years.

He pushes the shopping cart past aisles of things he doesn't need, that nobody needs.

Focus, Oscar. Focus.

With his gaze fixed on the piece of paper in his hand, he purposefully makes his way to the correct department. In the cart, he loads colorful packs of diapers, different sizes of bottles, some rubber nipples, packs of wet wipes, and the rest of what is on his list. At the baby food aisle, he nearly loses his cool. There's so much choice. What type of powdered milk will he need? He feels a trickle of sweat running down his back and rests his upper body on the trolley. He has to stay cool, and he forces himself to read the labels on the jars: lactose-free, gluten-free, soy-free... A panic attack announces itself; a second drop of sweat makes its way from his neck to his belt. Without looking, he throws a few cans of powdered milk haphazardly into the cart and then pushes it on towards the exit.

"Ah, a young dad?" the smiling woman behind the counter asks. She's wearing a yellow blouse and her lips are pink and full. Her nails are painted red. The combination hurts his eyes.

He forms his mouth into a smile. It took him years, but now he knows how to behave in public. It's not so hard once you know the rules.

"Not yet," he says. His voice is pleasantly soft.

"Ah, expecting, are you? And already so well prepared!"

He nods as he puts his purchases back in the cart. "I like to plan ahead," he says, his eyes hidden behind thick-rimmed glasses. His vision is perfect, but this way he's less easy to recognize, he hopes.

"I know what you mean. I'm just like you," she replies approvingly. "That wife of yours is lucky to have you."

Fortunately, the woman keeps her mouth shut after that remark, but when he pays her, cash, he feels her eyes burning on the scars on his hand.

"Will you be okay with these things? Should I ask someone to help you carry them? We also deliver to your home."

Damn. He shakes his head in exasperation and snatches the receipt from her hands. He then quickly pushes the cart out into the car park.

Nauseating woman. Meddler.

Why did everybody treat him as an inferior member of society? As if they were so much better than him. He tips the contents of the cart into the trunk and drives with his loot to the house seventy miles away.

He doesn't know when his child will be born, but one thing is certain: when the time comes, Oscar will be ready.

Julie

The most delicious smells drift up the stairs and force me down to the source of all that goodness. I've changed into linen pants and a turquoise top that Tom says reflects the color of my eyes. My hair is still wet. I've just combed it through without bothering to use a blow dryer. Smelling of coconut and Acqua di Gio, I walk over to Tom, who's putting the finishing touches on a big pot of fresh guacamole with diced tomatoes.

"Can I help?"

"No." He smiles. "Everything is under control."

He's already set the table on the balcony, I see. So sweet, with napkins and even a candle. As if it's going to be a romantic dinner with Eloise.

"Sit down. Would you like something to drink, madam?" asks Tom, with a white kitchen towel folded over his left arm. He bows slightly. I burst out laughing.

"Are you going to be so obliging all evening? Eloise won't believe her eyes!"

He chuckles. He's as fond of Eloise as I am. "May I offer you the aperitif of the house?"

"Yes, you may. Surprise me!"

"At your service, ma'am."

Moments later, he returns with two virgin mojitos. Satisfied, I smell the scent of mint and lime and we clink our chilled glasses. I feel a tingling in my stomach. It's not the baby; she's keeping quiet. For a few weeks now, I've been feeling her move, a very special sensation. At first, it seemed like little air bubbles bursting in my belly, but that soon changed into real kicks.

"Hey, lovebirds! Is there room for a lonely stranger at that table?" Across the street, with her back against the wooden fence of the horse pasture, stands Eloise in all her glory. She's wearing a beautiful green dress with large colorful flowers, her black hair is tied back on her head like a sculpture in an intricate arrangement, and she's almost collapsing under the weight of the many bags and sacks that she must have brought in her Mini Cooper.

"Wait, I'll come and help you!" Tom shouts downstairs.

I chuckle and sink back in my chair, enjoying my mojito. After some fumbling on the stairs, the two of them come tumbling in. I struggle to get up from my chair to give Eloise a hug.

"You're about to explode," she says, pushing me back into the chair. "I come with gifts!"

"Yes, I noticed that," says Tom, holding the bags in his hands. "Shall I put them here so I can make you a mojito? Virgin or regular?"

Eloise looks at him with one raised eyebrow.

"No virgin, then," concludes Tom. "One regular mojito, coming up!"

He puts the bags down next to Eloise's chair and makes his way to the kitchen.

Eloise looks at me approvingly and says, "You look happy, girl."

"I am," I agree. And that's the truth. Right now I'm truly happy, together with my two favorite people, with good food and a chilled beverage. Since Mom died, I know that happiness is to be found in moments like these, that it's not something you feel all the time but that it's a rather fleeting feeling, like a soap bubble with beautiful colors that can burst at any moment.

"I'm so glad you gave him a chance. You guys really fit together."

I grin. "How's Daniel?"

Eloise grimaces. "Good." Her self-confidence is as low as her mouth is big. With all her outward show, she's very insecure on the inside, which manifests itself in her choice of men. But this isn't the time to call her out on it.

"He's taking me to London in October."

"Wow! London!"

"Yeah, nice, isn't it? He attends a conference on Saturday, but the rest of the time we can spend together. I'll finally be able to keep him in my bed!"

I cringe unconsciously, unable to imagine sharing a man with anyone else. Luckily, that exact moment Tom presents Eloise with an ice-cold mojito and serves fresh guacamole with nachos to go with it.

"At your service, ladies. Help yourselves."

We won't be told twice.

"Tom, this is really lovely," I sigh. I feel like I'm in Mexico, especially with these temperatures. It's the beginning of August and one heat wave follows another.

Eloise presses her glass against her sweaty forehead in reply. "Where's that cute kitty of yours? Isn't it far too hot for her, too?"

I look at Tom, who shrugs his shoulders.

"I really don't know. She hasn't come home for a few days now and I'm starting to get worried. I rang all the doorbells in the street this morning to check if anyone has seen her, but to no avail. I just hope she's not locked up in a garden shed somewhere. In this heat, that would be terrible." He looks a bit sad. Dolly isn't even two years old and a real fluff ball; he's very attached to her. I, too, have lost my heart to the little cat.

"She'll turn up, dear. Nine lives, you know," I say, though I'm not nearly as sure as I sound. If the creature really is locked up somewhere, her chances are nil. "Did you ring the doorbell of the upstairs neighbor, too?"

"I did, but nobody answered," replies Tom. Our plan to invite him has still come to nothing.

"Time for presents!" exclaims Eloise, pulling a pink paper bag from the pile of gifts. She takes her role as godmother-to-be quite seriously.

Two hours and many mountains of wrapping paper later, Tom and I have a complete set of baby equipment.

"I don't think I'll ever have to buy clothes for that child again," I laugh.

"Oh, just be careful. A baby grows out of everything quickly. My sisters' children could often only wear something once and then it wouldn't fit anymore. And I'm responsible for my goddaughter's image. My reputation is at stake, so leave the clothes department to me!"

I get up to hug her. "You're the best friend ever, thank you! By the way," I say conspiratorially, "we've chosen a name."

"No! Tell me!"

"My lips are sealed. You'll have to be patient for another two months."

"Oh, come on. The first letter, then?" tries Eloise.

"Nope."

"The second?"

I laugh. "No way, just wait and see. After Dad, you'll be the first to know, I promise." No matter how grumpy he is, he's still my dad.

***

"This was lovely, guys," Eloise says, grabbing her bag and putting her stilettos back on; she had taken them off with a deep sigh after we'd showed her the nursery.

"That child of yours is so lucky. You've built a nice little nest here."

"Except for the stench," I remark.

Tom rolls his eyes. "Yes, yes, I'll get on it right away. Can I walk you to your car, Eloise?"

"No need, it's right in front. Bye!"

And she's gone.

"I'm going to try and lure Dolly out again," I say after waving Eloise off from the balcony. I walk up the stairs to the bathroom with a box of cat food in my hand. The bathroom window has been left open since Dolly went missing and I can't understand why the drain still stinks despite the ventilation. Shaking my head, I step into the bathroom and immediately close the door behind me. The smell is starting to spread to the hall and I absolutely want to avoid my bedroom stinking, too.

"Dolly!" I shout, rattling the box in the open window: "Dolly! Come on!" I stop rattling for a moment and prick up my ears, but apart from a solitary cricket there's nothing to be heard, so I try again. "Dolly!" Where *is* that cat?

This goes on for a few minutes: rattle, call, rattle, listen. But to no avail. I can't shout too loudly, as it's already quite late. It also frustrates me that I can't see anything; the window is just above eye level with a small cupboard underneath that Dolly uses as a step. I look around for a way to climb higher. If I hoist myself halfway up the toilet bowl and support myself with my hands on the cupboard, I might be able to peep through the window with my head or at least stick the box of cat food through it, I think. Grunting, I place one leg on the toilet bowl. I'm just about to add the second leg; flamingo-like, I'm halfway there when Tom steps into the bathroom.

"What the hell are you doing?"

"I wanted to get a little closer to the window. Maybe she can't find her way back but will hear us calling from there."

"Come off it, you're pregnant!"

"I'm pregnant, not sick," I protest, but I clamber down anyway.

"Let me try," says Tom and he puts his leg on the pot. He's tall enough to stick his upper body through the window.

"Do you see anything?"

"No, it's too dark, but it stinks much worse out here than it does inside. I don't think it's our drain."

An anxious feeling creeps up on me.

"Give me your phone," he asks with an outstretched hand.

I reach for the phone lying on the sink and hand it to him. With one hand he balances his body with his long fingers, and with the other he shines out the phone's flashlight. Suddenly, something startles him and he almost drops the phone.

"Do you see anything?"

"No, it was another cat frightened by the light, I think. Not Dolly." He shines his beam of light across the rooftops again and stops abruptly. I look at him expectantly, but he just stares into the dark night.

"Did you see anything?" I ask softly.

"No, it's too dark. I'll have another look tomorrow in daylight," he replies. He steps down from the toilet bowl and closes the window. "Let's go to bed."

The Day

9:00

Fascinated, Oscar stares at the glass. A wasp throws its tiny body against the glass wall. Helplessly, the insect bounces from left to right, from top to bottom, over and over again. The pleasure of the small amount of Coke that lured it into this situation is long forgotten. It wants to be free and fly high up into the clear blue sky where it will be seduced by the next delicious smell. But not if it's up to Oscar. He has hermetically sealed the top of the glass with a saucer and feels strangely calm.

He's in control now.

Not them.

No, no.

He slides the glass to the middle of the table and makes a sandwich. Calmly, he applies a layer of butter to the slices of brown bread, followed by a slice of cheese on one and smoked ham on the other. All the preparations have been made, and now he just has to wait for the right moment to make his move. He can't wait to see the look in her eyes.

How would she react? He can think of nothing else these days. In his fantasy, he first sees her eyes grow big with surprise, only to be seized immediately after by pure, primitive fear. The fear you feel when you know that something terrible is about to happen. The fear that Oscar has felt several times when Rutger was waiting for him in the toilets. She shouldn't have abandoned him.

He puts the last piece of bread in his mouth and eats it quietly while staring at the glass. The wasp has almost given up its fight and struggles only slightly. He waits until the ripples in the liquid subside and empties the glass into the sink.

Then, in one powerful movement, he lands the glass on the exhausted wasp's body.

Through the window he sees Julie returning from the market.

It's time for action.

10:00

Tom waits for Julie to go to the market before he climbs on the roof. She may be a newly graduated vet, but she's also pregnant and irritable and sometimes an emotional wreck. The heat doesn't help, of course. Last night, in the dark, he wasn't quite sure, but now there's no doubt: Dolly's dead and her body lies on the roof.

It's only morning, but on the black roof it's already scorching hot. With a haze before his eyes, he wraps the little cat in her favorite blanket. Her swollen body stinks; he has to make an effort to swat away the flies, but otherwise she looks unharmed. She must have been lying here for a while. No blood. No injuries as far as he can see. He doesn't understand. Dolly was in perfect health. What happened to her? How did she end up dead on the roof?

Shaking his head, he wraps Dolly in a towel, puts the sad package in a big shopping bag, and walks to his car. He wants to take Dolly to the vet before Julie returns. He wants to spare her for a while. The pavement has absorbed the heat and it rises to his legs. Sweat is already running down his back. Luckily, he has air conditioning. He stretches out his arm towards his car, the key in his hand, and stops abruptly.

"No!" He yells it out loud, unable to suppress his disbelief.

Not again!

Desperate, he puts the bag with Dolly in it on the hot asphalt beside the car and brings his hands to his head, his fingers entwined in his hair. What the hell is going on here? He walks around the car, inspecting it on all sides. Then he looks around, but the street is deserted. In the pasture, the horses stand under the shade of an oak tree, looking at him languidly. He is alone. As he walks to the driver's side again, he rubs his eyes. He hardly dares to look, but he's seen it perfectly well the first time.

On the side of his car, his freshly washed shiny car, four letters scream at him: "SLUT." They laugh at him, taunt him, shout at him in their rude, harsh way, without pity, filled with hatred. This time the vandal has made a job of it and the word is indelibly scratched into the blue paint of his Golf.

Despite the heat, Tom is freezing cold. This is no longer a coincidence. Someone is out to get him, but who? And why? And why the words "whore" and "slut"? It doesn't make sense.

He puts Dolly on the floor in front of the passenger seat and starts driving, his brow furrowed. This must have something to do with Julie. But why? Julie didn't exactly have a turbulent love life before she met him. At least, not that he knows of. Her previous relationships were uneventful. He knows that she occasionally went home with someone or vice versa, usually a fellow student. Did she step on anyone's toes? Maybe one of those guys wants more from her than she does from him? She's not hiding anything from him, is she? Could there be a connection with the anonymous phone calls she received? And with her punctured bike tires? His frown deepens and he steers through the bends faster than he should.

He decides to call her from the car; she needs to be aware of what's going on. While he waits for her to answer, he sees a woman looking at him strangely and it takes him a few seconds to realize that she's not looking at him but at the message he's carrying on his car. He feels his cheeks turning bright red.

Julie doesn't answer; he'll try her again after he's seen the vet.

Ten minutes later, he's pulling onto the driveway. The vet is very understanding when she takes Dolly from him.

"I'll examine her as soon as possible," she says kindly. "In this heat it's not uncommon for pets to die, so you mustn't blame yourself. Do you want to say goodbye?"

Tom stands before her with drooping shoulders, tears welling up in his eyes. He swallows a large lump and takes one last look at Dolly. The woman takes the green collar from her fluffy neck and hands it to him.

"So sorry for your loss. I'll call you as soon as I know more."

Empty-handed and with a heavy heart, Tom gets back into his car, his swearing car.

"What a shitty day this is," he says aloud to himself as he sets his GPS to the police station.

11:00

The police station is a large white building. The parking lot, where only a few trees provide some shade, is packed and Tom has to make several detours to find a spot. The sun is burning, his t-shirt is sticking to his body, and his courage is seeping out of his pores as he enters the building: a crowded waiting room without air conditioning. Perfect. Behind Plexiglas sits a tired-looking policeman with a moustache, sweat beading on his forehead.

"Yes?" the man asks wearily.

"I want to report an act of vandalism," Tom replies, for the second time in three months. The police station is a lot busier this time.

The officer pushes an A4 sheet under the Plexiglas.

"Fill it out and hand it over, please."

None of the plastic chairs are free, so Tom takes up position against a wall, next to a notice board warning of burglars and pickpockets. There's a smell of sweat and polyester in the room. He's about to put his name on the document when his phone beeps. It's a text message from Julie. At last.

Hey, sorry, I didn't hear my cell. Home now. Everything okay?

Just a little while longer, I'll call you later, he sends back, relieved that she's home. He's a bit worried, but doesn't want to tell her about Dolly and the scratches on his car with all these people around him. It'll have to wait.

Okay appears on his screen.

He fills in the form to the best of his ability, which isn't easy standing against the wall. His pen gives up several times. He's about to throw in the towel when a chair becomes vacant. When the document is completely filled in, he hands it back to the officer, who silently throws it on a pile.

Most of the people in the waiting room are tapping their phones absentmindedly, just as he is, while others are reading magazines. One man seems to have fallen asleep. Occasionally, an officer comes in to take the next person out of the waiting room, but there are still at least ten people before him.

Tom closes his eyes and lets his thoughts flow. What possesses someone to write swear words on the car of a stranger? The more he thinks about it, the more he's convinced it's a personal attack. But those words, "slut" and "whore"... Supposing they're directed at him, who could hold such a grudge? An ex-girlfriend? In his mind he goes down the list, but there's no one he has a quarrel with. He's never broken up with anyone, so none of his exes could blame him. Maybe it was one of his students? Every year there are a few giggly girls in his class, and sometimes one of them gets a crush on the young music teacher. Perhaps they're dealing with the resentment of a teenager whose love is unrequited?

A shiver runs down his spine. There was one student who showed a more than healthy interest in him during the past school year: Isabelle. She had dark long hair that was almost pitch black and invariably hung like a curtain before her eyes. From under her eyelashes, he could feel her gaze burning on him in every lesson. One day, he found an anonymous love letter behind his windshield wiper. He'd been sure that it came from her, although she'd never mentioned it to him. He decided not to do anything with it, as he didn't want to get her into trouble. He kept the letter, though. Maybe he should hand it over to the police after all. Come to think of it: shouldn't he wait to file a report until he has more information? The vibrations of his phone interrupt his train of thought.

"Tom, this is the veterinary practice of Dr. Ramaekers. I hope I'm not disturbing you?" It's the assistant, not the vet.

"No, go ahead."

"I've just had a cursory look at Dolly and it doesn't look like she died of the heat."

"Oh? Was she sick?"

"I'm sorry to say this, but she's been strangled."

"Strangled?" The word bounces around in Tom's head. Dolly has been strangled. His car has been scratched. Julie's tires punctured. What the fuck is going on here?

"Tom?"

"Yes, yes, sorry. I'm, um. Strangled, you say?" His ears are ringing. Strangled. Slut. Whore. He feels his knees going weak.

"Yes, you'll have to report it to the police."

Police.

"Tom?"

"Yes, I'm still here. You caught me a bit off guard. I, um, thank you."

He has to see Julie. Now. He has to talk to her. This can no longer be a coincidence.

"You're welcome. Good luck."

Tom hangs up and immediately calls Julie, but she doesn't answer. Damn. He looks around the waiting room again and then walks out. The police can wait. He needs to see Julie first. Then they'll come back and file a complaint together because this is too much for him to handle alone.

12:00

Despite the air conditioning irritating his eyelashes with a cold blast of air, the hollows of his knees stick to the seat upholstery and he feels his t-shirt getting wet with sweat. His hands clasp the steering wheel tensely as he maneuvers the car through the streets on autopilot. Meanwhile, he tries to clear his thoughts. Someone has strangled Dolly and written a hateful message on his car. Twice. Presumably it's the same person who's targeting him or Julie or both. He bites his upper lip. His car, his cat. Julie's bike tires. Did they piss someone off?

Against his better judgment, he hopes that this will all turn out to be a huge misunderstanding, even if it doesn't bring Dolly back. He blinks his eyes to get rid of the image of the strangled cat and tries to picture Julie as she looked this morning: wearing a long grass-green dress and a straw sunhat.

Julie isn't a classic beauty—her mouth is too wide and her jawline too strong for that—but she has something noble in her profile and she radiates a freshness that Tom drinks with his eyes every day. No matter how noisy she can be at times with her eternal chatter, she energizes him by being who she is. Pure and honest, and almost always barefoot. With the most beautiful smile ever. He can't imagine anyone would want to harm her. Of course, he knows she has a dark side, too, as he's not an idiot, but...

The parking space in front of their flat is still untaken. The neighborhood is so quiet during the holidays that it wouldn't be difficult to scratch something on a car unnoticed, he thinks. One of the horses whinny. If they could talk, he would surely know more now. He sprints up the stairs two steps at a time and opens the door of the duplex.

"I'm home!"

No answer.

"Julie?"

No answer.

He puts his hands around his mouth and calls out, "Are you upstairs?" But it remains silent. On the kitchen counter is a glass bowl with sliced fruit, covered with plastic wrapping. The sliding doors to the balcony are closed, but that's not so strange; they keep them closed during the day to keep out most of the heat. Only when the temperature drops at nightfall do they open them again.

Puzzled, he wonders where she could have gone. *Maybe she was tired of waiting? Or she went back to the market because she'd forgotten something?*

Sweat runs down his back and he decides to take a shower. She'll be here soon. Upstairs, he takes off his clammy shorts and t-shirt. At the sight of the bathroom window, he has to fight back some burning tears. He has to tell Julie about Dolly. He turns on the shower and welcomes the cool water on his skin. With his eyes closed, he holds his face under the spray and lets the warm, salty tears mingle with the cool water. "Go on," the water seems to encourage him. "Let the sadness flow, nobody can see you." And so he does. He cries for his little cat who didn't do any harm to anyone and who trusted him. He should have protected her, should have been more alert. In his mind's eye, he sees a big hand pressing itself around Dolly's neck and how she fights for her life.

"You mustn't blame yourself," the vet had said. But he does. Dolly died a horrible death and not a day will go by without thinking of her when he stands in this bathroom.

He turns off the tap and roughly dries off. What possesses someone to hurt, to kill, such an innocent animal? A shiver runs down his spine in the warm bathroom. What kind of hatred would consume a person to do such a thing? And how did Dolly's body end up on the roof?

He steps into the bedroom and opens the wardrobe looking for a clean t-shirt. As he gets dressed, he calls out "Julie?" again, hoping she's come home while he was in the shower, but it remains silent downstairs. He checks the screen of his phone, but there's no message from her. This isn't good. The fact that she hasn't left a message isn't like her.

With his hair dripping, he walks back downstairs. Everything is as it was before. On the counter he sees Julie's purchases: fresh cabbage lettuce, *Coeur de Boeuf* tomatoes with their summery scent, a bowl of strawberries, and half a watermelon. He puts everything in the fridge, opens the window to the balcony, and sits down at the table with his cell.

Hey, I've been home for a while. Where are you? he types. He keeps staring at the screen to see if she responds, but it remains blank. His stomach starts to flutter and he decides to always confide in her immediately from now on.

Suddenly, he catches sight of the place where the baby's car seat, one of Eloise's presents, had been this morning. He had already taken most of the things to the nursery, but had left the car seat there. At least he thought he had, because it's gone. Would Julie have carried it upstairs? He had urged her not to do so. There was no reason for it, as it wasn't in the way or anything.

A strange tingling sensation creeps from his neck to his spine and he decides to take a look in the baby's room. He knows he's being paranoid, but given how his morning has gone so far, he prefers to give in to his instincts. He climbs the stairs again and opens the door. His hand is on the door handle as his brain tries to comprehend what is being projected onto his retina, adrenaline rushing through his veins.

"Goddamn," he says softly, then louder: "Goddamn, goddamn!"

One Hour Earlier

The time has come. This is the moment Oscar has been waiting for all these years. He saw how Tom almost fainted when he saw the message Oscar had left on his car. How he left with his dead cat. It took the guy a lot longer to find it than Oscar had anticipated.

He hadn't intended to kill it, to be honest. The animal was stupid enough to slip into Oscar's kitchen through the neighboring balconies. At first, he'd wanted to put the cat back outside, but then, when he touched its fur, he was overcome by a sudden fury that made him lose it completely. All he could think of was Nivens, and how unfair it all was. When he regained his senses, the cat lay lifeless in his lap and he felt euphoric, as he does now.

Everything is ready. He only needs fifteen or maybe twenty minutes. He isn't nervous, but rather has a sense of anticipation for what's to come, like on the day before Christmas. He takes a few deep breaths. With each breath, he fills up more with his alter ego Floris and lets Oscar fade into the background.

He knocks on the door of Julie's flat, a gift basket in his arms.

"Hello, I'm F-Floris, the upstairs neighbor. I just came to say hello," he stutters when the door opens. Hesitantly, he stands in the doorway, his face half hidden behind the basket.

She welcomes him with a broad smile. "Floris! What a surprise, come in!" She holds the door open, her big belly protruding defiantly. "I was just about to make some coffee. Would you like a cup, too?"

"Yes, please, that's very kind." Shuffling, he enters the flat through the small hall into the living room. "Is your husband not at home?" he asks, though he very well knows the answer to that question.

"Tom? No, he had to go out for a while, but he'll be here soon. You shouldn't have done that." She points to the basket in his arms. In the cellophane is an assortment of fruit and biscuits.

"It's just a little gift," he mumbles, landing his cargo on the table.

Being a nurse, it was no problem for Oscar to get hold of ketamine and midazolam. He has the stuff safely in his vest pocket. He casually takes a packet of biscuits from the basket while Julie is busy with the coffee, barefoot. That she doesn't recognize him makes him both furious and proud of his metamorphosis.

He's in complete control of his body. His breathing doesn't quicken for a second now that he's so close to his prey, and his palms feel dry, despite the heat.

"Sit down, sit down," Julie says as she puts two cups of coffee on the table. "Milk or sugar?"

"Both, please."

The moment she turns around again, he drops the ketamine in her cup. It's a drug that has a quick but short-lived effect.

"You have as much of a sweet tooth as I do, apparently," Julie laughs as she puts milk and sugar on the table a little later.

Oscar doesn't like sweet things at all, but wants to be sure that the anesthetic is given enough time to dissolve.

With a sigh, Julie sits down at the table. "I'm so glad you took the initiative to come here. We were planning to invite you, you know," she says with an apologetic smile.

"No problem. With a baby on the way, of course, you have a lot on your mind."

"That's true, but it's no excuse. I only realized a few weeks ago that you'd moved in here. I think I saw you on the stairs once."

"Yes, that was me," says Oscar. He strains not to stare at her face, mesmerized by those green-blue eyes he knows so well, the freckles around her nose, the dimple in her cheek, the wide mouth. He wonders how long it will take for the drug to take effect, but for that, she must drink first.

"Have you lived here long?" he asks.

Julie brings her fingertip to her mouth while thinking. "Um, let's see. I've lived here for almost six years. It's my flat. Tom moved in at about the same time as you."

He feigns interest. He knows that, too. He puts milk and sugar in his cup and brings it to his mouth. "Cheers!"

"Cheers," says Julie. She imitates his gesture and drinks her coffee. "We haven't lived together long. Only since we found out we're expecting."

"Oh my," says Oscar. He hopes the ketamine will do its work soon; small talk isn't his thing.

"It wasn't really planned, that's why. But now we're very happy that she's coming."

So it's a girl. Too bad. He would have preferred a boy.

Suddenly, Julie starts nodding. "Oh dear, how strange, I'm a bit tired I think. The heat…" she mumbles, her forehead furrowed. "I think I'd better lie down for a while. Sorry, Floris, we'll have to—" She grips the table with both hands and looks at him with her eyes wide open for a moment before her head slumps forward with a thump.

Showtime.

Quickly, he takes a needle and some empty ampoules from his pocket. He grabs her under her arms, pulls her from the chair, and carefully lays her on the floor. He routinely ties off her arm and fills some tubes with her blood. Then he takes the ampoule of midazolam, a long-acting drug, and, averting his gaze, pulls her dress up a little so that he can insert the needle into her buttock. The sight of her tanned thigh momentarily throws him off-balance, but he quickly recovers.

Ready.

Now she'll be unconscious for several hours. He carries out the rest of his plan at top speed and runs to the nursery to grab some things. Not too much—just enough to arouse suspicion. Then he checks Julie's pulse: it's steady. Good.

He washes the cups and puts them back in their place, and wipes all the surfaces he has touched with a cloth. He puts the baby's things in a car seat that's on the floor and hangs it on his good arm; he carries the gift basket downstairs in the other. He checks that there's no one in the street and then he puts everything into his car, which is waiting out front.

Quickly, upstairs again. Now comes the hardest part: he has to carry Julie down one floor. He has a wheelchair waiting in the hall, but he has to get her there first. Now he'll find out if all those hours at the gym have really paid off.

He takes a deep breath and takes hold of Julie under her arms again, bracing his legs and hoisting her upright. Given her belly, he can't just put her over his shoulder, so he has to take her in his arms, like a baby. The pain in his joints is unbearable, similar to when he just came out of anesthetic after the fire. Breathing heavily, he puts one foot in front of the other purely by willpower, walks with his load out of the flat, and drags her down the stairs straight to the wheelchair.

Sweating, he lowers Julie into it. He suppresses the urge to rest for a moment; it's too risky. He puts a grey wig on her head and throws a checkered blanket around her. This makes it look as if there's an old lady in the wheelchair. There's little chance of anyone seeing him, but you never know.

One last time, he runs up the stairs to get her sandals and handbag. His eye catches a small suitcase in the hall of her apartment and on impulse he tucks it under his arm. Back downstairs, he puts the suitcase and the handbag on her lap and opens the front door. He rolls out the wheelchair with Julie in it.

He often drives with a patient to an appointment outside the hospital and the fact that he has a wheelchair in his car isn't unusual. His Peugeot Partner is equipped for it. He rolls the chair up the ramp, into the car, and then closes the door.

That's that. Time to take Julie to her new home.

12:30

It looks as if the frog on the wall is laughing at Tom as he casts his eyes around the room. Either Julie has decided on a whim to return a load of baby stuff to the shop, or something is very wrong. The yellow changing mat that was on the dresser is gone. The mobile above the cot is no longer there. He takes a few steps into the room and feels his knees buckle. A sense of total disbelief comes over him. He peers over the edge of the cradle and sees only the mattress; the yellow sleeping bag that was inside, the mysterious gift, is gone. With trembling hands, he turns to the dresser and opens the drawers. His suspicions are immediately confirmed: only empty space is left where some of the clothes used to be.

This can't be true. What kind of absurd joke has he got himself into? Did they fall victim of a theft? The baby stuff theft? He stands in the middle of the room, his hands on his head and no idea what to do. Then he gets a hunch. He walks into the master bedroom and pulls open Julie's part of the wardrobe. At first glance, everything seems to be there, but how does he know what is and what's not in the laundry at the moment? If Julie had left for some reason, what would she have taken with her?

Of course!

He hits himself on the head. Her suitcase. She set it up last week to be prepared if the baby came early, and it contains everything she needs to stay in the hospital. He bounds down the stairs and looks wildly around the hall, but no matter how hard he stares, there is no suitcase to be found. Completely flabbergasted, he drops to the floor against the wall.

She's gone. Julie's gone. She's taken her suitcase and the baby's things and he has no idea why.

Once again, he grabs his phone and calls her number.

"Hello!"

His heart leaps at the sound of her voice.

"I'm not here right now, but feel free to leave a message after the beep!"

Despondent, he hangs up again. The only other person who might know where and why she's gone is Eloise. He looks up her number in his contacts. The phone trembles in his hands; he's already sweating profusely.

"Yes?" replies Eloise after a few seconds.

"Eloise, I, uh, I..."

"Tom? Is everything okay?"

Tears prickle in his eyes and a lump the size of a tennis ball obstructs the words he wants to say. Eloise doesn't sound as if she expected him to call and that can only mean one thing: Julie isn't with her. A loud sob leaves his throat involuntarily.

"Tom! What's going on? Is something wrong with Julie? With the baby? Talk to me!" she shouts in panic over the phone, but he doesn't manage to say anything.

"Take a deep breath and calm down," Eloise says, trying to soothe him.

He does what she says and lets the oxygen flow through his lungs. Breathe. Breathe. Above all, keep breathing.

"Julie's gone," he says, trying to wipe his tear-stained face with his t-shirt. His mouth is sticky and he's terribly thirsty, but he can't move and remains sitting on the hall floor as if paralyzed.

"What do you mean 'gone'? Where did she go?" says Eloise, worried. "Is everything okay with the baby?" she asks again.

"I don't know," Tom replies in a hoarse voice. "I came home an hour ago and she was gone. She took some clothes and her suitcase and some things for the baby. I don't understand."

It takes a few moments for Eloise to reply. "There must be some explanation. Did you have a fight or something?" she tries to reassure him, but Tom hears the desperation in her voice. She knows Julie would have phoned her if they had.

"No, not at all. This morning everything was fine. She went to the market and I had to do some, um, shopping myself and when I came back she was gone. So was all that stuff."

"Did you try to call her?"

"Yes, of course, but I can't get through to her. Her phone goes straight to voicemail. Either she's somewhere without service, or her phone is turned off."

***

At the other end of the line, Eloise stares indecisively at her toenails, on which the nail stylist has drawn bright pink flowers. She had just dressed and was planning to have "lunch" with Daniel, which meant ordering room service at the Hilton. After a few seconds, she makes up her mind.

"Stay where you are, I'm coming. Give me half an hour."

***

Relieved, Tom hangs up. Two can do more than one. Against his better judgment, he tries Julie's number again, to no avail. His hands are shaking and the adrenaline continues to course through his veins, as if his body knows it must remain on high alert. But what can he do except wait? Waiting for a sign from Julie, waiting for Eloise. He knows he has to call Julie's dad, even if he's the last possible option where Julie could have gone. He would rather do that with Eloise present, and besides, it seems improbable to him that she would go there without telling him.

Would she really have left of her own accord? It seems so unlikely. Unless she saw something that frightened her so much that she wanted to leave immediately. But what? What did he do? No matter how hard he tries, he can think of nothing he did wrong. Unless she's found out that he lied about Dolly? But he hasn't; he just kept quiet about finding her. Besides, if he'd done something wrong, she'd throw *him* out of her flat, wouldn't she? It's *her* flat, damn it!

No, this is bad.

He hoists his body up from the cool floor and sits at the table, the volume of his phone turned up to maximum, while he looks through photos he has taken of Julie. There are fewer than he thought. Most of the pictures were always taken by her; her phone is full of silly images of them together. The last photo Tom took of her was at the seaside about two weeks ago. She was standing with her feet in the surf, the bottom of her white dress soaked and stuck to her legs. Her hair was bleached by the sun and she'd tried to put it up, but the wind kept releasing little tufts from the elastic, making her look so untamed that she had melted his insides with love. He grows weak again at the sight and shakes his head in disbelief.

"Julie, for God's sake. Where are you?"

13:00

29 Weeks and 4 Days Pregnant

I dream about the beach again. This time, Mommy has a pink bandana in her dark curls. Daddy isn't there; his lounge chair is empty except for a newspaper. Together with Mommy, I build a sandcastle and I'm busy filling my Hello Kitty bucket. The pit I dig gets deeper and deeper. The sun is burning, sweat is running down my cute toddler cheeks, and the sand is rubbing my knees, but I don't give up. I fill up the bucket and empty it into a big pile, over and over again. I shovel and build and shovel and build. Higher and higher becomes the pile, and deeper and deeper becomes the pit.

A dark cloud slides in front of the sun, but I don't notice it. A chilly wind rises over the ocean, but I keep on working. More clouds gather, rumbling in the distance. I look up to Mommy, but she's no longer there. The pink bandana is being carried away by the wind, like a graceful bird, in the direction of the ocean. It gets darker and darker, and in a panic, I look around, searching for my mom. I call out. I turn and put my hands over my eyes.

"Mom! Mommy!"

The distant roar gets louder and mixes with the sound of the waves crashing on the beach. The water closes in around my sand pile and I step backwards, startled. I tumble around my axis as the clouds and the sea move further and further away from me. I no longer know where is up and where is down. I fall deeper still, into the blackest black, until I disappear into the bottomless nothingness, where no light ever shone and no shadow ever arose.

***

I wake up with a groan. My limbs feel heavy and there's a pounding behind my eyes. Carefully, I try to open them, but the light is too bright to do any more than squint. I put my arm over my eyes and try to take a deep breath, but my chest feels like a bag of cement is lying on top of it.

What happened? Where am I? It smells strange in here.

I try to remember where I was before I fell asleep, but can't get past the image of a summery fruit salad. Right, I'd made that for Tom and me.

Tom! I want to say his name, but nothing more than a hoarse shriek comes out of my throat. I swallow and try again.

"Tom?" I whisper, my arm bent over my eyes. I wait tensely for a sign of life, but hear nothing. Apart from the buzzing of blood in my ears and a slight hum that I can't quite place, a total and absolute silence surrounds me. I rub my eyes with both hands and try to open them again. This time I turn my head slightly to one side so that I'm not looking straight into the bright light. My vision is still blurred, but I can see a wooden chair next to the bed I'm lying on.

My confusion increases and I frantically rub my eyes again, hoping to dispel the haze. What is this place? Slowly, I detect the outline of a room: grey walls and a low ceiling with a fluorescent lamp flickering softly, producing the hum I'm hearing. I try to sit up, but a wave of nausea bubbles up and I immediately sink back down.

I don't know where I am or why. My memory is failing me and a sudden fear surges through my body. The adrenaline makes my fingers tingle and my vision sharpen. Instinctively, I place my hands on my belly, where they are greeted by a few gentle stubs that almost make me cry with relief. With renewed energy, I sit up straight, my bare feet on the carpet in front of the bed.

Where is my handbag? I need to find my phone. I peer around the room and locate my sandals on the other side under a staircase. I follow the steps upwards with my gaze; they seem to end in the ceiling. Under the stairs, I recognize a kitchen model I've recently seen in IKEA. It's the most basic one, with white cabinets, an electric hob, and a sink. Next to it is a small fridge. On the green carpet is a simple table with four chairs around it.

No handbag in sight.

A modest sofa divides the small room in two. Directly opposite the bed on which I sit are two doors, to the left of which is a low cabinet with a TV on it. It's overflowing with DVDs.

I look around in amazement. Against the wall to the right of the bed, I discover a chest of drawers with a yellow changing mat on it. Something tingles at the back of my neck. This is bad. My mouth is dry as a bone, my tongue sticks to the roof of my mouth, and my eyes widen, searching for an answer.

Why am I here? Where am I? Where the hell is my phone? And why are there no windows here?

Shaking, I try to get up. At the foot of the bed is a cot with bars, an old model. I take a few steps in the direction of the cot and then, with a groan, I sink to my knees. Hanging over the bed is a mobile with yellow chicks. In the bed, there's a cute white and yellow striped sleeping bag. They're my own things. They were in the nursery a few hours ago.

I get down on my hands and knees and feel the bile rushing up, but it doesn't get beyond my mouth. My face twitches at the disgusting taste and I feel tears running down my cheeks, but I immediately pull myself together. There is something very wrong, that is clear, but crying and whining won't solve a thing.

I bring my hand to my neck out of habit; I still have my necklace on. Gratefully, I clench it in my fist. Whatever this is, I'll get through it. I just need to use my brain and not panic.

I push myself up and walk to the kitchen. I let the water from the tap run over my hands. I splash some on my face and rinse my mouth. Something itches in the hollow of my arm, and with a frown I pull a small round bandage off my skin.

"What the…" I curse. Someone has injected me with something or taken blood. Anger flares up inside me and I head for the concrete stairs and walk up with determination. It's been long enough now. I need to know what's going on.

The stairs end at a metal hatch. I brace myself and push, but it doesn't budge. With my back against the wall and knees buckling, I put both hands against it.

"Come on! Open up!" I shout in frustration, but to no avail. Eventually, I arch my back and push against the hatch in an ultimate attempt to get the thing open, but it's hopeless. I can't hold onto anything and my legs are too weak to do this.

Discouraged, I descend the stairs again.

Think, Julie, think!

How did I end up in this place? What are the baby's things doing here? Where is my handbag? And why do I feel like I've been under a train? I also notice the car seat that was just sitting in my living room. What have I got myself into?

Think!

I went to the market, I remember. It was warm, as it has been for weeks. I was wearing my green dress. I look down for a moment and see I'm wearing the same dress. Is it still today, then? Without a phone, I'm lost. I have no idea of the time. I look around and discover a wall clock above the TV. It's one o'clock. In the afternoon? At night? How long have I slept? And why? Maybe I fell ill at the market?

In my mind, I go through the route I took. If I just go through my morning chronologically, I'll probably remember what happened.

I parked my bike and first stopped at the bread stand, I remember. There I bought a loaf of bread and a croissant, which I ate on the spot. I strolled past the flower stand and briefly considered buying sunflowers to put in a large vase in the living room, but it was so hot that I decided against it. They would hardly have survived the ride home. My last stop had been the fruit and vegetable stand and then I cycled home again. Yes, I cycled home. Definitely.

I lean my back against the counter and look around the room. What had I done when I got home? My head is pounding and my throat feels dry.

I cut up fruit and put it in a bowl.

Was Tom there, too? I don't remember. I have to sit down, so I take a seat on one of the chairs. My hands are trembling and my lips are dry. A glass and jug of water are on the table, but I don't dare drink from them.

I shake my head. No, Tom wasn't there.

My breath falters. I remember something. Someone.

Damn it, Julie! Who? Think!

Tears are welling up in my eyes. I haven't felt so helpless since the day Mom died. I have to remember. I have to. I run down the list; who could've been in the flat?

Eloise?

No, it was a man. I squeeze my eyes shut and try to see him in front of me. Was it Dad?

No, definitely not. Someone from the university, then?

I grit my teeth in frustration. The image won't focus. Was it someone I know?

With a jolt, my head flies upright. An image shoots past like an old slide; I just have to get it straight. It costs me so much energy. Why do I feel so sick?

And then, suddenly, I see it: it's a hand. A mutilated hand.

13:15

"When did you last see her?" Eloise has waltzed into the flat in a cloud of scents that is almost visible and turned on the coffee machine without asking. "And where are your mugs?" she continues in one effort, raising her elegantly epilated eyebrows.

Tom gratefully hands over the reins. As he pulls open a kitchen cupboard, he answers, "This morning, around ten o'clock, when she left for the market on her bike."

"And everything was okay then?"

"I think so," he says, but a slight tremor can be heard in his voice.

"No quarrel?"

"No quarrel."

"Or an argument, perhaps? About the baby?"

"No, really nothing. There was nothing at all."

Eloise frowns. "I've called Julie a couple of times now. Something's not right. She'd never just take off, not without telling me." She looks at Tom with squinting eyes and he feels uneasy under her gaze.

"Where do you think she's gone?" he asks, pouring coffee into her cup and making tea for himself.

Eloise shrugs. "The only possible place I can think of is her dad's house. We'll have to call Mr. Meskens. I don't understand why you haven't told him yet, Tom."

They take their cups to the balcony. Tom sits down at the table with a sigh; luckily, a little wind has picked up to cool his heated brow.

"He doesn't like me, I'm afraid."

"Who? Mr. Meskens? Yes, and? This is about his daughter, isn't it?" says Eloise in surprise as she sits down.

"He is indeed a stern man, but when it comes to Julie, he's a soft-boiled egg."

"Yes, I know that, but we... Let's just say he's not very happy with his son-in-law and I'd rather not call him if it's not really necessary."

"And you didn't think it's necessary now?" she exclaims.

"Yes, of course! I just wanted to wait until you arrived. I don't know what to do anymore," he replies, his hands entwined in his hair in frustration. Tears prickle in his eyes again.

She looks at him inquiringly. "Tom, are you sure there's nothing else?" she asks, more gently this time. "If you want me to help you, you have to tell me everything."

He takes a sip of his tea. "I don't know, Eloise. Yes, something happened, but I don't know if it has anything to do with this."

"What is it?" she asks again suspiciously.

He sighs. With a lump in his throat, he tells her how he found Dolly on the roof and that he took her to the vet without saying anything to Julie.

"So that was the stench we smelled? Why didn't you tell Julie? She's a vet herself, isn't she?"

"I was going to, of course, but not right away. I wanted to protect her, I guess?"

"She can take a beating," Eloise replies, offended. "This is Julie, you know, not some frail little nymph."

"Um, yes, I know. I meant well. But in any case, when I was at the police station—"

"Whoa! Wait! Rewind, mister. So you were at the police station?"

He looks up, startled. "Yes, I... So that's another story," he stammers, confused.

"Tell me," she urges him, looking compulsively into his eyes.

Tom puts his elbows on the table and supports his head with his hands. Eloise makes him nervous; she makes him feel like he's done something wrong. "I was going to report an act of vandalism."

"Go on?"

"A few months ago, before I moved in here, my car was scratched while parked out front. I had the damage repaired, but..." He hesitates for a moment, just enough for Eloise to realize there's more to it. Her dark eyes bore deep into his.

"Tom, tell me, man! What is it?"

His face turns red and he feels his cheeks glow. "A few weeks later, someone wrote 'whore' on my windshield and this morning something happened again," he says resignedly.

"What, then? What happened?" She impatiently drums her long nails on the table top.

"This time the car had 'slut' scratched on it. I'm surprised you didn't see that, by the way."

Her mouth falls open. "Slut and whore?"

He nods slowly. "Slut and whore. The first time it said 'whore' and this morning it said 'slut'."

"That's really too bizarre. Do you think someone is targeting you? Or your car? Or Julie?"

"I don't know. I'm not so sure it was directed at me."

Now it's Eloise's turn to fall silent. She drinks her coffee thoughtfully, looking out over the fields in the distance.

"This doesn't make sense," she mutters, more to herself than to Tom. He can see from her face that she, like him, is struggling to think of an explanation.

"What are you thinking about?" he asks.

"I wonder if you think someone's targeting Julie with those scratches."

He shrugs his shoulders. "I don't know what to think. But you'll have to admit that they're strange insults to a man and Julie has... Well, before we were together, she was..."

Eloise slaps the table so hard that the cups jump up. "So, yes! You think someone says 'slut' and 'whore' to Julie by scratching it on your car!" Her eyes are on fire and Tom cringes. "If you think that, then you don't know Julie Meskens, Tom. No way. We're going to stop this nonsense here and call her dad. Give me your phone."

He takes the phone out of his pocket, unlocks it, and puts it in her waiting hand. She quickly scrolls through his contact list, selects "Julie's Dad," and pushes the phone back into his hands.

"Call him."

His hands are shaking again. He holds the phone to his ear and swallows heavily.

"Yes?" says the deep voice of Jean-Pierre Meskens warmly in his ear.

"Um, Mr. Meskens, good afternoon. This is Tom speaking."

"Tom? Yes?" The warmth disappears and gives way to a cool interest.

"I... um..."

Eloise flaps her hands impatiently, making her bracelets tingle. "Come on," she says quietly.

"I was wondering if you'd heard anything from Julie," Tom says.

It remains silent at the other end of the line.

"Hello, sir?" Tom asks, worried.

"I don't think I quite understand your question," replies Jean-Pierre Meskens. "Why do you ask me if I've heard anything from my daughter if she's living with you?"

Tom swallows and explains the situation. That Julie went to the market and came home, but since then she's been missing, along with the baby's things and her suitcase.

Mr. Meskens makes no attempt to conceal his contempt for Tom. "So, you've had a fight and my daughter has packed her things. Well, boy, I have no idea why you're calling me. I'm the last person she'd want to admit she'd made a mistake to. And if I can give you some advice: leave Julie alone. If she left, I'm sure she has a good reason. Call her friend Eloise; Julie will be there. Oh, and if you hear from her, tell her my door is open."

"Eloise? No, she's not there. Eloise is here with me now. We're really worried, sir," replies Tom, bewildered, but he's speaking to the big nothing.

"Did he hang up?" asks Eloise with big eyes.

Tom nods and puts the phone down on the table, defeated. He knew Julie didn't have a great relationship with her dad at the moment, but that he would react like this... "She's not there, either. Now what?"

Eloise bites her lip. "I think we'd better call the police."

13:30

29 Weeks and 4 Days Pregnant

I remember now: the last person I saw was our new neighbor. He had introduced himself as Floris and looked like he couldn't hurt a fly.

What has he done to me? And why? Is he some kind of madman and was it just bad luck that I lived in the same building as him? I don't know him, do I? I rack my brain looking for any point of reference, but I can't place the pale, disfigured man with the shaved head and thick glasses. Although... His posture gives me that strange feeling of déjà vu, the way he tried not to be noticed despite his tall, broad stature.

That creep has kidnapped me! Where did he take me? My eyes fly around the room again, looking for a clue or a way out. What is he planning to do with me? Is this one of those basements you read about in the papers?

My hands keep trembling. I try my best to stay calm, but it's damned hard. Simultaneously, I feel anger. Why the hell would you kidnap a complete stranger from her own flat? How was he even able to? He must have drugged me, but with what? What kind of poison did he give me? I'm pregnant, damn it! Is that why I feel so sick? If he gave me roofies or something similar, it could take several hours for me to recover. I try as best as I can to pull any knowledge I have of sedation from my brain. I can only hope he's given me something that won't harm the baby.

With a jolt, I realize that he knows I'm pregnant. He can't *not* have noticed. And all these baby things being here... He can't be after the baby, can he? My hands reach for my belly as panic surges through my body again. Where is he? What's he waiting for? The not knowing takes over from the fear.

"Hey!" I shout. "Where am I? Let me out of here, goddammit!"

Silence.

I'm going mad. I begin to roar again, my voice unrecognizable from the rage in it.

"Floris! What the fuck is this? Let me out of here, I'm fucking pregnant!"

More silence.

Again, I see that mutilated hand before me. It had a lot of scars all over it—from burns, I guess. He was also limping a bit; I even felt sorry for him when he stood in my flat. He seemed so vulnerable despite his height.

The silence weighs on my chest and takes my breath away. I know I have to calm down and so I let my thoughts wander to Tom. If it's half-past two now, he's probably looking for me, worried. He must be wondering where I am and why I've taken all that stuff with me.

Despondent, I kick the table leg and lie down on the bed again. I can't do anything except wait for Floris to show up and tell me what's what. Or to come and torture and then kill me, of course. I start chewing my hair.

***

Perhaps I've fallen asleep again—the anesthetic makes me weak and distorts my perception—but a little later I hear a noise coming from the stairs. I jump up and put my arms around me in some weird form of protection.

The hatch opens; I feel the warm air blowing into the back of the room as his big feet step down the stairs. His left foot follows a second later. Slowly he comes down, cautiously. I'm startled when I see that he has a taser in his hand.

"Stay away from me! Stay away!" I shout in panic, but he continues unperturbed down the stairs until he stops at the bottom. I stiffen in fear and crawl against the wall, trapped like a rat. "Bastard! Get away from me! Leave me alone!" I sob, feeling the tears running down my cheeks.

My baby, my girl, what's he going to do to me? What's he going to do to her?

But he doesn't do anything and just keeps staring at me like I'm a monkey at the zoo. I stare back and for several minutes nothing happens.

Then he says, "Drink, Julie, there's nothing wrong with that water."

I shake my head.

He walks to the table, the taser in his hand, and pours a glass of water. Then he opens the fridge. "There's fruit and some yogurt, if you're hungry. I'll bring you a hot meal every day, and there's bread and spreads. If you need anything else, you can write it down here." He holds up a notebook and a pencil and puts it down on the table. I don't understand.

"Why am I here? What are you up to?" I ask, although it's almost unintelligible.

He doesn't answer and pulls open one of the doors, the one closest to the kitchen. "In here is the bathroom where you can shower and change. I've brought some of your things, as you've already seen." He nods his head towards the wall. I recognize the small suitcase that was ready to be taken to the hospital.

Okay, so he didn't bring things just for the baby, but also for me. Why?

"I don't get it. Are you going to keep me here as a pet or something?"

Again, he's silent, as if he hasn't heard me. His eyes remain hidden behind the thick glasses. He pulls open another door. "And here's the toilet."

"Floris, say something! What are you up to? You won't get away with this! Tom will have called the police by now. You can let me go now. Nothing has happened yet," I try again.

"The TV isn't connected to the cable, but I bought you some DVDs. I can also get you some books. Just write down what you want to read," he continues calmly, as if he were a campsite manager presenting the facilities I can use during my holiday. From behind his glasses, he looks at me penetratingly, even defiantly. Powerlessness rushes through my body. I can't stop it and I start roaring like a lunatic while banging my hands on the mattress.

"Bastard! Let me out of here! You're crazy!" I scream. I want to pounce on him but my instincts stop me.

He waits patiently for me to finish. "Call out as much as you want. You're underground and there's no one around, so no one can hear you. I'll be back tomorrow and I hope you've calmed down a bit by then."

I cover my face with my hands and feel warm tears flowing. I'm trapped here, in an underground cage, and have no idea why. At best, Floris is a madman hiding me in a basement for his own amusement; at worst, he's a murderer who wants to make his prey suffer for as long as possible before he's tired of them. In both cases, I'm seriously screwed.

I peek at him through my fingers as he walks back up the stairs and disappears through the hatch. At least I have peace of mind until tomorrow morning, if he's telling the truth.

I wonder what Tom's doing now. And Eloise. And Daddy. Would they be looking for me? Do they understand that I didn't leave on purpose? I hope so.

14:45

For the second time that day, Tom parks his car in front of the police station. This time he walks to the entrance with Eloise by his side. She'd insisted on coming along and had followed him in her Mini. She looks back at the four letters on the side of his Golf and shakes her head.

"This is not good, Tom. This is really not okay."

The nerves squeeze his throat, so he pushes open the door for her without answering. There's a different officer at the counter now and this time they don't have to wait. As soon as the word "missing" is mentioned, Tom is taken straight to an interview room. Eloise stays in the reception area waiting for him. This all feels so surreal.

Tom plays with the plastic cup of water that's been placed on the table in front of him and waits. After a few minutes, the door swings open and a man enters who introduces himself as Chief Inspector Van Dijck. It doesn't escape Tom that the inspector is taking him in with an alert gaze; without words, the interrogation has already begun. Despite his small stature, the man radiates authority; it reassures Tom somewhat he can put his concerns in professional hands.

"Tell me," begins Van Dijck. "Who do you want to report missing?" Although he acts briskly, his attitude is concerned and interested, and Tom explains what happened that afternoon, how he came home and found the flat empty. Van Dijck nods and writes something down in the file in front of him.

"What was Julie wearing when you saw her this morning?"

Tom describes her green dress and sandals.

"Did she take her handbag?"

He nods in reply.

"Cell phone?"

"Yes, but I've tried to call her several times and it goes straight to voicemail."

"Okay, if necessary, we can use that to try to determine her location."

If necessary? Tom thinks. *Why not right now?*

"Have you had words?"

"Words?"

"Yes, did you have a fight before she left? A disagreement?"

"N-n-no," Tom stammers.

"Why do you regard her disappearance as suspicious?"

He tells the chief inspector everything: that she's pregnant, that the flat is hers, that there's no reason for her to leave. He also tells him about the scratches on his car and her punctured bike tires.

The man disappears for a moment to trace their previous report and Tom thirstily empties his cup of water. He stares at the empty screen of his phone.

Julie, where are you?

His hands don't stop trembling.

Van Dijck re-enters and sits opposite Tom again.

"I'll have someone investigate the vandalism on your car. If I understand correctly, you reported scratches earlier. Why do you think there's a connection with your girlfriend's disappearance?"

"I don't know. She'd heard someone shouting in her flat"

"*In* her flat?"

"No, I mean, she was home alone when she heard someone calling, but she didn't know who it was nor where it came from," Tom stuttered.

Van Dijck makes another note. "You just said 'her' flat. Don't you live together?"

"Yes, but only since recently." Tom feels his cheeks turning red, as if he's been caught in a lie. Those stupid hands won't stop shaking either; he puts them on his lap under the table, but Van Dijck seems to see and take everything in. Outside the interrogation room, loud noises can be heard; someone's being taken somewhere against their will. Tom swallows and tries to explain, without any hiccups, why he's moved in with Julie.

"So the pregnancy wasn't planned," Van Dijck concludes, and he continues to write in the file as if this is an important fact.

"No, but she was happy with it," Tom stammers. "I mean *is*. She's happy with it. She wasn't at first, but she is now. And so am I."

"Did she suffer from mood swings?"

"Yes, of course." He blurts it out before he realizes what he has said. "No! I mean..."

Van Dijck frowns at him and nerves race through his throat.

"She wasn't depressed, if that's what you mean, but she could sometimes go from one extreme to the other. *Can*. I mean can."

His red face is beginning to show beads of sweat and he's terribly thirsty, but his cup of water is empty.

"And according to you, there was no quarrel? Nothing?"

"N-no."

"So your relationship's all right?"

Van Dijck's question doesn't sit well with Tom at all.

"What does that have to do with—"

"Routine questions. Please answer."

"Yes, our relationship was fine."

"Could she have met someone else?"

Tom looks at him in bewilderment. "No! Of course not, she's seven months pregnant!"

"Did she have money problems?" Van Dijck continues coolly.

"No, not at all."

Van Dijck nods and makes some notes in the file. After a few more standard questions, he ends the interrogation.

"All right, we'll file a report about the disappearance, but I have to tell you that there's not much we can do at the moment. Julie's an adult, there are no signs of forced entry, and she has taken her belongings with her. If you want my opinion, she's probably confused because of the pregnancy hormones and the stress that the situation has caused."

Tom is quite sure that this isn't the case and he fights to hold back the tears. Van Dijck bends over the table paternally and looks him in the eyes.

"She'll turn up again, son. Less than one percent of disappearances are really worrying."

"But—"

"Give her a little more time, and if she doesn't turn up by tomorrow, we'll put the missing persons unit on her case."

***

"So they're not doing anything yet?" Eloise asks him when they're outside again, her dark eyes wide.

"No, for the time being she's only flagged."

She bites the little piece of skin next to her nail bed. "Tom, I'm really worried."

"Me too."

"Shall I stay with you tonight? Until she returns?"

He nods gratefully. He doesn't want to be alone now with his thoughts. They descend deeper into darkness every hour.

I can't believe this is happening to me. As soon as the hatch closes, I run up the stairs and try to push it open again, but in vain. Furious, I look for a way to escape. I search every inch of my cell with my hands, looking for evidence of a hidden exit, a loose stone, or anything else I could use. The grey cement walls seem solid, but I must try to find a way out. I open all the cupboards and drawers and throw the contents on the floor. If I find something sharp enough, I might be able to use it as a tool, or a weapon. But I can't find anything. In the bathroom, all I find is a toothbrush, toothpaste, a plastic hairbrush, a few towels, and some flannels. The kitchen drawers are empty, and the cupboards, too. No knives, scissors, or other sharp objects. What did I expect?

Think, Julie, think.

My suitcase! It's a small travel bag that I use as hand luggage on the plane. I'd prepared it to take with me to the hospital, for the delivery. I hadn't put that much in it yet, but I liked to be prepared.

Hopeful, I throw the thing on the bed and pull open the zip. Floris has been smart enough to check the contents: everything is mixed up. I find pajamas and clean underwear, but no toiletries bag and therefore no sharp objects.

There are a couple of baby onesies in it. I pull one out, cream with a soft polar bear on the front, and press it against my chest. My vision blurs and the room spins around me; everything seems to be moving away from me, as if I'm looking through upside-down binoculars. My heart is pounding in my throat and my fingers are starting to tingle. It's a panic attack, but knowing that doesn't make it any less bad. I put my head between my knees until the room comes to a stop. The last thing I want to do now is lose my mind. I try to think of Tom, who must be looking for me. The police are surely looking for me, too. Soon, the hatch will open and they'll get me out. Then everything will be over.

My breathing calms down; my head clears. I turn my attention to the suitcase again. It's a fancy thing with little pockets everywhere. My hope of finding something flares up. Frantically, I start to open all the zips, but the pockets are empty. I don't give up; I feel every nook and cranny of the rough fabric until I hit a bump in the lining. It's something small, the size of a tampon, which it very well could be. Nervously, I search for a way to reach the thing with my fingers, my hands shaking so much I can't make it out. I grit my teeth in frustration. This isn't going to work. I have to control myself and be systematic.

Calm and controlled.

I close my eyes and take a deep breath, then I calmly start examining the travel bag, starting at the seams. It doesn't take long before I find the small hidden zip, on the inside of the bag, just below the coarse seam of the main closure. Carefully, I open the compartment and put my hand inside. It's a small space, ideal for hiding something of value. My hand closes around something that feels cold. It's metal, not a tampon. My heart skips. Is it a pocketknife? Am I really that lucky? I quickly pull the thing out of the bag and open my hand.

No, it's not a pocketknife. It's a nail clipper.

I pry the thing open and am almost jubilant when I see that it has one of those mini-files attached to it. It's extremely small, but at least it's something. I immediately try out my new tool on a piece of wall under the bed so that if I manage to make a hole, he won't see it right away. I roll over on my side and put the tip of the file into the wall. A small hole appears and I start scratching back and forth. Grey dust falls to the floor, but no more than a few shallow scratches appear. I apply more pressure and try to make a hole. It doesn't work. I try another place. I know nothing about basements. What are they made of? Bricks? Cement? Frantically I start again, but the result remains the same.

My knuckles are scratched and I feel exhausted. What am I doing? If I'm in a basement, how on earth am I going to dig a tunnel with a nail file without him noticing? Even if I manage to pry the stones out of the wall, where am I going to put them? And how thick is the wall? I must save my strength. Think.

I sit up straight and pull myself onto the bed. I'm really exhausted. The wall clock indicates a little past four o'clock.

I'm tired.

So tired.

Captured

Julie

29 Weeks and 5 Days Pregnant
Day 2 in the Basement

The light is on in the basement. I don't know if I can turn it off myself. The darkness doesn't appeal to me anyway, so the bright fluorescent lamp stays on all night. Again and again I wake up with a jolt, at first not realizing where I am until the musty smell of the basement penetrates my nostrils. Again and again, reality crashes into my consciousness. I've been kidnapped. I would prefer the worst nightmare to my reality, but unfortunately, I'm not dreaming.

I wonder if the police are already looking for me. Every little sound makes me prick up my ears, my gaze fixed on the hatch, hoping that it will fly open with a bang and a team of armed men will burst into the basement saying, "Police, you're safe."

But nothing can be heard except the constant hum of the fluorescent tubes.

What would Floris want from me? Ransom? I have no money. Apart from my flat, I have nothing of value. Neither does Tom. My dad? Yes, Dad has money, but he's not really rich. At least I don't think so. I realize that I don't really know. He has a small road haulage company, but it could have become quite big by now. We don't speak to each other that often, and certainly not about his work. Could that be it? Could Floris have had it in for my dad and therefore moved in above me? That could be. How much would Dad be worth? The more I think about it, the more I start to believe that money is the reason I'm here. That's good news, because then it's in Floris' interest that I stay healthy and well, right?

I try to imagine my dad's face when he gets the ransom call. Poor Dad; he doesn't deserve this. His work is his life, especially since Mom's gone.

I turn on my side and think back to the time when the two of us lived together, when we moved to the city after her passing. The look in his eyes when he dropped me off the first day at my new school: a look that said both "sorry" and "please don't make this harder than it already is." I know he did what he could. I know the choices he made had stemmed from his clumsy way of dealing with loss—a loss so huge he had to drag himself through the days. He couldn't carry the weight of my grief on top of it. I knew that even then. But if I hadn't had Eloise, who never left my side from the first day of school, I don't know if I would've made it through adolescence alive. She had immediately approached me and taken me under her wing as a matter of course. Only later did I understand that she'd been used to doing this at home where she and her elder sister had to help raise their younger siblings. I must have looked really helpless. Even then, she always managed to look great with little money. She tried to impart her sense of style to me too, but it never worked. I enjoyed accompanying her on her weekend rummages through second-hand shops. That way, I could escape for a few hours from the depressing atmosphere at home. Eloise always found some designer skirt or blouse that she managed to combine in spectacular fashion. Afterwards, I would treat her to pizza or McDonald's, because she couldn't afford it.

But all that seems so long ago now. It's six o'clock in the morning and my second day in the basement has begun.

Tom

With Julie's picture, Tom and Eloise had gone around to all the doors of the neighborhood together, but nobody had seen anything or been able to tell them anything. Then they had another photo printed hundreds of times at the copy shop. At every bus stop, in every café, and on every lamppost, Julie's smiling head was on display. Each time he taped the A4, he looked her in the eye and needed a few seconds to breathe out the increasing pressure on his chest. They'd gone to the train station, to the market, to the university, to Billy's of course, even to that children's shop where Julie's bike tires had been punctured. Eloise called everyone who might know something. The result was zero.

Then the gynecologist's secretary called Tom because Julie and he hadn't come to their appointment and she couldn't reach Julie. Immediately afterwards, he called the police again. They had to take this seriously: twenty-four hours had passed and Julie wouldn't let her appointment go. She was always looking forward to seeing the baby on the ultrasound.

Now, the case has gained momentum: the police are doing their own neighborhood investigation and are talking to everyone. Just moments ago, Julie's face came on TV. "Have you seen this woman?" along with the phone number of the police. It gave him goosebumps.

Tom was interrogated again, and so was Eloise. He had to tell the police where he was and what he'd done that morning—a formality, according to them. But Van Dijck asked him if anyone could confirm his alibi, which no one could for the hour between his drive home and the moment when Eloise arrived. At the police station, he had seen Mr.

Meskens, Julie's dad, although he'd hardly recognized him. The big man sat slumped on a plastic chair waiting in front of the interrogation room. Tom wanted to go up to him—they were in the same boat, after all—but he didn't dare and walked past him. He would call him later.

Now he's back home, exhausted. The adrenaline that kept him going the past few days seems to have worn off.

It's quiet in the flat, the emptiness filling the room and pressing down on his head. Eloise has gone home. He misses Julie, he misses Dolly. His whole world has turned into a horrible nightmare in three days.

He sits down on the stool behind his piano and bows his head, his hands on his lap. Slowly, he lifts them up and touches the keys with his fingers. The lonely living room fills with delicate sounds. He closes his eyes. The musical notes swell and fall again, like waves on a beach. He allows his mind to be carried away by the music and opens his eyes only now and then, just to let the tears that are pressing against his eyelids evaporate.

The doorbell rings, causing him to abruptly stop playing.

"Chief Inspector Van Dijck," he hears through the intercom and a moment later the man is standing in the living room with a number of people from his team.

"Good evening, is there any news?" Tom asks nervously.

"No, not yet. Sit down, I want to ask you some more questions. These people can do their work in the meantime," says Van Dijck, pointing to his colleagues.

Tom looks at him, not understanding.

"When a disappearance is worrying, we always do a search. I explained that to you this morning," says the chief inspector. His tone is friendly but firm and he hands Tom a document. Right, he'd been told. He remembers. He sits down at the table with his knees buckling and reads the paper only briefly before signing it.

"Are you looking for something special?" he asks as Van Dijck hangs his jacket over a chair and sits down.

"Anything that could indicate malicious intent," says Van Dijck, his gaze fixed on Tom. "If there's something you want to tell me, you'd better do it now, Mr. Van de Velde."

Tom looks at him in bewilderment. What's the point of that? He has nothing to hide, has he? And since when does he call him Mr. Van de Velde?

"What do you mean?"

"What I just said."

He doesn't understand a thing. Have they received a tip-off or something? His hands are clammy and his tongue sticks to the roof of his mouth. Nervously, he licks his lips.

"I-I don't think so. I don't quite understand..."

"Did you have an argument with Julie Meskens?" Van Dijck asks, as if he hasn't already asked that question twice.

"I've already told you that, haven't I? No, we had no quarrel. Everything was fine." He doesn't understand a thing. What does Van Dijck want from him?

"That's not what I heard," growls the chief inspector. His dark hair is combed forward in a crest. The hairstyle reminds Tom of a duck's ass.

"Oh?" Tom swallows, not liking his tone.

"I have a witness who claims to have heard regular arguments coming from your flat."

"Who says that?"

"That's irrelevant, Mr. Van de Velde. I'll repeat the question: did you have a fight before Julie disappeared, yes or no?"

"No!"

"You deny that you shouted at her?"

"I never have and I never will," Tom stammers with growing unease. If anyone ever yelled, it was Julie. When she was angry, she always made that very clear.

"So you also deny that you called Julie Meskens 'whore'? That you shouted that at her?"

"I certainly deny that! That didn't come from here!" cries Tom and he feels his cheeks getting warm. Had he told the police about what Julie had heard? He doesn't remember. The scratches? Yes, and the bike, too. And Dolly. But the shouting? He never heard the shouts himself.

"Not from here, you say?"

"No, Julie told me that a few times she heard someone shouting very loudly, but she thought it came from the neighbors."

"I was told a different story."

"What, then?"

"That there were regular arguments in your flat."

Tom grips his head with both hands. What is this? "Am I a suspect now or what? Do I need to get a lawyer?"

Van Dijck continues in a milder tone. "If you have nothing to do with Julie's disappearance, you have nothing to fear and we'll be able to take you off the list soon enough. It's best that you just cooperate and then this will be over in no time."

Tom nods and rubs his hands over his stubble.

"I didn't yell at Julie," he tries to explain calmly. "The words 'slut' and 'whore' did get written and scratched on my car while I was parked out front. You already know all that, because I reported it."

"I do know that, but you understand that we have to investigate every trace. You claimed that you had no relationship issues; this testimony makes us question that.

Moreover, another witness told us that Julie wasn't as happy with the situation as you would have us believe."

Tom is speechless. Who would say such a thing? He doesn't have the time to go into it though, because at that very moment, one of the investigators calls Van Dijck away.

"One moment," he says, getting up and following the investigator up the stairs. Tom is left bewildered. He stares at his hands, feeling confused. Is he a suspect? Do they think *he* scratched his car? That would be a disaster, because it means that they wouldn't be looking for the person who kidnapped Julie. Because that's what happened, he's sure of that now.

He has no time to develop a real panic because Van Dijck re-enters the living room. In his hands he has a plastic bag containing something that looks like a t-shirt. A bloody t-shirt.

"Tom Van de Velde, I'm arresting you in connection with the disturbing disappearance of and possible violent crime against Julie Meskens," he says, handcuffing Tom. "You'll come with me now."

Julie

30 Weeks Pregnant
Day 4 in the Basement

I'm alive, but that's the only good news. I feel so alone. It seems as if time has slowed down; the minutes crawl by.

The first time Floris came in with the food, I threw the plate against the wall as he walked back up the stairs.

"I don't want your filthy food, pervert!" I shouted as the mashed potatoes dripped down the grey wall like flakes of foam on the beach. "And I don't eat meat!"

He shrugged his shoulders, continued up the stairs, disappeared through the hatch, and left me alone. I was hungry, but at that moment I still thought that I would soon be able to escape from my prison after the ransom had been paid. What a nice dream that was.

The next afternoon he came back and calmly scraped the leftovers from the floor and the wall as if nothing had happened. He put a new plate on the table for me: fish this time.

"I don't want your food, let me out of here," I shouted, but in hindsight I wasn't doing myself any favors. He clearly didn't care whether I liked his food or not. I knew that eventually I would have to eat, if not for myself then for my baby. How long would she be able to rely on my reserves if I only drank water? What deficits would she get? At home, I took extra folic acid, but I don't have that here. I do know that bananas are rich in it, so I reluctantly ate one. The fish stayed there all evening and all night, smelling awful. Cod, I believe.

The silence drives me crazy, yet I stubbornly refuse to look at the DVDs or ask him for books. This isn't my house;

I don't live here. I'm not going to make myself comfortable. I wait.

Doubt slowly creeps in. Is this really a kidnapping for ransom? Then wouldn't he take a picture of me with a newspaper or something? And record a spoken message or video to prove to my dad that I'm in good health? That's how it goes in movies, but this isn't a fiction. This is reality. *My* reality. And my reality is apparently not about ransom.

It's about *me*.

In some sick way, he's convinced that what he's doing is right. I can tell by the way he looks at me: as if I've brought all this down on myself. He seems to think it's my own fault. He lets me suffer just by holding me here. He doesn't do anything else. He doesn't try to touch me or threaten me.

More things become clear to me: the cursing I heard at home…that was Floris, of course. A shiver runs down my spine when I realize that he's been calling me "bitch" and "whore" and whatever else while I was home alone. My brain goes into overdrive and makes one connection after another: the scratches on Tom's car… also his work. But why? Why Tom's car? Is it Tom he is after, instead of me? And does he want to punish Tom by kidnapping his unborn child and me? No, I shake my head. That's not it. I feel it. His hatred is directed at me. I must've done something to him once. To him, or to someone he knows and loves. But how can that be if I've never seen him before?

After a restless night, I have made a decision this morning: if I want to get out of here, I have to save my strength and eat more than yogurt and fruit. But I haven't eaten animals for years, and I'm not going to start now. So, finally, I write a note for him and place it on the table.

***

It's already evening when I hear the hatch open. He comes down with a new tray and puts it on the table. I stare at him from the bed. My hair is greasy and I'm still wearing the same clothes: the green dress I wore when I went to the market—the last time I saw the sunshine and breathed fresh air. I can see how he unconsciously wrinkles his nose at the smell of fish, sweat, and unwashed human being that undoubtedly hangs in the room. I also see that there is fluff growing on his head and that he has stubble. His hair is as white as a baby's. The stubble on his chin is also white, as is the skin on which it grows. This makes a sharp contrast with his dark eyebrows. His eyes are hidden behind those idiotically thick spectacle lenses.

He takes the tray with the untouched food from the table and sees my note. He carefully puts the tray down again and looks in my direction. Then he takes the note and reads: *I'm a vegetarian.* That seemed like more than enough information.

He gives me another one of those looks that make me feel like dirt and disappears upstairs. He takes the tray with yesterday's fish, but leaves the rest.

When he's disappeared, I curiously go and see what he's brought me: vegetable soup with spaghetti strings and a piece of baguette. He's probably given up on cooking for me and kept it simple, but right now I'm as happy as a child. I hungrily dip the baguette into the soup and empty the bowl in no time.

Tom

The police detained him for two days but then had to let him go. They'd found a t-shirt with bloodstains in the back of his wardrobe. Tom has no idea how it got there and whose blood was on it, but according to his lawyer, the police assume that he killed Julie during an argument. Whether this was intentional or not, the investigation will show. Afterwards, they say, he must have hidden her body somewhere, together with some clothes and things for the baby, to make it look like she had left on her own. According to Chief Inspector Van Dijck, he had had enough time between his visit to the police station and Eloise's arrival in the flat. It doesn't look good.

Never before did he feel so helpless as when the cell door closed behind him and he could no longer look for Julie. When he had to appear before the examining magistrate, he almost passed out from panic that he would be locked up again. But now he's standing here, at the bus stop, breathing in the fresh scent of the rain. He's free, although he has to remain "available" for any subsequent hearings. What a nightmare. Julie's been missing for five days now and Tom is the only suspect, as far as he knows.

He's reluctant to go back to the flat, but where else can he go? He wants to call Eloise, but of course his cell phone is dead and he doesn't want to show up at her shop unexpectedly. They can't talk there anyway.

Fate decides for him. In the distance, he sees the bus approaching, and a moment later, he's dry and bumping up and down the potholed streets. With his fingers, he taps his thighs. Through the windows, he sees the city sliding past. He knows the streets and neighborhoods like the back of his hand, but it's been a long time since he took public transport.

It's raining harder now. A woman fights with her umbrella, her hair blowing in the wind, a dogged look on her face. An older man watches the scene from his balcony and smokes a cigarette. Tom feels as if he's watching a movie instead of the world around him—a world he no longer feels part of. He doesn't belong to the "ordinary people" anymore; he's a suspect in a missing persons case, a murder, perhaps. His name is in the newspaper. Even if it's only his initials, he's tainted. The kind of man you keep away from your children. He sighs. Is this who he'll be from now on? An onlooker who looks at everyone else's happiness without ever experiencing it? Despite the warmth in the bus, he's shivering; he isn't dressed for this wet weather.

With an iron clamp around his heart, he puts the key in the lock. Quickly, he walks into the flat, but the hairs on his arms rise when he's confronted with the place where Julie may have fought her last battle. Silently he says her name: "Julie?" The atmosphere weighs heavily on him. He cautiously steps into the living room and scans it with his eyes. The traces of the search are still visible: cupboards and drawers are open, the carpet lies rolled up in a corner, the table and chairs have been pushed aside.

His piano looks undamaged and he slides his hand tenderly over the smooth, dark wood. If only he could turn back time, if only he hadn't driven to the vet that day, Julie might still be here. He sits down on the piano stool, runs his hands over the keys, and begins to play. One thing, after all, that wasn't taken away from him. He automatically feels lighter; he stretches his back and straightens his shoulders. Faster, his long fingers move, his head nods along to the beat of the music and soon his body takes over from his head. Not a thought or emotion intrudes; no sorrow, no joy, no pain.

Tom no longer thinks about what's happened to him or to Julie. Finally, his head is silent and only his hands speak.

When the doorbell rings, his heart almost jumps out of his chest. The same happens every time his phone rings: he's overwhelmed by the hope that Julie's been found, followed immediately by the fear that she's no longer alive.

But it's not the police. It's Eloise, who has slipped away from the shop for an hour. Hearing her voice through the intercom, his legs go limp with relief. When she steps into the flat, a color bomb seems to go off. She jumps around his neck.

"Tom, this is really surreal. Tell me this is a mistake." She has dark circles under her eyes.

"I'm afraid not."

"On the news, they said that traces of violence were found in your flat and that's why you were arrested. Is that true?" She looks around at the mess he hasn't yet cleaned up.

Tom covers his face with his hands and nods. A shiver runs down his spine.

"But what did they find?" asks Eloise. Her eyes are wide and she bites her lower lip.

"They found blood," he replies softly, almost in a whisper. He still can't believe it. Apart from the t-shirt, the forensics lab had also discovered a pool of blood next to the dining table that had been hastily mopped up. In the kitchen sink, they found bloodstains, and then they discovered a bloodstained mop in the dumpster downstairs.

"As if I would ever do anything to Julie," he continues. "I love her and I miss her and now I'm sitting here and I can't do a damn thing."

Eloise slaps her hand over her mouth. "Jesus, if they found so much blood, what the hell happened to Julie?" Tears spring to her eyes. "Oh, Tom, what if she's dead?"

"I can't think of anything else, and I don't understand it. I mean, why would someone kill Julie? And why would that person take her things? And the baby's? That doesn't make any sense!"

Eloise shakes her head. "No, that doesn't make sense. But neither does the fact that they suspect you."

He shrugs his shoulders. "I get it, it's usually the partner," he says bitterly. "And according to the police, witnesses claim to have heard us arguing regularly."

Eloise's head flies up with a jerk. "Is that true?"

"No, but it's my word against theirs."

She looks at him sharply. He senses that she's not yet sure whether to believe him or not. "Nice neighbors. What shall we do now?" she asks.

They sit down at the table. He wants to grab her hands, but holds back. "I have no idea. I keep racking my brain to find out where she could be, what could've happened, but I have no idea. Someone took her, Eloise. In broad daylight. And because the police suspect me, the bastard walks free," he says with clenched jaws.

Eloise's lip begins to tremble. She's usually so strong, but now all her strength seems to have drained away.

"Hey, come on, don't cry. Please. I just feel so powerless, you know? I'm glad that you at least believe me. You do believe me, right?" he asks.

"I believe you," she says with a nod, but her head is bowed. She picks at her painted nails, bright pink this week. "Is there anything I can do?"

Tom folds his hands behind his head and thinks. Eloise is the only person in the world he can trust, who knows he's innocent. Jean-Pierre Meskens, Julie's dad, is convinced that Tom has killed Julie. His parents believe in his innocence, of course, but they live too far away and can't just leave their shop behind. He also suspects that his dad is afraid that the whole affair will damage the reputation of his business, Woonboulevard Van de Velde. His brother and sister have their own lives and he doesn't expect much from them. And he doesn't have many friends; he just likes to be alone.

"There is something you can do," he begins.

She looks at him questioningly.

"Do you remember when I told you about Dolly? That the vet said she was strangled?" He starts speaking more softly. Eloise nods in agreement and leans across the table closer to him. "And what I told you about the scratches on my car?"

"Hm?"

"You didn't believe at first that those swear words were meant for Julie. How do you feel about that now?"

Eloise sighs and sits up straighter in her chair. "I don't know. I find it so hard to believe that someone would say something like that to Julie. I mean, she did have a lot of flings. You know how she was. *Is*. Shit. But she's never cheated on anyone, as far as I know, and she's on good terms with all her exes. I guess. It just doesn't make sense."

"I agree, but there's something else: every time I wasn't home, she heard shouting from somewhere nearby; that's probably what those so-called witnesses heard. I don't know how many times that happened, but she told me they were swear words like 'bitch' and 'whore' and so on. That's a bizarre coincidence, isn't it?"

"That is indeed strange. And she had no idea where it came from?"

Tom leans even closer to her, and she mirrors his posture. "The funny thing is, she thought it came from our upstairs neighbor, but because he lives alone, she suspected the family next door. But, Eloise, what if it *was* our upstairs neighbor?"

"What, then? He may have been talking on the phone with someone, right?"

"Sure, he may have, but don't you think it's a strange coincidence? The exact same words? Besides, he never opens the door when I knock. Isn't that strange?"

"Yes, it is, but if your upstairs neighbor shouted at Julie and scratched swear words on your car that were directed at her, why did he? She didn't know him, did she?"

"No." Tom slumps in his chair. That's a gap in his theory: there's no motive. Why would a complete stranger do such a thing? They hadn't even met the man yet. That he didn't open the door is no proof. But it's the only clue he has.

"You know so many people. Can't you find out who this man is?" he asks.

Eloise hesitates. "Isn't that something for the police?"

"Of course, but they think they've already found who did it," he replies in frustration.

"All right, I'll see what I can do. You never know, you might be right," she says, putting a gentle hand on his. Then she gets up and straightens out her purple suit. "I have to go back to the boutique. Have you eaten yet?"

He shakes his head. Not hungry.

"You have to eat, Tom. I'll go to the supermarket later and then we'll eat together tonight, okay?"

He nods. "Thank you." As much as he usually likes to be alone, he now finds it horrifying.

As soon as Eloise is out of the door, he runs up the stairs for the umpteenth time to knock on the door of his upstairs neighbor. There's something off with that man. Any innocent person would spontaneously offer to help, wouldn't they?

But this time, too, there is no answer.

Back in the flat, he grabs a stack of photos of Julie and runs downstairs with the posters under his arm. Someone must have seen something.

Julie

I've decided not to mention his name anymore. He's a monster. A nameless monster. As much as I want to know why he's holding me here, I don't want to ask him anymore. I don't want to give him that pleasure. Besides, every time I ask him a question, he doesn't answer and points to the notebook.

Since I started eating again, I feel my strength returning. I use the notebook to write messages for him. For example, I asked him for folic acid tablets and he gave them to me a few days later. That gave me a greater sense of control than I've had in days. I also asked for a newspaper, but that never came.

I think he has a job with changing working hours and therefore comes at different times. Given his knowledge of anesthesia, he may well be a doctor or a nurse.

The not knowing drives me crazy. Are they looking for me out here? Do they have any idea what happened? I've also realized that it will look suspicious that I've disappeared with some of my clothes and the things for the baby. I fervently hope Tom won't get into trouble, that they'll believe him when he tells them I didn't disappear voluntarily. If *he* even believes it.

I don't know. Have I made it clear enough that I was happy to be with him? Now that I think about it, I'm afraid he might have some doubts.

And Eloise? She also knows that I would never be with Tom if I hadn't gotten pregnant.

Damn, this isn't good. What if they think I've left? Who knows, they may not even have called the police yet!

No, that's not possible. It really can't be. I would never do such a thing without confiding in Eloise and she knows it. Doesn't she?

I have too much time to think. That's the problem. Maybe I should ask him to bring some books.

I'm racking my brain as to what strategy I can use to get him to let me out, because escape isn't an option. I've examined the room from top to bottom and there's not a single hole to be found. I've hidden the nail clippers with the little file under the mattress; it may come in handy. I curse every movie I've seen where a prisoner escapes by using their creativity. Nonsense. It's all bullshit. There's nothing I can do.

He hates me, so I'm thinking maybe that'll change when he gets to know me better. And who knows, maybe I'll get through to him if I find out more about him. Maybe he was abused as a child? Or did he grow up without a mom, like me? What if he's not a monster at all, but a man who has never known love? Then a charm offensive is the best strategy, right? I have to show him what I can mean to him, show him that I'm a human being made of flesh and blood. Someone he can love and who loves him. Or so I could make it seem.

I feel the baby kicking and my new plan gives me some courage. I'm going to get out of this, damn it.

Pieter

Investigative journalist Pieter De Saegher bends closer to the mirror and brushes his finger over the spot where a beer bottle hit his nose. The scar is a memory of a bar brawl at Billy's that he tried to defuse. Depending on the temperature, and on his mood, it changes color. Sometimes you can hardly see it; other times, it flares up bright red, like today. The erratic stripe is reminiscent of the mark on Harry Potter's forehead, but without the magical power.

He combs his black hair with his fingers. He's thirty-two but looks ten years younger. He dresses like a teenager with his ripped jeans and dirty Adidas trainers. His fellow journalists sometimes refer to him jokingly as "the rock star." He thinks that's funny because he's never sung a note or played an instrument in his life.

On his way to the office, he reflects on the conversation he just had with Jean-Pierre Meskens, the dad of the missing girl Julie Meskens. He recognized the desperation in his eyes. It was the same distraught look he saw in his parents' eyes, every time his older sister, Tinne, disappeared. Tinne had first come into contact with drugs when she was fifteen. Pieter was eleven at the time. He remembers the many fights at home, the nights his mom slept on the couch while his dad drove through the neighborhood, past all the places she could be. He also remembers the small flashes of hope they had each time Tinne was hospitalized and remained clean for a few weeks.

Until the next relapse.

But most of all, he remembers the day his mom called him. By then, he was living on his own. He'll never forget the visceral scream that came through the phone before she told him, sobbing, that Tinne's body had been found. Stabbed by her boyfriend. In a dark, smelly alley. Some stories just don't end well.

Since then, Pieter has taken up every missing persons case that comes his way with more than his usual professional zeal, if only because he understands what's going through the minds of the family. Fortunately, it doesn't happen often that a case is really disturbing. Moreover, he's always able to maintain the necessary emotional distance.

Until now.

Not only is the Julie Meskens case unsettling, but also, in this particular case, he knows the victim well.

When he was a student, he sometimes worked at Billy's and later it became his favorite bar. In the beginning of his relationship with Ellen, his ex, he used to hang out with her there every Friday, but Ellen didn't see the charm of the pub as he did, so after a while he went there alone. He knew everyone there anyway. Julie and Eloise. And Tom, who's now suspected of having done something terrible to Julie. Pieter has never exchanged a word with him. Is he a murderer, as Julie's dad thinks? Could be. Of course, he knows that the partner is usually the perpetrator. There were no signs of forced entry, and no fingerprints other than those of Tom and Julie and some of their friends, who all have alibis. It's not so hard to imagine a man panicking and killing his girlfriend, especially when you know that they hadn't been together long before she turned out to be pregnant. The couple had even been separated for a while.

Pieter had gone to Billy's and questioned everyone who knew Tom or Julie, looking for anything—anything at all— that might shed light on what had happened to her, but he hadn't learned anything new. He already knew from his own experience that Julie wasn't the saint her dad described—not that he would write about that. His job was to report on the investigation and to sketch a profile of the perpetrator, but Pieter wouldn't have become a journalist if he didn't have a natural critical eye.

No, Tom Van de Velde wouldn't be the first man to suddenly get cold feet about an impending birth; on that, he had to agree with Julie's dad. His theory runs parallel to that of the police: that Tom panicked and did something he might regret. But what if that isn't what happened? Then maybe Julie's been kidnapped and is being held somewhere. He clenches his jaw. Or she's been murdered and the culprit's still out there.

In one swift movement, he turns his Peugeot into the parking lot and walks into the office building. Unconsciously, he rubs his upper arms, which are sore from last night's training session. At five foot seven, he's not exactly an imposing man, but anyone who dares to underestimate him will soon regret it. His talent in Krav Maga takes care of that, a martial art where only effectiveness counts, not grace. He started practicing the sport after he was beaten up during an investigation into a corrupt politician. The only thing Pieter De Saegher expects from a martial art is to be able to fend off his attacker in such a way that they'll think twice before making another attempt. Elegant arm movements are of no use to him.

He puts his laptop bag under his desk and plops down on his chair. As he does every day, he first reads the memos in his mailbox and goes through his e-mails. There's a message from his editor-in-chief. Sales figures are falling every week. *So*, he writes, *as long as the body of Julie Meskens isn't found, I expect all the details about the life of Tom VdV. Who are his exes? What do his pupils say? Find someone who's prepared to hang out his dirty laundry.*

Pieter sighs. He hasn't found anything to hold against the timid music teacher. Even Jean-Pierre Meskens couldn't tell him anything concrete. If the guy really did kill his girlfriend, it was very clever of him to have the presence of mind to get rid of her body without anyone seeing anything. Also, it was a very smart and cunning move to remove her personal things and those of the baby from the flat to make it look like she'd gone off on purpose. This doesn't fit with Pieter's image of Tom, which is confirmed by the schoolteacher's friends and colleagues. But there must be something to it. Maybe he can get him to do an interview and find out more?

Now Pieter has to work out the interview with Jean-Pierre Meskens. He puts on his headphones and starts typing.

Tom

It's been one week since Julie disappeared. The adrenaline rush that the search had initially given him wore off after a few days and was followed by a grief so enormous that it paralyzed him.

Every day is a new struggle trying to keep his head above water. He feels he keeps sinking deeper. In the street, he sees Julie's face blowing across the pavement, or flapping on a lamppost. Still not a single valuable tip has come in, yet he continues to wander through the city every day with his stack of posters. It's all he can do. The realization that it's not enough destroys him.

He rubs his unshaven cheeks and is startled when his phone rings. It's the only moment he feels alive, when his heart is pounding in his throat and panic races through his body. Could she...? Is she...? Did they...?

But it's only Eloise.

"Have you read it? That bastard of a journalist! What a jerk!" Her shouting startles him, and he holds the phone away from his ear. He hasn't read the papers, as he knows the media reported extensively on his arrest, but he has just enough self-respect not to lose himself in the image of his own face with a black bar over his eyes.

"What is it? What are they writing that I don't know yet?" he says when she finally takes a break to breathe.

"It's Julie's dad. He gave an interview to Pieter—you know, the journalist who comes to Billy's every Friday to drink and thinks he's Robert Smith from The Cure," she roars. "Jean-Pierre Meskens portrays you as a wastrel, a loser, a profiteer who gets a girl pregnant and then kills her. What kind of man does that? How did he get that idea into his head?

You're her boyfriend, goddamn it. The father of her child; his grandchild!"

Tom sighs. He knows what kind of man Jean-Pierre Meskens is. A broken man, just like him. A man who thinks he's lost everything. Whose life has no meaning now that his greatest treasure has been snatched away from him. His only treasure.

"Can you blame him?" he replies. "If I had a scapegoat, I would also project everything onto that person. Which reminds me: do you have any news about Floris De Wachter? The upstairs neighbor?"

"No, nothing concrete yet. I'm working on it. But, Tom, you can't let this go! You have to tell your side of the story!"

"And talk to the press? No, Eloise, I won't. They'll twist my words and I don't have the energy for it anyway."

There's silence on the other end. Tom knows that she knows he's right, but doesn't want to admit it yet. He hears her breathing in and out, fast.

"Okay, then don't. But don't read the paper, all right?"

"No problem. Will you come over later?"

"Of course, and I'll bring you something to eat."

Tom walks out of the flat and goes downstairs. Eloise's story about the newspaper reminds him that he hasn't emptied the mailbox since Julie went missing. He stands in front of the two mailboxes; the lower one is his and Julie's. The upper one belongs to the neighbor. Who is this man? The guy has irregular working hours. Tom has only heard him at night or very early in the morning this week.

The corner of a white envelope peeks out of the man's letterbox and Tom's fingers itch to pull it out. Would he?

No. He ignores the man's mail and opens his own box. A thick packet of mail falls out; he needs both hands to keep the envelopes from falling, and with difficulty he closes the box again. At that moment, the frosted glass of the front door catches his eye. It looks as if something has been stuck to the outside. Puzzled, he puts his pile of mail on the stairs and opens the door.

First the smell hits him in the face, although he doesn't immediately understand that there's a connection. His eyes register the large brown stain on the glass, but only after a few seconds does he realize that he's looking at a turd. A horse's, presumably, given the pieces of straw sticking out of it. The turd is just wet enough to stick, and must have just been flung against the door. Tom peers into the street, which is empty. Whoever did it has gone.

He shrugs his shoulders despondently. Whatever. He picks an advertising leaflet out of the pile of mail, removes the biggest chunk of feces with it, and then throws it in the garbage. Then, with the remaining mail in his arms, he trudges back upstairs to fetch a bucket and soap.

It's only a few hours later that he plucks up the courage to open the mail. Most of the envelopes contain threats. With growing amazement, he reads one accusation after another. He's clearly no longer the anonymous boyfriend. Unbelievable how people stick their noses in private affairs that have nothing to do with them. And how they jump to conclusions. What happened to the phrase "innocent until proven guilty"? The letters tell him in no uncertain terms that he's being "watched" and that "if I see you, I'll cut you open from top to bottom."

He bites his lip. So they know where he lives. That means they'll probably also… He gets up, opens his laptop and checks his work e-mail.

Yup. There they are.

Dozens of e-mails from obscure web addresses such as *takingmattersinmyownhands67* and *iwilldestroyyou666* fill his inbox.

However, one e-mail stands out from the rest.

Julie

Every morning when I open my eyes, I want to close them again so I can remain in that wonderful dreamy state of ignorance, but I'm living an actual nightmare. That, unfortunately, is my reality. Why is this happening to me? I can't stop wondering.

I started my new approach: the charm offensive. I showered and put on clean clothes. I even took the sheets off the bed and put them in a pile at the bottom of the stairs. It feels good to behave like a human again, to take control of my own hygiene. It's not much, but something is better than nothing.

To gain his favor, I put on a DVD, *Ghost*—a movie that reminds me of my mom. It was her favorite. Luckily, she's no longer here to endure this; she would have gone crazy worrying.

I try to be strong and hang on to every ounce of hope I can muster, but it's hard. If little Hannah didn't give me a reassuring nudge now and then, I wouldn't know what to do. He knows that very well. He knows that I wouldn't kill myself out of desperation. I could do it; the plastic knives he gives me at dinner have sharp teeth. But I don't intend to. That I'm still alive after more than a week in captivity means I have a chance. It's as simple as that.

When he comes down the stairs with my daily meal, he looks surprised at the pile of laundry on the floor. I stare at him in innocence.

"Good afternoon, Floris. Would you be so kind as to wash my sheets? If I'm going to be here for any length of time, that will be necessary." I smile amiably. "Oh, and I've put a note on the table for you with a list of books I'd like to read."

His stubble has grown. I notice that, here in the basement, he doesn't have the hunched over posture he had in my flat. There he looked a bit pathetic, with his limp and his scars. In here he doesn't—not at all. He's tall, at least six feet, and looks strong with broad shoulders. He radiates confidence. Either my imprisonment made him confident, or he's a good actor. Or maybe it's a combination of both.

He doesn't say a word; instead, he puts the tray on the table, puts my note in the pocket of his jeans without reading it, and disappears upstairs with the laundry. I empty my plate, feeling glum, and lie down on the bare mattress. I don't resume the movie; the memories of my mom are too painful.

When night falls, I expect him to return with clean sheets, but he doesn't. This is probably one of his ways to make me realize how much he despises me.

Why does he hate me so much?

Lacking clean sheets, I gather up all the dry towels I can find and improvise a blanket in which I wrap myself like a doll. Fortunately, there's no lack of warmth in the basement. It's the second week of August and it's probably warm outside. Down here, it stays cool but not too much. And in case I feel cold, there's even a heater that I can regulate myself, should I need it.

Strange, isn't it? On the one hand, he hates me, but on the other, he provides me with every comfort. Or did he not build this basement for me?

No, of course not, I think. This shelter has been here longer than I have. I fall asleep with my arms cradling my belly.

Tom

"Forget her. She was never yours" was the strange message in the e-mail. It was sent from a Hotmail address consisting of only numbers. The tone was so different from the other e-mails and letters that a shiver ran down his spine. What did it mean, Julie has never been his? Whose was she, then, if you could say something like that of Julie? Because as far as Tom was concerned she didn't belong to anyone. Or was that not what the sender meant? He'd immediately called the police; he'd also delivered the threatening e-mails and letters to them. They were going to investigate it, they said, but he didn't have much faith in them.

"What if that e-mail came from the man who kidnapped Julie?" he says to Eloise.

Tonight she's wearing a cream-colored blouse with a plunging neckline and a dark blue pencil skirt with a slit, her idea of business attire. Before Tom met Julie, Eloise and he had already become friends in Billy's. Once, she spontaneously joined in the singing when he played an Elton John song on the piano. She's wonderfully impulsive and he loves her like she were his sister. No, he loves her more than his sister.

She puts her arms, which are jingling from the many bracelets, on the table and looks deep into his eyes. "I don't know, Tom. I really don't know. How are you? Are you holding up okay?"

He barely sleeps and only just manages to get food down. Where has his life gone? He misses Julie so much that it hurts. He's slowly going mad.

"I'm fine. Now, tell me what you know." She'd told him on the phone that she had more information about the neighbor.

"I don't know what you expect from me; I'm not a detective," she replies. "I did my best and looked up his name online but nothing came up."

"No, I noticed that, too." That was the first thing he had done. "And your clients?"

"Nobody knows him."

Tom lets his forehead drop to the table and he sighs deeply; this isn't what he had hoped for.

"I followed him, of course," she continues, and Tom's head immediately rises again.

"Eloise, you shouldn't have! That's far too dangerous!" he exclaims.

"I know where he works," she continues calmly.

"Okay..."

"He works in the hospital. I saw him go in there."

"Maybe he was visiting someone?"

Eloise shakes her head. "I went in myself and a little later I saw him again, but in one of those nurse's uniforms. He really works there."

"So he takes care of sick people," Tom mutters. "Not exactly a job you'd expect from a kidnapper or murderer."

"That's true, but there's something else. I don't think he's the man you're looking for." She looks apologetic now that she has to subvert his theory. "He's disabled."

Tom frowns; he's never seen Floris in the short time he's been living in Julie's flat and so he doesn't know what he looks like.

"How so? What did you see?"

"He walks with a bit of a limp, and one of his arms is full of scars. Really full. He's had an accident or something. I don't think he's capable of kidnapping or killing Julie and carrying her out of the flat. You know what she's like; she would never be overpowered without a fight."

Discouraged, he shakes his head.

"No, you're right." Whatever happened, Julie didn't walk out of her flat of her own accord. The blood found by the police indicates that she was either unconscious or dead. And a dormant body feels extra heavy. He remembers the time he jokingly carried her across the flat threshold on the day they officially moved in together.

"Whoever kidnapped Julie, that person must be strong."

They're both silent for a moment. It seems like a dead end.

"What did the police say about the scratches on your car? And about Dolly?"

He shrugs. "They don't see any connection. At first, I thought that this Chief Inspector Van Dijck was on my side, that he believed me, but since they found the blood, he keeps looking at me as if I'm not worth living. I think they suspect I scratched the car myself to draw suspicion onto someone else."

"But they don't have anything on you, do they? I mean, that there was blood in your flat doesn't mean you did anything wrong, does it? Julie could've let anyone in, and a neighbor is the most plausible option."

"I know, that's what my lawyer says, too, although there's that bloodstained t-shirt, but that could easily have been planted there. As long as they don't have any hard evidence, they can't touch me. But that's not the point; the problem is that they aren't looking for her in the meantime. They're so damn sure of their case. They've turned my car inside out looking for evidence, but haven't found anything. At least, that's what I think. That I have no alibi for that one hour doesn't help either."

"Yeah, they asked me about that: what time you called me and when I was with you."

Tom looks straight at her and smiles a little. "Who would have thought that one day you would have to be my alibi?"

"Yes, indeed. What a mess." Eloise's nails are the same pink color as the last time he saw her, only now the polish is flaked off in several places.

"What else do they say about me in the newspapers?"

She bats her eyes. "Tom..."

"Okay, never mind. I get it."

"It's tabloid gossip. You know how it goes."

He nods. Although his job is the last thing on his mind lately, the question of whether he will still have one in September flashes through his mind. Even if he was released, his picture has been in all the newspapers. What parent would want to put their kid in a classroom with a creep? He can't even blame them.

***

Eloise's gone. It's getting dark outside. He lies on the bed and moves his fingers over an imaginary piano. His thoughts go back to that strange e-mail. *Forget her.* Does that mean she's dead? He shivers. If the e-mail really came from the kidnapper, what has he done with Julie?

The doorbell rings. His heart jumps out of his chest. At this time of night, he expects no one but the police. He runs down the stairs of the duplex and answers the intercom.

"Tom? It's Isabelle. May I come in for a moment?"

Isabelle? Which Isabelle? He hesitates for a moment.

"From school," says the voice. *Oh no.* He automatically pushes the button to let her in. And immediately regrets it. Isabelle is the pupil who was in love with him. What's she doing here?

"Isabelle, what...?" he says, frowning.

"May I come in for a moment?" She smiles sweetly at him and he's too polite to send her away.

"Yes, of course. Would you like something to drink?" When he doesn't know how to respond, he lapses into pleasantries, to his own annoyance.

"No, I'm fine. I just wanted to talk to you."

He leads her to the table and they sit opposite each other. She reaches out her hands to his, whereupon he quickly pulls away and places them safely in his lap. Her smile disappears for a moment, her slender hands brush her long hair behind her ears, and then she looks straight into his eyes.

"I... I thought you might need a friend in this difficult time," she says softly, as her eyes drop to the table top.

"Isabelle... I..." He doesn't know what to say. The newspapers already portray him as a perverted music teacher; the fact that she's come here late at night probably doesn't help.

"You know how I feel about you. I understand that you can't reciprocate those feelings, but the thought of you going through all this alone..."

Oh, God. Is she serious?

"That's very sweet of you, but maybe it's not such a good idea because... you know." Who knows, she might have come here at the behest of a tabloid; it wouldn't surprise him, however innocent she looks.

The girl isn't discouraged. "That you're a suspect? I know you're innocent; you would never do such a terrible thing. I just know it. I've been thinking about you for days; every hour of the day I wonder how you're doing, if you aren't too lonely, if you eat enough." She swallows and looks at him again with those brown eyes of hers.

She's probably telling the truth. She's still in love with him, or maybe even more so now that she thinks she can "save" him. He has to get her out of here, and fast. The risk is too great.

"Isabelle, if you want to help me, please leave. I'm suspected of my girlfriend's murder and it doesn't look good when a pretty student of mine pays me a visit. Do you understand?"

Her cheeks turn pink and he could slap himself when he realizes that he has unwittingly complimented her, but she's understood the message and gets to her feet.

"I understand. Stay strong, okay?"

He nods briefly and gets up as well. He walks her down the stairs into the hall. A sweet smell follows her. Vanilla. When she's almost at the door, she turns around again and blows him a kiss. He clenches his jaw and wants to turn back, but then he notices the outline of a man standing in front of the door through which Isabelle slips outside.

However bad Tom looks, Jean-Pierre Meskens looks even worse: the skin of his cheeks is sunken and flaky, his eyes bloodshot. It's as if he hasn't slept since Julie disappeared, which Tom can only imagine.

His empathy is short-lived, however, for within seconds the man stands before him, trembling with rage.

"You..." he says between gritted teeth. "You've got some guts, kid."

He is half a head taller than Tom, who backs away carefully. In his hand he holds a phone, the screen pointed at Tom.

"But now I have proof. If the police don't do their job, I'll do it myself!" He's taken a photograph of Isabelle blowing a kiss at Tom. If that goes to the press, he's doomed.

"It's not what it seems!" he protests. "I haven't done anything to Julie!"

Jean-Pierre Meskens brings his face a few inches from Tom's. "You're worse than a murderer. At least admit what you've done, coward. Be a man!" he shouts.

Tom swallows. The man's convinced that he's facing the murderer of his daughter and unborn grandchild; nothing Tom does or says will change his mind. He closes his eyes, ready to take the blows.

"Do what you want," he says. "I don't care anymore. Just beat the crap out of me."

But nothing happens. After a few seconds he opens his eyes again, just in time to see Jean-Pierre Meskens walking up the street.

Defeated, he's left behind in the hall with the shouted accusations forever etched in his mind.

Julie

I put on one of the CDs from the TV cabinet: it's the music from *Schindler's List*. I don't know if he did it on purpose, but there isn't a single CD with happy songs in this place. I pull my legs up under me on the sofa and rock to and fro, fighting back tears. What have I done to deserve this? Why haven't they found me yet? Are they even looking for me? It's hard not to lose hope. I feel that I'm slipping into self-pity, but as soon as I hear him fumble at the hatch, I wipe away my tears. I don't want to show him how I feel. I don't want him to know.

He carries a large bag of clean sheets and orders me to sit at the kitchen table while he makes the bed so he can keep an eye on me. Then he takes two books out of the bag and puts them on the table. Again, he disappears without a word.

Perhaps that's the greatest punishment of all: having no one to talk to. Or at least, no one who talks back. I always thought I was okay with being alone. Was that an illusion? I yearn for a good conversation.

I reach out to the books to see their covers: they're library books with a barcode on them. I swallow and take a closer look. The name of the library they come from is printed on the barcode.

I swallow again, and can't believe what I'm seeing. Is this a coincidence?

My flat is at least fifteen miles away from the village I grew up in and I don't know where he took me, but these library books come from my old village library; it's written on them loud and clear. Are we in my hometown? If so, did he just bring me here by chance or is there more to it? And is he really that stupid to give me this information unknowingly? Or does he *want* me to know where I am? Why? Who was this basement built for? Could there have been girls in it before me and is he a Dutroux type after all? What does he want with a pregnant woman?

I have so many questions that my head is spinning. I can't go on like this. I have to get him to talk.

Tom

He is suffering from palpitations, probably caused by lack of sleep and regularity. The days are getting shorter; the summer holidays are slowly coming to an end. The family in the house next door had just left for their holiday when Julie disappeared, and this morning he saw them returning home. Bikes on the roof, tanned arms and legs. They probably don't know a thing; they have no clue what happened here. Everything seems so normal; the world keeps on turning. But nothing is normal anymore for Tom. Will it ever be again? Day after day, he feels he's slipping further away.

Jean-Pierre Meskens did go to the police with the photo of Isabelle and they interrogated Tom again. Fortunately, after some investigation, they abandoned the trail. Isabelle will have told them the truth: there has never been anything between them. The press would have loved it, had it been otherwise.

His phone rings again: an anonymous caller ID. He's put it on vibrate in case it's Eloise, because he only gets threatening phone calls these days, or calls from journalists wanting an interview. After the horse manure that was stuck to the front door, he also got a portion of that in his mailbox.

He's so tired that he's fallen asleep on the sofa, but unfortunately this rare moment of peace doesn't last long. The sound of shattering glass, followed by screeching tires, jolts him out of his sleep and he jumps up, startled. He's just in time to see a red SEAT Ibiza speeding away. A dark hole adorns the window of his Golf. How on earth do these people know where he lives and which car is his? And what possesses them to make his life even more miserable than it already is? He swallows angry tears. He has to go out on the streets, put up posters, talk to people. Call out Julie's name. He can't just sit here.

Armed with a piece of cardboard, a dustpan, and brush, he walks down the stairs. His legs feel like lead. Each time, he imagines how Julie was carried downstairs, injured. How's it possible that the investigators didn't find any blood here? Was there even any?

Shaking his head, he walks out to survey the damage. The driver's side window has been smashed and most of the glass has ended up in his car. He puts the largest pieces on the pan and tries to sweep up the rest with the brush. He folds the piece of cardboard against the opening and checks that he hasn't left anything of value in the car. When he turns around to walk back to the front door, his head flies backwards. Before he realizes what's happened, he's lying on the ground. It takes a few moments for the pain to gallop into his head, then he reaches for his eye. At the edge of his consciousness, he hears footsteps rushing away.

"Dirty murderer!" someone shouts.

And then it's quiet. A bird whistles, or maybe he hears the sound only in his head.

Someone has knocked him down. He opens his eyes and looks around, trembling, but there's nothing to see.

"Help," he says softly. A sharp pain makes him shift his attention to his left hand. In his fall, he's dropped the dustpan with the glass on the ground and planted his hand right into it. He stares at his palm and sees blood gushing out like from an overflowing sewer.

Immediately, his vision goes black.

No, don't faint.

Not here, not on the street.

He feels he's drifting off, but forces his mind to stay conscious by concentrating on his breathing. He has to stay calm and, above all, not look at his hand.

He cautiously tries to stand up but his head is spinning, so he holds the car for support. Leaning forward halfway, he pushes the dustpan under the Golf with his foot; he'll sort that out later. The world spins around him. He can't stay here; he has to go inside. What if his attacker comes back?

Taking small steps, he crosses the street, holding his good hand over his throbbing eye while he raises the bleeding one as high as he can. Still, he can't avoid leaving a trail of bloody drips behind him.

Don't look at the blood.

Relieved, he reaches the front door. In the hall, he catches his breath, but not for too long: he has to stem the blood. With trembling legs, he climbs the stairs.

He's back in the flat, in the kitchen. Black dots dance before his eyes as he runs water over his hand.

Don't look, don't look.

He wraps a kitchen towel around it and then flops down on the sofa.

Ice. He needs ice for his eye, but first he needs to rest. The black dots grow larger; he feels his mind slipping away. How wonderful it would be to never wake up again.

Loud banging in the distance forces him to leave his daze. The pain shoots through his head like lightning and he groans. His hand is throbbing and the towel is full of brownish-red stains. He stumbles to the intercom, pushes the button to let Eloise in, and lies down again.

"What happened to you? Tom! What happened? Your eye! That blood!"

He mumbles something in return and she immediately springs into action, grabbing an ice pack from the freezer and putting it on his throbbing head. Then she peels the bloody towel from his hand.

"Tssss," she says, removing the shards of glass one by one. "You have to go to the hospital with this, you know."

"No, I'll stay here," he says.

She fumbles around, runs up the stairs to the bathroom, and then comes back with disinfectant and bandages. As she dresses his wounds, he explains in a few words what happened.

"Bastards," Eloise hisses.

She gives him a painkiller, which he swallows with some water, and comes and sits next to him, laying his head on her lap.

Slowly he's becoming human again. The pounding in his head subsides, although it hurts to keep his eyes open, so he closes them again. The warmth of her body, the beating of her heart. It calms him, but at the same time makes him long for Julie's warm body against his. Will he ever see her again? How did he end up in this situation? Two weeks ago, he was a young father-to-be and now he's nothing. He's so alone.

Eloise strokes his hair gently, as if she can read his thoughts. With his good hand, he grabs hers.

"Please stay here."

Julie

31 Weeks and 1 Day Pregnant
Day 12 in the Basement

The more I think about it, the more I fear he's after my baby, although I don't understand why. This is bad news, because if I'm not important to him, what will happen to me after I gave birth? I can't deliver my daughter in this basement, not under any circumstances. That would be the death of me.

My belly is growing enormously now that I do nothing but rest. Hannah is moving a lot and that reassures me, but she's breech. I can feel it in my pelvis. She has plenty of time to turn, but I do worry. What if she doesn't turn properly in time? Or what if I give birth too soon?

I'm not squeamish, or afraid of a home birth. My medical knowledge is a big plus, but I don't want my daughter to be born in captivity. I don't want her first breath to be one of musty air. I don't want him to touch her. I have to get out of here while I still can, while I'm mobile. If my belly keeps growing like this, I'll hardly be able to get through the hatch, so running would for sure be out of the question.

I need some exercise, but I can't do more than pacing and some yoga on the floor. It's so stuffy in here. I miss the daylight. I miss my flat. I miss Tom. Much harder than I could ever imagine. Just a few months ago, I absolutely didn't want to live together with him. What an idiot I was.

The hatch is grating again; I'm no longer alone. My need for human contact is so huge that I'm glad he's here. Now I can try and use my charm offensive again.

He comes down the stairs with my daily meal and I want to get up to greet him. "Good afternoon, Floris." But with a movement of his hand, he directs me back to the bed at the back of the room.

I try again. "What's for dinner today?"

He puts the tray down and looks at me with a gaze that gives me goosebumps, with those thick glasses of his.

It seems as if he's just worked out: he's wearing black Nike shorts that fall just above his knees with a white sleeveless shirt on top. I can see now that his entire left side is scarred. It's as if thick cables run over his shoulder and arm, down his leg. He looks imposingly large, but I don't let his physical appearance scare me.

If only he spoke to me now, I could try to get through to him. There must be some compassion under his white armor.

But he says nothing and keeps staring at me.

A feeling that I dismissed when we first met creeps up on me again: do I know this man? He hates me for some reason, so doesn't it make sense that we've met before? I stare back in curiosity and immediately notice that he doesn't like that because his eyes move back and forth nervously. I can't tell what color they are, but given his white skin and hair, they must be blue or green. My brow furrows as my brain tries to match this image with someone I've met before, but before I can dig deep enough, he turns and walks back up the stairs.

"Vegetarian lasagna," he replies before disappearing through the hatch.

Hallelujah. He spoke.

Lured by the smell, I sit down at the table and start to eat, but the feeling that I'm onto something doesn't leave me. There's only one boy I've ever known who was so blond and pale, and that was Oscar. But I haven't seen him since I was fourteen or fifteen, and I'm sure he doesn't hate me—just the opposite. I was the only one who stood up for him at the time.

Come to think of it, he didn't wear glasses. And he didn't have dark eyebrows, although those may have been dyed. What would have become of him?

As I eat the lasagna, I think back to the time when I lived in the village, the time when Mom was still alive, before she was hit by a car on that fateful February day. The driver was probably drunk, but was never caught by the police. Mom was on her way home from work. She couldn't drive and went everywhere by bike. That day she had picked up a chocolate cake in the shape of a heart from the bakery, because it was Valentine's Day. It was a dark evening and it had been raining. Mom had been to the hairdresser's and wasn't wearing her helmet. If only she had. She hadn't died immediately. After a passerby found her by the side of the road, she was rushed to the hospital where Dad and I stayed day and night for a week, hoping she would wake up from her coma.

That time in my life is like a black hole to me; I remember little or nothing of the week in which our lives changed forever. People came to visit and there was a lot of crying. Women I didn't know hugged me, probably friends of Mom's, and food was made for us that we barely ate.

After the funeral, I stayed with my grandparents so that Dad could empty our house. He didn't want to stay there anymore. He wanted to leave the village because he couldn't bear the thought of driving past the place where his wife had suffered so much every single day. The place where the chocolate cake caused a nuisance for days because of the many pigeons it attracted. I let it all happen, as if in a daze. We moved to a new house in the city and I started all over again: a new school and new friends. I never saw my old friends again—only Tobias, whom I ran into once at a music festival. What became of Oscar, I don't know. I hope for his sake that he got away from that horrible mother of his. What a witch she was.

I finish my lasagna and take my folic acid tablet. There's not much I can do for Hannah, but I can keep her healthy, so I'll keep doing that for as long as I can. I'm hanging on to every bit of control I have. Another nine weeks she'll be safe with me. Another sixty-two days, to be exact. Hopefully that'll be enough to get us out of this. I lie back on the bed with one of the library books and read until I fall asleep.

In my dream, Floris comes in with a chocolate cake. When he cuts off a piece for me, the filling oozes out: it's a thick syrup of what looks like raspberry jelly. I dip my finger in it. It's sticky and I lick my finger, but instead of sweet deliciousness, I taste the woeful taste of blood.

I wake up gagging. The feeling that my dream is trying to tell me something won't leave me.

Pieter

"Shall we begin, then?" Journalist Pieter De Saegher switches on his tape recorder. The three of them are sitting in Julie Meskens' sun-drenched flat: Pieter, Tom, and Eloise. That was Tom's condition for agreeing to the interview: Eloise had to be there. She's the one who persuaded him, he says. Since Julie disappeared, people who want to take matters into their own hands have harassed him. A few days ago, he was even knocked down in front of his own door, resulting in a black eye and a slight concussion. That was the last straw.

Pieter observes the young music teacher and feels that Tom is doing the same with him. They may have known each other from Billy's, but they never exchanged more than a friendly nod. Moreover, Pieter doesn't know how much Tom actually knows about the brief romance he had with Julie— long before she started anything with Tom.

Although it's summer, Tom looks as if he hasn't seen any daylight for months. His pale face is covered with stubble. His left hand is bandaged and he has a yellowish bump above his right eyebrow. His eyes are red-rimmed. From crying? Possibly. But that doesn't mean he's innocent. He could just as well be burdened with guilt.

Pieter decides to start the interview on a relaxed note.

"So tell me, how did you meet Julie?" he says, taking out his notebook.

Tom coughs. "I play the piano at Billy's every Friday, as you know. I'd seen her there a few times, but I'm not much of a hero at socializing." He pulls the corner of his mouth into a crooked smile, but it doesn't reach his eyes. "It was only after... um, when I met Eloise that I got to talk to Julie."

Tom looks quickly in Eloise's direction and Pieter has the feeling that he isn't being told the whole truth. Is there more going on between them? He makes a short note and continues.

"What appealed to you about her?"

"Actually, I found her too noisy, especially when she'd been drinking. I thought she was acting up." Again, he looks at Eloise, this time with an apologetic look. "But one evening we got to talking. I'd played a song that she liked and she came to tell me that." He shrugs. "It's not that I fell in love with her immediately, but from that moment on I began to look forward to our conversations. I liked the fact that she wanted to be a vet. If I didn't faint at the mere sight of blood, it would've been something for me, too."

Eloise laughs a little and rolls her eyes. "And he's not exaggerating," she says to Pieter. "Tom is an incredible wimp." But the warmth in her voice doesn't escape Pieter.

"You can't stand the sight of blood?"

"No, not at all. I faint at the slightest speck."

"And you told the police this? After they found that blood?"

"Yes, of course. But I can say what I want, can't I? That doesn't make it true."

Pieter nods and takes notes. Not only does Tom not strike him as the type to coolly dispose of a corpse, but also he simply couldn't do it, given that *he* would be knocked out. If that's true. But Eloise confirms his story. Why would she do that? Unless the two are in league...

"Have you two ever been more than friends?" he says at the outset. Tom and Eloise look at him in bewilderment. Eloise is the first to react; she looks at Tom for a moment and then turns her gaze to Pieter. Her dark eyes take on a haughty expression. The warmth is gone.

"One night. Before Tom was with Julie."

Ha! Want to bet the police don't know that yet? He looks at Tom questioningly, but he remains perfectly still, even though his pale cheeks have now turned a bright shade of red. Jesus, that boy is an open book.

He decides to drop the subject to avoid ending the interview prematurely and takes a different tack.

"Good. Back to Julie. What do you think happened?"

Tom shakes his head. "I haven't the faintest idea."

"You must have a suspicion, right?"

"None. We've talked about it so many times." He nods his head in Eloise's direction. "But we can't think of anyone who would want to harm her. She was probably unlucky. The wrong place, the wrong time. Some monster must have been watching her."

Then Tom tells Pieter the whole story again. About the anonymous phone calls, the punctured bike tires, his car that was scratched, and finally, about Dolly.

So Julie might have been stalked.

"What did the police do with that information?"

"They've investigated it, but they haven't found anything. There's nothing to indicate that it's the same person. The phone calls are untraceable, and I could have scratched up the car myself." Tom sighs. "I can hardly blame them. I would suspect me, too."

Pieter rubs his hair, which stands up in spikes. He knows Chief Inspector David Van Dijck. He's a good man, and very thorough. He's probably under enormous pressure to find Julie Meskens. Dead or alive. Dead, probably, since she's been missing for almost two weeks.

"And you really have no idea who was stalking her?"

Tom shakes his head in denial.

"Suppose you *have* to say a name, of someone whose behavior seemed strange to you in recent months. Who would that be?"

Tom thinks for a moment. "If you were really forcing me to name someone, I'd tell you to look into our upstairs neighbor."

"Why?"

Tom tells him about the shouting. "I suspected him right away, but Eloise did some research on him and discovered he is disabled, so we eliminated him."

"Name?"

"Floris De Wachter."

"And the police have spoken to him?"

"Yes, I think so. They spoke to everyone in the street, including him. Apparently they didn't believe him to be suspicious." He shrugs. "I believe he's home, by the way. I heard footsteps a moment ago. You can always try to speak to him, though he never answers the door. He's kind of a loner, I think."

Pieter nods thoughtfully.

"I got a strange e-mail, too." Tom digs up the printout and hands Pieter the sheet of paper with *Forget her. She was never yours.*

Pieter looks at it for a moment and then turns his attention to his phone, which is vibrating. It's a message from Serge, his contact at the police.

"Excuse me a moment," he says as he opens it. He reads what it says and then quickly puts his phone away. "I'm sorry, I have to make a phone call," he says as he walks to the front door. "I'll be right back."

Tom lets him out. As soon as he's in the corridor, Pieter reads the message again and then calls Serge's number.

"Pieter here, do you have more details?"

"Hi, P. A fisherman found the handbag in the canal near tavern De Roeispaan."

"And you're certain that it's Julie's bag?" He keeps his voice as low as he can.

"In any case, it's exactly the same one. It will now go to the lab for further examination."

"Shit."

"Yes, it doesn't look good for that girl. Pregnant and all."

"Indeed. No other news?"

"Van Dijck is still putting his money on Tom Van de Velde, who's said to have had an affair with a pupil."

"Okay, do you know anything about threatening e-mails to him?"

"Yes, IT is working on it. Most of the e-mails are harmless—idiots with nothing better to do than waste our time. If anything turns up, I'll let you know."

Pieter met Serge twelve years ago when his sister, Tinne, first disappeared without a trace for several weeks. Serge was the only one who took him seriously every time Tinne disappeared. It was never too much for him. He was an incredible support. First for his parents and later, when they could no longer cope, for Pieter, who became the one dealing with his sister's many encounters with the police.

After Tinne's death, Pieter and Serge stayed in touch, the older inspector and the young journalist having developed a close friendship. Serge provides him with information when Pieter asks for it, in good faith. He knows Pieter will never betray that trust.

He stands in the hall of the building, gritting his teeth. It's not his job to give Tom the news about the handbag; he's a journalist, not a victim support worker. Besides, Tom will find out soon enough, and the best thing he can do now is help find Julie.

With a dogged expression on his face, he walks all the way up the stairs to the top flat and knocks on the door. Although he hears some shuffling inside, nobody answers. He tries again.

"Hello? Floris?"

He listens tensely, but the man keeps quiet. Damn. He tries again.

"Mr. De Wachter? My name is Pieter De Saegher, I'm a journalist for *De Gazet*."

Again he listens at the door. Does he hear someone breathing?

"I would like to ask you some questions about the disappearance of your neighbor Julie Meskens."

Yes, he definitely hears someone breathing, but that someone clearly has no intention of opening the door. Strange. Most people are eager to read their opinions in the newspaper, in his experience. Unless they have something to hide.

"I'll slide my card under the door. Call me if you have time," he says. Then he walks down the stairs again.

Just before his knuckles hit Tom's door, he hears the unmistakable sound of a door on the top floor opening briefly and then softly shutting again.

Tom

Her legs are spread before him as her body lies dead still. Gently, Tom sits down next to her on the bed and touches the tip of her nipple with his finger. He touches the goosebumps on her breasts. His finger begins to make small circles around the nipple, bigger and bigger, until he reaches her other breast. Her breath falters as his finger aims for the other nipple, but he pretends not to notice and continues his journey. Again, he circles over her soft skin. Every now and then, he lightly scratches her skin with his nail. She smells like no one else: of flowers and the sea at dawn. And her hair smells like the sun. He presses his face against it and breathes in, as deeply as he can. When his finger slides down her belly via her navel, she moans a little. His erection gets harder. He wants her, but even more he wants to please her, so he continues his journey. His finger has arrived at her Venus mound and curves around it towards the soft inside of her thigh. A shudder goes through her body as he starts stroking her there. He decides to put his other hand to work and takes one of her nipples between his thumb and forefinger and starts pinching it rhythmically. Gently at first, but then harder and harder. She begins to squirm.

"Shh, don't move," he whispers.

Her mouth twitches into a smile for a moment. She plays along.

His one hand squeezes her breast and with the other he moves from her thigh to the spot where he feels the heat radiating. Very lightly, he runs his finger over the little hairs, hardly touching them. Again, a moan escapes her mouth. His finger gently moves on until his fingertip touches her lips; he caresses the little slit between them and feels his finger getting wet. Gently, he pushes his finger inside her. He puts his knee between her legs so that his erection presses against her thigh. He runs his tongue along her stomach in search of her breasts. Her back arches, her pelvis rises, but he's not done yet. He wants to play some more, so for a moment he sets his teeth in her beautiful neck, nibbling it. Then his mouth finds hers and she kisses him back eagerly.

"Oh, Tom, now, now," she moans and turns to him.

He looks at her face.

Eloise.

Tom jerks out of bed, his heart bouncing like a basketball, and he looks around in a daze. He's at home, in the bedroom. He tries to get his breathing under control and stands upright in the room, his hands in his hair.

What the hell kind of dream was that?

He still has a slight erection. Why did he dream about Eloise? He shakes his head and starts talking softly to himself.

"It was Julie, for sure. It was her body, her smell, her face." Only at the very end did Julie change into Eloise, but why on earth? He'd never had feelings for Eloise since that one time, or at least not in that way. They should never have slept together. That was a mistake. A mistake they never told Julie.

Why? He didn't even know Julie when it happened. And there was never really an opportunity to bring it up. It didn't seem relevant at all. In despair, he sinks back down on his bed. With hindsight, it's always easy to see where you've made mistakes, but then it's usually too late to correct them.

Julie
31 Weeks and 4 Days Pregnant
Day 14 in the Basement

The days are so long in here. So little happens. I asked him for some DVD series. He brought *House M.D.* and a puzzle with two thousand pieces. That'll keep me busy for a while.

I sleep a lot, and I have neither the courage nor the inclination to change my situation. The lack of daylight makes me feel depressed. My circadian rhythm is disturbed because I don't produce cortisol, but this knowledge doesn't give me the power to change anything. I feel that I'm slowly reaching my breaking point.

Time and again I try to make him talk, but it doesn't work. This way, it's difficult to show him that I'm a human being of flesh and blood with feelings. With a past and hopefully a future.

I'm not afraid anymore, not as long as I'm pregnant. I know he won't hurt me, at least not for the time being. Time is both my greatest ally and my worst enemy. The longer I sit here, the closer I get to giving birth, and the more I put Hannah in danger. And myself.

When I asked him if we were in my home village, he just grinned. As if he'd given me those library books on purpose so that I would know. If I die in here, it doesn't matter, of course. I realize it more every day: I won't get out of here alive unless someone finds me.

How small my world is. Sometimes it feels as if I'm already dead. I float around like a polar bear on an ice floe in the middle of the ocean. You can hardly call this living, here, under the ground. My days are all alike. Only the food is different. At first, I thought I was trapped under his house.

How else could he provide hot meals? But now I suspect he doesn't prepare the food himself. It's a bit too similar to the kind of food you get in hospitals. He buys it and keeps it warm, or takes it home from work. I'm going to tell him that I'm not getting enough vitamins this way, and that I need to go outside to get some.

There he is again. The hatch opens. I feel the warm air flowing in and breathe deeply: soil and grass, wonderful. In my mind's eye, I walk barefoot in our old garden, the blades of grass tickling the soles of my feet, the sun warming my skin. Along with the smell of grass, something else blows in: I smell basil. And tomatoes! Gratefully, I stretch my neck to see what's on the tray.

Slices of fresh tomato and mozzarella are arranged on a plate, topped with an abundance of basil. Next to the plate I see a miniature plastic bottle of balsamic vinegar and a piece of baguette. My mouth is watering.

"That looks delicious, Floris, thank you," I say from my regular spot on the bed. I'm still trying to thaw him despite everything, but he never talks to me. No more than is absolutely necessary. It's become a habit that I go to my spot on the bed as soon as I hear him. He warned me that he would put me on a chain if I didn't and he means it. There is a ring in the wall next to my bed.

"Really, thank you. I was just about to ask you to give me fresh vegetables more often. The baby needs them." I have noticed before that I can get his attention by talking about the pregnancy; he doesn't care about anything else. I can tell he's listening to me as he places my food on the table, so I continue. "Could I please go outside just once to get some daylight on my skin? For the vitamin D?" I beg.

He remains motionless beside the table with yesterday's tray in his hands.

My hope is growing. Usually, he runs straight back up the stairs, so who knows? Maybe I'll get through to him today.

"You can blindfold me and tie my hands, I don't mind. It's important for the baby, Floris. For her development." For a moment I think I see a glimpse of connection, but I'm not sure what gives me that feeling. Are his shoulders less tense? Does something change in his gaze? But just as quickly the moment is gone and he turns around towards the stairs.

I look at him in resignation. How am I ever going to break through that armor? What if I don't succeed? I rub my eyes and stand up listlessly, my lunch has lost all its appeal for me, but I realize that I have to eat anyway and sit down at the table. I break a piece of the bread, put it in my mouth, and poke a slice of tomato with my plastic fork.

The plate wobbles a little. There's something underneath that unbalances it. Curious, I lift it up and am surprised to see a newspaper clipping. Immediately, I push the food out of the way and unfold the article. Tears fill my eyes when I read the headline.

Boyfriend of missing Julie Meskens arrested.

"No!" I exclaim. I wipe away my tears and start reading the article:

The police have arrested Tom V.d.V. (27). His pregnant girlfriend Julie Meskens (24) disappeared without a trace from their flat on August 3rd.

Initially, it was assumed that the young woman had packed her things and left after an argument, but this proved not to be the case. Forensic investigation in the couple's flat shows that there was violence, possibly an argument that got out of hand.

According to a witness, the couple often argued and sometimes had harsh words.

Tom V.d.V. is currently being questioned and will appear before the investigating judge tomorrow.

Tom

He can't shake off the thought of Eloise in his bed. The harder he tries not to think of her body, the more clearly he sees her before him. He's disgusted with himself. He feels as if he's cheated on Julie. He's decided to keep his distance from Eloise for a few days, but the loneliness weighs on him.

Soon it will be Julie's birthday and they were going to spend the weekend in a B&B at an organic farm. He hasn't cancelled the reservation because it would mean he no longer believes she'll come back. He wants to continue believing, and hoping, although he realizes how naive that is.

He's being interrogated again today and is almost grateful for the distraction. His lawyer is waiting for him in the interrogation room.

"How are you?" she asks with concern.

"I'm all right, just too much time to think," he replies. He feels her studying him, her eyes sliding inquisitively from his chipped nails via his drooping shoulders to his pale face.

The door opens with a swing and Chief Inspector Van Dijck enters. His face is grim. He has a thick file under his arm, which, before he sits down, he slams down on the table between them. Then he puts his elbows on the table and stares at Tom, who nervously clicks his fingers. He opens the file, takes out a photo, and slides it across the table towards Tom.

"Do you recognize this?"

The photo shows a sandy patch of ground with some grass on which a brown handbag lies. Julie's handbag. Tom gasps. He jumps up.

"Where did you find this? Is it Julie's bag? Have you got her?" he shouts desperately. Still being stared at by the chief inspector, the man doesn't react to his outburst and continues to observe him coolly. Tom glances sideways at his lawyer but she doesn't answer his gaze.

Van Dijck again takes a photograph from the file, this time of a man. It's a mug shot. The man has the kind of puffy pale face of someone who rarely sees daylight. His eyes are small, probably blue. They're deeply sunken beneath light-colored eyebrows and a high forehead. The little hair he has is blond. The grin he gives the camera makes Tom shiver.

"Do you recognize this man?"

Only then does Tom realize that this face might belong to the guy who kidnapped Julie, or worse. His body turns ice cold as his hands tremblingly reach for the photograph to take a closer look. He studies the full lips, the stubble. "I've never seen him before. Is he... Do you know more?"

"We have new evidence that points in the direction of this man. We were able to trace this e-mail to his IP address." Van Dijck passes him a sheet of paper.

Forget her. She was never yours, Tom reads, trembling. Oh, Julie. He starts to stutter. "Who is he? What's he done to Julie? Did you catch him?"

Van Dijck looks at him sternly again, although Tom thinks he sees a hint of compassion in his eyes this time. "Yes, we've arrested him. We're doing everything we can to get him to talk. Given the evidence we've found against him, it shouldn't take long."

"Evidence? Have you found anything? At his place?" Tom's voice skips.

But the chief inspector is already back on his feet. He holds out his hand to Tom, who accepts it in astonishment. "I'm afraid I can't tell you anything about that yet. As soon as we have any news, I'll let you know."

And he's gone.

Tom runs his tongue over his parched lips, uncertain whether he should be relieved or terrified.

Pieter

The guy arrested by the police is called Rutger Stevens, a man who has a lot up his sleeve. Pieter goes to the office kitchen to pour a cup of coffee. Serge has told him that Stevens is claiming to be innocent, although the evidence against him is piling up.

He should be relieved now that a suspect has been arrested, but he isn't—far from it—because there's still no trace of Julie and his gut feeling about the upstairs neighbor continues to haunt him. Out of frustration, he started knocking on doors himself. He's talked to neighbors, fellow students of Julie, colleagues of Tom, customers of Billy's. He questioned everyone who even remotely knew who Julie was.

How is it possible that nobody saw anything? According to the police, there were one or more witnesses who had heard Tom and Julie arguing, but Pieter hasn't met anyone who could confirm this. Is that story even true? Or did someone deliberately lie? He asked his contact at the government to trace the data of the upstairs neighbor. He has to do something to get rid of the restlessness, of that itch that tells him they've overlooked something.

His boss isn't too happy about it all. There was an irate e-mail in his inbox. The article about Tom was too soft, he said, and moreover it was no longer relevant now that he had turned out to be innocent. Pieter's senior colleague Hannes was given the task of drawing up a profile of Rutger Stevens and Pieter is ordered to write an article about unsolved disappearance cases because the chance that Julie's still alive is small.

Once back in his seat, he absentmindedly starts leafing through the old photographs and interrogations. You never know, he might find a link to this case. He takes a sip of coffee, puts on his headphones, and starts to work his way through the chunks of text. Occasionally, he checks something in Julie's file lying next to him, but his eyes never venture much from the computer screen. It's the typical De Saegher way, his colleagues know. He can work for hours, determined to find what he's looking for.

"You're rubbing your nose again, De Saegher." It's two hours later and Hannes is standing in front of his desk, frowning at him. Pieter takes off his headphones.

"I can't let it go, Hannes. There's something wrong with that girl's upstairs neighbor."

"The one with the burnt left side? You don't really believe that, do you?"

"I'll stop believing it when I can speak to him, but that man is quasi-invisible. Why is he being so secretive if he has nothing to hide?"

"Because he's a strange bastard," growls Hannes. "By the way, the police have got the culprit, haven't they? Have you seen what this guy has been up to? He has a season ticket at the prison and happened to be out pending his trial for rape two years ago. He fits the profile perfectly."

Pieter sighs and shrugs his shoulders. Hannes is right. He'd read the Rutger Stevens file in a hurry. The details will be in tomorrow's paper and will cause quite a stir.

"Here, this has just been delivered for you." Hannes hands him a large brown envelope.

At last. The information about Floris De Wachter. He knows very well that he's violating the man's privacy by requesting his details, which is why he hasn't received the documents by e-mail but by courier. They took a long time getting here. He waits until Hannes has his back again and then rips open the envelope.

This file is all he has now, and if there's anything hidden in the letters dancing before his eyes, he'll find it. If his gut feeling is right, this is his chance. The headphones cover his ears again so he can concentrate. The murmur of his blood helps him to focus.

Already on the first page he discovers why it took so long to receive the information about Floris De Wachter: the man has changed his name. He reads with increasing amazement about Oscar Plessers, the boy who nearly died in a fire and was maimed for life.

Then an address catches his eye. Frowning, he takes out Julie's file to check whether his suspicion is confirmed.

Yes, it is.

Well, there *is* a connection between Julie and her upstairs neighbor. Would the police know that? Surely, they must?

His fingers trace the scar on his nose as he leans back in his chair.

Julie

31 Weeks and 6 Days Pregnant
Day 16 in the Basement

I'm cleaning up. Not that I make a big mess on my own, but it gives me something to do. I have my daily routine now: get up, shower, make the bed, have breakfast with yogurt or fruit, put on a DVD, wash my underwear (he won't get that from me), read, and wait for him to come with dinner. That's the highlight of my day, I must admit. The routine gives me control and that's what I need to not lose my mind.

It's easier now for me to understand why Dad snatched me away from my familiar surroundings. It was his way of keeping control over what had happened to us. As long as he could decide where we lived, which school I went to, which clothes I wore, who my friends were, and what I would study, he felt he could handle the situation. And if he could handle the situation, he could handle life. Whether that life was worth living or not was of secondary importance.

Part of the dining table is now occupied by the puzzle I was given. First, I sorted the pieces by color, then I laid out the corners, and now I'm starting on the outer edge. Anything is better than thinking about Tom, but this time I can't stop thinking about him.

That newspaper article. I've re-read it at least a hundred times to try and understand what happened.

He's in prison. Locked up. Alone. Just like me. Tom is in prison; I'm in prison. Imprisoned. Trapped. It becomes a mantra that I replay over and over in my head. How can Tom find me if he's also locked up? What "traces" have they found? I don't remember fighting with Floris. No, the police would've found traces of his presence anyway, which wouldn't be surprising, considering he was the upstairs neighbor.

For the umpteenth time, I try to remember what happened that day, but I can't get any further than him standing at the door with a basket. The article is from four days after my abduction; could he have withheld it on purpose? I have no way of knowing whether Tom is still in custody, but I assume the worst.

I'm in big trouble. I won't be released in exchange for ransom and the police are probably only looking for my corpse.

I take out my notebook and start digging back into my childhood, from my earliest memory, writing down all the names of people I've known. The key must be there.

Julie
32 Weeks Pregnant
Day 17 in the Basement

Today, according to my calendar, is August 19th: my birthday. I'm now twenty-five years old and have been locked in a basement without daylight for seventeen days.

My request to go outside has so far been ignored. Will I ever see the sun again?

Poor Tom, the preparations for the new school year will start about now. Normally it's a time of new beginnings, new possibilities., with new exercise books and sharp pencils, the smell of paper, the roar of voices in the corridor. I sigh when I realize that his reputation is in tatters. Even if he's released, he won't be teaching again this school year, if ever.

I've filled the back pages of my notebook with the names of all the people I've ever had an argument with, but I can't figure out who he is... except the one name that keeps going around in my head: Oscar—however improbable it may seem.

Oscar was an albino boy with white hair and almost transparent skin. His eyes were very light and his eyelashes and eyebrows nearly invisible. I must admit that I, too, thought he looked a bit spooky, but I never bullied him, unlike some of my friends. He used to have a crush on me, I guess, but there was no question of us dating or anything. I felt sorry for him and often defended him. And yet... the more I think about it, the clearer I see that Floris could be Oscar, but in a muscled and mutilated version with dyed eyebrows and glasses. I'm not sure whether it's a good idea to confront him with my suspicion. Suppose it's him... how would he react?

Here he comes again. I brace myself on the bed and hear the hatch open. The heat seems to be over and a cool breeze makes the hairs on my arms stand up. Or is it the sight of him? I swallow and I can't imagine that this big, muscular man is the spindly Oscar I used to know. But I don't have many options, so I take my chance when he walks over to the table with the tray.

"Floris? It's my birthday today."

No reaction.

"I feel so alone down here. Don't you want to keep me company?"

Stiff silence, as always. I don't want to call him by what might be his real name right away because I'm afraid he'll clam up, so I try a different tactic... one that I hope will get through to him.

"Did you know that I just graduated as a vet? That's what I wanted to be all my life. I was crazy about animals from a very young age."

He puts down the tray and looks at me through his glasses, but stays quiet.

"My dad was allergic to most pets, so I never had one," I continue, "and when Tom came to live with me, his cat Dolly moved in, too." His shoulders stiffen and his mouth pulls into a line. "Do you think it's possible to get me a pet here?" I try. "A kitten or a guinea pig or something?" He turns and starts walking towards the stairs, but I'm not ready yet. "Or a rabbit, maybe? A white rabbit?" I say innocently.

He stops abruptly and turns to me. Although I can barely see his eyes, I can feel them appraising me. Oscar once told me about his rabbit and I've spent the last few hours trying to remember what it was called until it just popped into my head.

"I would name it Nivens—after that rabbit from *Alice in Wonderland*, you know? Because, like Alice, I'm underground," I conclude. His motionless stance makes me nervous and an involuntary giggle escapes from my mouth. The sound brings him out of his trance and a grin slowly creeps over his face. Painstakingly slowly, he takes his glasses off his nose and walks towards me. My heart is pounding in my throat. It's him. It is really him.

"Oscar," I whisper hoarsely and his grin widens. It's as if he's been waiting for this moment.

"That took you long enough," he says. He stops a few feet in front of my bed and crosses his arms, standing there like a white giant. I swallow and pretend to be a lot braver than I feel.

"I'd made the connection before, but I couldn't believe it was you. I mean... why, Oscar? What did I ever do to you?"

"You have time to think about that now, don't you?"

I want to keep him talking and start prattling: "I thought we were friends, and I always defended you. Do you remember that time at the Christmas market on New Year's Eve? I intervened then, didn't I? There was nobody to stand up for you, nobody at all. Only me. My friends all thought I was crazy. They thought you were weird. But not me, Oscar. I didn't think you were weird at all. Why on earth are you doing this? What have I done to you?" Tears spring to my eyes and I feel so small.

He's still standing in the middle of the room, but the grin has disappeared from his face.

"Why don't you say something? Talk to me! Tell me what I did!"

His light eyes stare at me coldly and a shiver runs through my body. The baby starts kicking and instinctively I put my hand on my belly. His gaze follows.

"Oscar, please, tell me. Why do you hate me so much?"

He turns around and starts walking away.

"Oscar! Why did you shout those things at me in the flat? Why did you move in above me if you hate me? Why did you change your name? Oscar!" I can feel the desperation increasing with every step he takes away from me. "Oscar!"

He walks up the stairs. A few more seconds and he's gone.

"Oscar!" I get off the bed and run across the room, as fast as my big belly will let me. I don't want to cry, but I do anyway. "Oscar, don't leave me!" I call upstairs, but his legs are already disappearing.

Just before closing the hatch, he sticks his head back in and says, "I'll leave you alone, dear Julie. Just like you left me alone." And away he goes.

Pieter

The summer's been so hot that the asphalt melted in some places. Pieter, who hates bare legs and arms, especially those of other people, was relieved that this second half of August was cooler so that his jeans no longer stuck to the backs of his knees.

When he looked through the file that his government contact had sent him, he immediately noticed the old address of Floris De Wachter, Julie Meskens' upstairs neighbor. It turned out he had lived in the same village where Julie grew up. Moreover, the age difference between them was small, which made Pieter suspect that Floris must have known her. That the man hadn't mentioned this was strange, to say the least.

It became even stranger when he discovered that Floris' real name was Oscar Plessers, a name that set off alarm bells in his head. A quick search in the newspaper's database refreshed his memory: a dramatic house fire. He remembered the pictures of the white-haired boy with no eyebrows. The fire was an accident; it had been a foregone conclusion then. Just as Julie's disappearance was, according to the police, a foregone conclusion.

He had immediately called Serge to tell him about his findings, but the inspector told him that Van Dijck already knew. The detectives had followed Oscar's trail for a while, but when they got to Rutger Stevens, they had abandoned it. The evidence against Stevens was so overwhelming, Serge said, that there was no reason to pursue Oscar Plessers any further. "Believe me, Pieter," Serge had said. "We have the right guy in custody. If you only knew what we found at his house, you would agree with me."

***

Frustrated, Pieter types out his notes. His intuition points with red arrows to Oscar Plessers, but his hands are tied. Sometimes he regrets not having joined the police force, as he had originally wanted to, and this is one of those times. Serge had talked him out of it, saying Pieter couldn't handle the authority and hierarchy in the force. That may be true, but if he'd been a detective, he could at least do something from the inside instead of running after the facts as he's doing now.

His phone vibrates. It's Ellen, his ex. "Pieter, where the hell are you?"

Confused, he replies, "At the office, why?"

"It's past four o'clock. You were supposed to pick him up today, remember?"

The reproach overwhelms him and it takes him a few seconds to understand why Ellen sounds so irritated.

"Oh, shit! I forgot!" he shouts as he jumps up and takes his laptop bag with him on his way to the elevator. "I'm coming. I'll be there in fifteen minutes."

He hears Ellen grumble something and then she hangs up. He could slap himself. How could he forget that it's Monday, the changeover day when it's his responsibility to pick up Gabriel, his three-year-old son, from daycare?

Angry, he drives away from the office. Raindrops splash down on his windshield. He curses when he has to wait for a closed barrier. Ellen had stipulated as a condition for co-parenting that Pieter would accept his responsibility and make enough time available for Gabriel. It had seemed obvious to him at the time, but it's not. His parents live too far away to help out when needed, so he's largely on his own. Maybe he should hire someone after all?

No. He immediately dismisses the idea. Ellen would never accept that, and rightly so. She does have time for Gabriel, and her boyfriend, Maarten, is only too happy to play Daddy.

With a lump in his throat, Pieter drives into the car park and sprints through the rain to the entrance of the daycare center. He follows the arrows to the classroom at the end of the corridor. He sees Gabriel through the hallway window before the boy notices him, sitting on the lap of the kindergarten nurse who's reading him a story. His blond curly head rests against her shoulder and he has his thumb in his mouth, listening intently. Pieter takes a deep breath and blinks his eyes for a moment before he steps inside with a decided knock on the door.

"Good afternoon, sorry I'm late. Hello, little fellow." Gabriel jumps up and runs towards him, wrapping his chubby arms around him.

"No problem, Pieter. Just let us know next time, okay? We didn't know if he was staying with you or Ellen this week, so we didn't know who to call."

With his child in his arms, Pieter waves away her excuses. "I know, it's my fault. It won't happen again. Thank you."

On the way home, he wonders for the umpteenth time whether it was the right decision to fight for co-parenting, but one look at the curly head in his rearview mirror takes away that doubt. He'll have to work from home today.

Julie

What did he mean by "I'll leave you alone, dear Julie. Just like you left me alone"?

Again, I let my memories run through my mind like old slides. At least now I know whom I'm facing and I partly know why. Oscar feels abandoned by me. There's only one moment he could mean: after Mom's accident, when we moved without saying goodbye to anyone. Would he resent me so much for that? I try to understand him, but I can't. Anger claws at me, at my insides. My mom had died, damn it! What's there not to understand? The whole village knew what had happened, so it's impossible that he didn't know.

He has *no* right. We weren't even that close. At least not as far as I was concerned.

The puzzle is finished. On the table now lays a large picture of a mountain landscape with a lake. Only brown, blue, and green pieces—quite a challenge. But instead of joy and fulfillment, I feel panic. The puzzle has become whole while I fall more apart every day. Is this my life from now on? Will he be holding me captive forever?

To keep myself busy, I've started to count my steps. It's three steps from my bed to the bathroom and seven to the stairs. By counting, I keep my head and my body moving so I'm not brooding all day. I swear that if I get out of this, I'll go for a run every day. What a lovely thought.

I put the *House M.D.* DVDs on all day. I don't watch them, but they make me feel like I'm not alone. The chatter gives me that illusion and I cherish it. I also talk back to the TV. With every medical conundrum Dr. House is confronted with, I try to figure out what's wrong with the patient. It's ridiculous, but it makes me feel like I'm doing something with my medical studies. I feel so useless otherwise.

I haven't received any more newspapers since that one time. Oscar silently gives me my food every day, no matter what I try to do to draw him out. My charm offensive has officially failed. Now that I've unmasked him, I'll have to do things differently.

So I make up a new plan.

***

As soon as I hear the hatch open, I lie down on the bed. When he puts down the food tray and takes away the old one, as he always does, I keep lying there with my face to the wall. I hear him hesitate for a moment, but then he walks up the stairs anyway. The smell of food is coming my way, but I have to be strong now and hold on, so I groan slightly. I hear the hatch open and close again, but know he's still there.

He's testing me.

I didn't expect otherwise. Of course he doesn't trust me. It would be stupid of him to do so. So I groan once more and wait patiently. A slight noise betrays him, and soon the hatch opens again. Now he's really gone. Relieved, I exhale and roll over on my back.

I have some fruit which I saved and hid under my bed. I won't starve while I pretend not to eat. But food is about the only thing I look forward to here. It will be very difficult to resist. And the less I'm allowed to think about it, the more I do. All my guilty pleasures pass through my mind: paprika chips and green olives, M&M's.

Oh, M&M's...

Seven steps to the stairs, seven steps back. Three steps to the bathroom, three steps back. Think of something else. I eat a banana and concentrate on my belly. She's been very active lately, my little girl. I can't wait to hold her. But I'd better not think about that now, because it's doubtful whether I'll ever be able to.

Julie

32 Weeks and 3 Days Pregnant
Day 20 in the Basement

I make sure that my hair is damp all day long. Every hour, I run to the bathroom to splash some water on it so that when he finally, finally comes in, he sees me lying on the bed like a pathetic heap.

He puts the tray down and stands there for a moment. I left yesterday's food on the table untouched.

"Oscar," I whisper. I shiver and try to look as sick as possible. I hear him walking towards me. Suddenly, his hand is on my forehead, his warm breath brushing my face. It's been so long since anyone has touched me that the sensation, in combination with his smell, gives me an unexpected shock. My body reacts instinctively. I don't want this. I spring to my feet and throw up, right onto his shoes.

Startled, Oscar jumps backwards. He lets out a cry. I'm equally surprised by this unconscious act of my body; my faithful body doesn't abandon me. The whole room smells of my sour stomach contents and I flop down on the bed like a sack of flour.

"Help me," I groan.

Oscar walks backwards to the kitchen, his gaze fixed on me. Then he cleans up my mess and puts a damp cloth on my forehead. I let it happen and wait; it's up to him to make the first move.

He sits down at the table. Silently. I keep my eyes closed, so I can't see what he's doing, but I suppose he's looking at me and thinking about what to do with me, so I keep quiet.

After what seems like an eternity—I had almost really fallen asleep—he's standing next to my bed again.

"Are you in pain?" he asks.

I groan again and point to my head, my eyes half-opened. His gaze isn't worried, but rather focused.

He nods. "I'm going to get you a painkiller."

"No," I say. "Don't leave me, Oscar. Please."

He frowns and looks down at me before turning around and leaving the basement.

Yes.

A feeling of triumph races through my body and I let it. It may be a small step, but I'm happy with it. Because now I have his attention.

Pieter

The unpleasant feeling in his lower abdomen is growing. No matter how hard he tries, he can't get in touch with Oscar Plessers. He's stopped showing up at work. Has he fled? Then he must have something to hide.

Gabriel is lying in bed. Pieter read to him from his favorite book, *Frog is Frightened*, about a frog that hears strange noises around his house at night.

"But if there are any crooks here, you will catch them, won't you, Daddy?" the boy had asked, his eyes wide.

"Of course, darling. No villains come here. Go to sleep." He watched with awe as his son curled up and closed his eyes. So confident. If only he had that much faith in mankind, it would make his dreams a lot lighter at night. In what kind of world is a pregnant woman abducted from her flat? Not the kind of world in which he wants to raise his child. The photograph of Julie Meskens appears on his screen and he stares at the face with the green-blue eyes that is so familiar to him.

He walks to the kitchen and picks up a wineglass from the drainer. Since the divorce, he's lived in this small flat. It's not much, but it's his, although it doesn't really show much personality. He hasn't had the time to furnish it yet. He knows he should take a day to go to IKEA and buy a rug and some plants, but he hates the idea of being surrounded by people. Only Gabriel's room is ready.

He's just about to pour a glass from the bottle of red wine he uncorked yesterday when he has second thoughts. He's an investigative journalist, damn it. He should be following his instincts instead of drowning them.

He puts the cork back in the bottle and calls Lin, his regular babysitter. "Hey, Lin, it's Pieter. Sorry to call you last minute, but could you watch Gabriel tonight? He's already in bed, but I need to go out for a while."

What if this Floris, or Oscar, has kidnapped or killed Julie? What if she's still alive? Then they're losing precious time by focusing the investigation on Rutger Stevens alone, however much everything points in his direction.

While he waits for Lin, he goes through the details of the strange upstairs neighbor again. He writes down the address of his parents' house, the house that burned down, and waits.

Julie
32 Weeks and 4 Days Pregnant
Day 21 in the Basement

In my mind, I imagine how the interest in my disappearance is fading in the world outside. How the people at the bakery gossip about me. "Three weeks already, we'll never see her alive again. Poor woman, she was pregnant, too." It makes me furious to realize that my fate provides entertainment.

Just wait, I think. *Just you wait.*

It's only seven steps to the stairs. Seven tiny steps towards my freedom, but I must be given the chance to take them. The grey walls are closing in on me. I'm so tired of having myself as my only interlocutor. I'd hoped that Oscar would feel sorry for me. That he would get scared and take me to a hospital, but that's not going to happen. He's acting so coldly, even now, although he's come down to the basement as often as he can to check on me. I think he's taken time off work, or maybe he doesn't work. It makes it hard to keep up my feigned illness, so it's time for action.

"What are you going to do if I give birth?" I mutter in a weakened voice when he comes to put a new pot of tea next to my bed.

He doesn't answer.

"Do you know how to bring a baby into the world?"

He fills a flowered mug with lime tea and I can smell that he's put honey and lemon in it. He remains silent.

"I don't know why you're keeping me here, Oscar, but if you care about my baby, you should at least listen to me," I try again. I feel him hesitate. He wanted to leave but he stays put, so I continue.

"I was planning to give birth as naturally as possible, but if the baby's in a breech position, she may not survive. My medical knowledge will be of no use to you at that point. Is that what you want? A dead baby?"

He mumbles something. In three weeks, a white beard has covered his chin; it looks ferocious but I'm not afraid. It's time he faced up to reality.

"I don't understand what you're saying," I reply, propping myself up on one elbow. He no longer wears his glasses, which were part of his disguise, and his ice-blue eyes stare at me coldly.

"I know what I'm doing," he replies. "Stop asking questions."

I stare back and hold his gaze. Should I be reassured now? Is he really a doctor? Oscar used to want to become one, I remember. But that was the young, sweet Oscar, not this monster. He planned all of this, I realize. He's going to guide me through childbirth and then he'll take my child away from me and get rid of me. He clearly doesn't want to keep me in his life.

Seven steps. Seven tiny steps. I keep my gaze fixed on his, by now he must realize that I'm not ill, or at least not anymore.

It's now or never; there aren't many chances left, so I have to do it now. The adrenaline is racing through my body, I can't think, I can't doubt. I must count on him wanting to keep me in good health.

With a roar that releases three weeks of pent-up fear, rage and frustration from my body, I grab the heavy teapot and rise up to my full height. Before he realizes what's happening, I've already smashed my porcelain weapon against his head. Hot tea sloshes over my hands as the pot breaks against his skull.

I don't know if he's shouting, I don't know if he's grabbing his face with his hands, I only know that I have to run and I do. I run seven steps to the stairs with my hands on my belly and plunge onto the steps that I can feel under my feet but can't see. My gaze is fixed on the hatch and I rush towards it. I hear someone ranting, but my ears are ringing so loudly that I don't know whether it's me or him. With everything I can muster, I push against the hatch and it flies open with a bang. I can smell the fresh air and gasp for breath. I feel stitches in my stomach but have to keep going. My body is thick and bulky and I try to push myself through the hatch, but I can't.

I have to.

I have to get through it; otherwise, it's all over.

I feel my dress tear when it gets caught and manage to hoist my upper body through the hole. A hand grabs my ankle and I kick with all my might. I hear another roar and this time I know it's not me. For a moment my ankle is free and so am I. Quickly I turn around so that I can close the hatch, but there he is already. I have no time left. I have to run. Run.

I'm standing in some kind of shed. I walk to the open door and suddenly I'm outside. The grass comes up to my knees. I look up and see the sky; it's cloudy. I run on and hear him behind me.

Where am I? I see high treetops. I'm running through bushes.

I see a house and I recognize it immediately. It's Oscar's house, but it looks different. Uninhabited. Haunted.

My breath is wheezing and I feel sharp stitches everywhere. So... I really am in the village. My village.

I knew it.

No time to look. I have to go on. I run past the house. I know the way.

But it's too late. I feel his warmth behind me, and seconds later it seems like my skull explodes into a thousand pieces.

Everything turns black.

It's over. I've lost my only chance.

Pieter

Dark clouds slide in front of the moon. A few raindrops fall on his windshield. Concentrating, Pieter follows the GPS that leads him through the village, past the church square, the bike shop, the bakery. It's a typical village that, like the rest of the world, is making way for renewal. Where there used to be cobblestones, the asphalt is now as smooth as the surface of the pond, which lies dark and black. Old village houses make way for new builds and suburbs. The influence of the city is getting ever closer. The house of the Plessers family, however, is an exception. It lies just outside the village center, where the streetlights end and the dirt roads begin.

Pieter is unfamiliar with the route and curses softly as he maneuvers his car towards the house, over a bumpy road. He turns on his dipped headlights and drives on at a walking pace, his eyes focused on the road ahead. Suddenly, something jumps out in front of the car and two luminous eyes stare at him.

"Shit!" he shouts, hitting the brakes, but the animal—whatever it was—has already disappeared. A nervous laugh escapes from his mouth. What an idea to drive here in the dark. But he knows that if he doesn't, he won't be able to sleep tonight. What if Oscar is indeed holding Julie? So he starts the car again.

When he sees the house looming to his left, he breathes a sigh of relief. It's shrouded in darkness. He pulls the car over, grabs a large flashlight from the glove compartment, and gets out. Although he doesn't expect to find something, his heart is pounding harder than usual. With the beam of the flashlight ahead of him, he steps towards the house. He knows from the photos what it looked like before, right after the fire, but has no idea what to expect tonight. Has it been rebuilt or is it uninhabitable?

Curious, he approaches, the building looming black and sinister before him. The rain has stopped and, as if on cue, the moon comes out, allowing him to take in the outline of the house perfectly. No, it hasn't been rebuilt—at best patched up. Nobody lives here.

The image of the boy in the hospital bed flashes through his mind. This whole case gives him the creeps, but he can't put his finger on it. Yes, Oscar's mother was an alcoholic. Yes, she regularly fell asleep on the couch downstairs. Yes, it was possible that her burning cigar had caused the fire. Yes, Oscar had been badly maimed and that ruled him out as a culprit. So why did Pieter have doubts about his story? The facts proved it, didn't they?

He's not the only one with doubts. He found the same questions in the notes of the inspectors who had investigated the fire. They had no real arguments, except that Oscar hated his mother and therefore had a motive. That he had never expressed grief over her death. And the look in his eyes. An icy emptiness that gave them chills. But if Oscar really had something to do with it, why had he left the burning house too late? If he had planned the fire, he would've had time to get away, wouldn't he?

Pieter has no explanation for this. The only thing he can think of is that Oscar was either so ingenious that he'd deliberately stayed in the house too long to avoid arousing suspicion, which was very unlikely, or he was so stupid that he'd gone back inside to save something from the fire, which was even more unlikely, as nothing was found on his body.

"Or he simply had nothing to do with it and became the victim of a fire caused by his own mother. A mother who wasn't worthy of the name," he murmurs. But he doesn't believe that. It's the second time that the name Oscar Plessers appears in a possible crime; the chance of it all being coincidence becomes slimmer.

Determined, he walks towards the house across a carpet of wet leaves, looking for answers hidden behind the façade. A burnt-out car wreck stares at him sinisterly. The doorway of the house is boarded up. Although it's clear that no one lives there, he bangs his fist on the boards. He knows it would be better to leave this to the police, but the urge to do something is stronger than his fear. He listens with bated breath, but apart from the rustling of the wind, there's no sound. The smell of rotten and burnt wood gets hold of his nose. This is going nowhere. Discouraged, he starts to walk around the house. A quick inspection tells him that even the windows are boarded up. Here and there, he bangs on the wooden planks.

"Julie?" he calls, but it feels ridiculous and pointless, as if he's waiting for the echo of his own voice. The house is obviously empty and there's no legal way to get in. If he breaks in, he breaks every rule there is and Serge will never talk to him again.

He shines his flashlight hesitantly in the backyard. It's a large garden that hasn't been maintained for a long time. A path starts at the left of the house. He's here now, he might as well inspect the rest. It takes Pieter a lot of effort to get to the back of the garden without getting hurt. His trainers make sucking sounds on the muddy ground. The moon has disappeared behind a cloud again and his only source of light is the flashlight. Suddenly, there's a sound behind him. He stops, startled, and points the flashlight in the direction of the sound, but there's nothing to be seen. A hare? A rat? His heart is in his throat.

What if he's right and Oscar is indeed holding Julie prisoner here? Won't Pieter put her in danger showing up like this? And what about his own safety?

The image of the sleeping Gabriel appears before him, blond curls on the pillow. What kind of dad leaves his child to sneak around the house of a possible kidnapper—or worse: murderer—in the middle of the night? What if Oscar is hiding in the bushes and overpowers him? He clenches his jaw and stares into the darkness, ready to bring out his fighting skills, but there's nothing. The urge to turn around and get into the safe cocoon of his car is overwhelming, but he's just noticed a garden shed that's almost completely hidden from view. He's going to check it out and then he will leave, he decides.

He crouches down to cover the last few feet. He tries to make as little noise as possible, but the glow of the flashlight gives him away anyway. The wooden shed was once painted green, but the paint has flaked off and it looks neglected. He pushes against the door and, to his surprise, it gives way.

He's standing inside. Pieter shines his flashlight in all corners, over the floor, over the ceiling, but there's nothing. No mattress, no blood, nothing that indicates that someone was held here. Apart from some rubbish, it's completely empty.

He has to admit that his relief is taking over from his disappointment. No corpse is always good. Once more, he calls out Julie's name, but of course there's no reply. Relieved, he turns around and hurries along the path back through the garden past the house to the safety of his car.

His heart is pounding as he drives away. Only when the first streetlights come into view does his breathing stabilize.

With a deep frown on his face, he drives home again. His mission has yielded nothing, he knows, and yet something is bothering him. His subconscious has picked up something he can't place. Something that wasn't right, or something he should have seen. No matter how much he concentrates, it keeps floating around somewhere without him being able to grasp it.

Julie

32 Weeks and 4 Days Pregnant
Day 21 in the Basement

I can't move my arms; my fingers feel stiff and tingly. My legs, or rather, my ankles, are tied to something. My head is pounding. It feels as if there are bandages around it. A rag is blocking my mouth.

My eyes try to get used to the dark. I can't see anything, but I know that I'm still in the basement. It smells the same.

It doesn't take long for me to remember what happened. The teapot. The hatch. The blow to my head. I messed up. This was my chance and it's gone. He'll never trust me again. My eyes sting and I feel a lump in my throat. I want to touch my belly so badly, but I can't.

I feel so alone.

Sorry, dear Hannah. I messed up. I want her to hear my voice, but I can't speak. My only glimmer in this darkness is that at least now I know where I am: in a shelter under the garden shed of Oscar's old house. I'm back in the village where I lost my mom, the place I would never return to.

I remember something else: I only caught a glimpse of the house, but even in the twilight I could see that it had been damaged by fire. That explains Oscar's scars, I realize with shock. It must have happened after I moved. I wonder if it has something to do with his hatred of me, but I can't think of a single scenario in which I am to blame. Maybe his mom died in the fire? I want to ask him, but of course I can't.

Does he even know that my mom is dead? It would explain his harsh reaction to our leaving, if he doesn't. Could that be the case?

Just when my throbbing head is trying to get the facts of that terrible February day in order, I hear him coming back. I hold my breath. Maybe all is not lost. Maybe his revenge is based on a huge misunderstanding and I can put it right. Hope makes my body tingle and I tense up, waiting for the familiar sound of the lock being opened, but nothing happens.

The hatch doesn't open.

An adrenaline rush shoots through my body.

This is not Oscar.

The moment I have this thought, I hear my name. My name! Someone's here, looking for me! I start screaming with all my might, but the rag in my mouth muffles every sound. I want to bang on the walls and ceiling, but no matter how hard I yank and pull, I'm tied up on all sides. My body is tensed like a spring and the ropes cut into my wrists and ankles. Animal sounds come out of my mouth.

The footsteps move away again.

My throat is raw from silent screaming, my cheeks wet.

Minutes later, my body is still shaking.

It is silent again. Whomever came here looking for me is now gone. For the briefest moment I had hope, but that's now further away than ever.

I'm alone.

I'm alone.

I'm alone.

Tom

Each day seems both too long and too short. In the morning, Tom feels despondent thinking about the many hours that lie ahead. Whereas not so long ago he got hateful looks everywhere he went, now pitying glances follow him as he puts up new posters.

Julie's dead. That's the public opinion. And so is her unborn child.

Every night he fights against sleep to make the day last as long as possible, hoping that this will be the day Julie returns.

Her due date is in about seven weeks. He doesn't know what he hopes for more. That her body is found and he can know for sure what happened to her, what Rutger Stevens did to her, or to remain in this endless uncertainty.

To Tom's surprise, that journalist, Pieter De Saegher, kept asking him about Floris, the upstairs neighbor. He asked him if he knew that Floris came from the same village as Julie, and if Julie had ever told him about a certain Oscar Plessers, a boy with albinism. But Tom knew nothing of this.

It dizzies him that Floris and this Oscar guy are one and the same person and that he had changed not only his name but also his appearance before moving into the flat above them. And that he's now disappeared without a trace.

Did the police detain the wrong person and is Rutger Stevens innocent? And is this good or bad news?

He calls Van Dijck again, desperate for news—something, anything—but to no avail. The man can only confirm that the police have picked up the trail of Oscar Plessers, although he's still convinced that Rutger Stevens is the one who did it.

So many questions, so few answers. Who is this Oscar? Why would he want to hurt Julie? Is he keeping her prisoner somewhere? Did he kill her? He doesn't know.

Julie never spoke about her time in the village; it was a period that she'd ended after her mother's death. He calls Eloise with the news.

"You know, sometimes I wonder if we really knew Julie," she says. "That she never talked about her childhood and no longer has any contact with her friends from back then... that's weird, isn't it?"

Tom hums in the affirmative. It's not the first time that this thought has crossed his mind.

"Do you think she did something to that boy Oscar in the past? Bullied him, maybe? Or hurt him in any way?" she asks.

"I can't imagine, but children can be cruel to those who don't belong."

"Whatever it was, it must have been bad to turn him into such a monster," she continues.

"What if he already was a monster?" suggests Tom.

"Yeah, that's probably closer to the truth. I can't believe Julie did anything to him, to be honest. It was probably the other way around: he was in love with her and her only crime was that she wasn't in love with him, or something like that."

Tom nods, his excitement growing. Suppose Oscar became obsessed with Julie and has been stalking her for years... "If he's not quite right in his head, he might be very angry now that she's pregnant. It would explain why the words 'whore' and 'slut' were on my car. That way he punished both her and me."

Eloise bites her lip. "But what does that mean for Julie if he wants to punish her? That she's dead?" Tears spring to her eyes and Tom swallows a lump.

"That's a possibility," he says softly. "And if she is, I think he'll try to put the blame on me, so that way he kills two birds with one stone."

Pieter

Serge just called. The police have issued an APB: Oscar is now a wanted man. Not as a suspect, but as a witness. At least it's something, and Pieter feels some degree of hope.

He couldn't shake off the strange feeling that he missed something during his visit to the house last night, so he's driven to the village again. In the local bike shop, he found a childhood friend of Julie's.

"She was the only one talking to that goddamn white monkey," growls Tobias Machiels, as he puts a new wheel on a mountain bike that looks expensive.

"Were they good friends?"

"Not really. Julie always stood up for him, yes, but that was more out of a sense of justice. Although he had a different idea about that." The red-haired man laughs slyly.

"What exactly do you mean?"

"Listen, I've just told this to the police. Do we really have to?"

"Please. Two minutes, then I'll be off again."

The man sighs. "All right. Oscar was madly in love with Julie. Everyone knew that. He followed her around like a dog and thought nobody noticed." He shrugs his broad shoulders. "But it was innocent; he didn't stand a chance anyway. The guy didn't have all his marbles, you know."

"Julie turned him down?"

"I don't think it ever came to that, but honestly I'm not sure. I mean, we were kids."

Pieter nods and makes a note in his pad.

A customer enters the shop and Tobias wipes his greasy hands on a cloth. "Sorry, I have to get back to work."

So Oscar not only knew Julie, he was in love with her. He even stalked her. Back in his car, Pieter calls Serge again, who sounds agitated.

"Van Dijck has sunken his teeth into it, Pieter, we're working on it. Now let us do our job," he says.

But for Pieter, that's just not enough. Cursing, he drives back to the office.

***

Back at his desk, he picks up the old police file on the house fire and everything else he's collected over the past few weeks. It's time to bring some order to the chaos and get everything organized; maybe it'll help him find Julie.

Determined, he grabs a marker and writes two words on the whiteboard, "Oscar" and "Julie," with a vertical line in between. Some of his colleagues look on in curiosity. Beneath the names, he writes both their dates of birth and the places where they were born.

"Oscar wasn't born in the village," he mumbles. "He came to live there with his mother when he was four, so the first year Oscar and Julie both lived in the village was 1984." He makes a note of the year.

"From 1987 to 1992, they attended the same primary school, but Oscar was always a year ahead of Julie. They didn't have any common hobbies and, according to the villagers interviewed, Oscar and his mother were very much on their own. He had no friends. It's unclear when he met Julie.

From 1993 onwards, Oscar was placed with several foster families. There was no contact to speak of, although according to Tobias Machiels, Julie sometimes stood up for Oscar, which indicates she felt some kind of affection for him.

In 1994, Oscar was placed with Kirsten and Robert De Ridder for more than a year. According to them, he was an exemplary foster son, at the most a bit of an eccentric, which manifested in his extreme reticence, but otherwise perfect. They also gave him a rabbit to which he became extremely attached. The animal moved with him when he went back to live with his mother."

Pieter takes a breath and checks the file in front of him before continuing. He looks for reports by psychologists that might shed some light on Oscar's state of mind, but can find nothing. Meanwhile, several of his colleagues have left their desks, listening with interest.

"Then tragedy strikes: Oscar's house goes up in flames, presumably caused by his mother who fell asleep with a burning cigar. Oscar manages to escape but is badly burned, leaving his left side disfigured. This was on... Let me check the date..." He runs his finger along the text until he finds what he's looking for. "Aha, on the fourteenth of February, 1996." He writes the date on the board.

"That's also the last day Oscar spends in the village, because after his long hospital stay, he's placed in a children's home and nobody has seen him for years.

"Back to Julie. Let's see, she left the village, too, together with her dad. This was on... aha, in the same year." Pieter frowns for a moment and checks the information in front of him.

"Hm, this is quite a coincidence." He hesitates and looks again at both files. "According to my information here, Julie moved shortly after the house fire, following another tragic accident: the death of her mom. She was hit by a drunk driver on that same fourteenth of February."

One of his colleagues remarks, "Must have been a great Valentine's Day," and Pieter looks up, dazed, unaware that he has an audience.

"Yes, indeed. What a strange coincidence, no?" he murmurs. There's that niggle again.

"Julie's mom was probably hit around seven o'clock in the evening, but it wasn't until around nine o'clock that she and her bike were found by a passerby in the ditch. She was still alive then. The fire broke out around eleven o'clock." He knows there's no logical connection between the two, but writes both moments on the timeline anyway. "I don't know if it means anything, but it's certain that Julie and Oscar haven't seen each other for a long time, probably since the fire."

He searches the police report about the fire for the list of visitors to the hospital and scrolls it with his finger. The list is appallingly short. "There's hardly anyone on here except the police. Not even his foster parents sought him out."

They probably weren't aware of the fire, but still. He scrolls on. "Julie hadn't gone to see him either, by the way."

"Wow, that boy really had no one at all; that must have been very lonely," another colleague remarks.

Pieter looks at the eyebrowless boy in the photo: a transparent form that almost disappears in the white hospital sheets. As if he wanted to be invisible, which in a way he was. No one really cared about his fate, not even Julie, who had been there for him before. But she had a good reason. Would Oscar have known that Julie's mom had a fatal accident the same night his own died?

"How long had Oscar been in a coma?" he thinks aloud, searching through the papers with quick fingers.

"Ten days," he mutters, continuing to rub his hands through his hair, leaving it standing on end in all directions, "so there's a chance that Oscar didn't know what happened to Julie's mom." Pieter looks around at his colleagues. Nobody really answers, they just shrug and look at each other.

"Yeah, so," says Pieter in their place. "That might be the motive, guys."

"What, then?" asks Hannes, who has also joined. "That Julie didn't come to see him in the hospital ten years ago? That's why he's kidnapped her now, and maybe killed her?" He laughs. "I'd better watch out the next time my mother-in-law is in the hospital!"

Some colleagues chuckle along, but Pieter fails to see the funny side.

"Listen to me and think for a moment. This is a boy who's been on his own all his life. Who has no one but an addicted mother. Who's bullied and excluded time and again because of his strange appearance. Who goes from one foster home to another like a Pokémon card that's worth nothing. Who doesn't know what love is. Who on top of that gets maimed in a house fire and loses not only his mom but also his home. Suppose this boy has a personality disorder and can't form a realistic picture of a healthy, natural relationship. In this file, I see no one, no one at all, who has stuck their neck out for him. The only person who ever looked out for him and for whom he dared to have any feelings was Julie. And she of all people doesn't come to visit him at the lowest point of his life. Worse yet: when he's finally strong enough to return to the village, she's disappeared. How do you think an unstable boy like Oscar would cope?" He looks the team in the eyes one by one; they've fallen silent and look at him expectantly. "Don't you think it's possible that in his mind he felt betrayed by her?"

"But she was the only one who *did* care about him," protests Ilse, one of the junior journalists.

"That is precisely why he felt betrayed. All the others left him cold, except Julie. She was special to him. And she left him, alone."

"Okay, okay, I see where you're going with this," growls Hannes. "But it's a bit far-fetched, I think. What about Rutger Stevens? He's a dyed-in-the-wool rapist who sent an anonymous e-mail to Tom and in whose garage, according to the police, Julie's DNA was found. That's what I call a great suspect. On the other hand, we have Floris or Oscar, whatever we call the guy, who's kept quiet about knowing Julie and maybe also about being in love with her, who has now disappeared without a trace. I know who I'd put my money on, don't you? This Oscar has the profile of a stalker and got scared after he was interrogated. He knew full well that the police would find out he was hiding things, and that's why he ran. I'm still betting on Rutger as our man."

Pieter nods but his thoughts are already elsewhere. A few years ago, he researched stalking for an article. He sits down at his desk again and taps on his laptop until he finds what he's looking for.

"*Erotomania is when a stalker is under the delusion that the object of his affection is in love with him.*" Concentrating, he absorbs the information until a loud curse from Hannes makes him look up.

"That son of a bitch has an alibi, goddamn it!"

"What? Who?"

Hannes increases the volume of the television. The police have just released Rutger Stevens. At the time of Julie's disappearance, he was caught on a security camera in a deserted car park behind a warehouse, miles away, and seen getting involved in a shady deal with some other figures just as shady as he is. Shady, yes… but not Julie's kidnapper.

Julie

32 Weeks and 5 Days Pregnant
Day 22 in the Basement

The pent-up anger hangs around Oscar like a dark aura. With a dogged expression on his face, he unlocks my cuffs so I can finally go to the toilet. I hardly dare look at him. He has a cut above his eye from the smashed teapot. He seems okay, apart from a few red marks. The tea was no longer hot enough to do any serious damage.

In the bathroom, I take the cloth from my mouth and splash water on my face. There's no mirror and I wonder how pale I must be after all these weeks down here. I feel the bandage; there's a big bump on the back of my head.

Back in the living room, I sit down at the table where a new tray is waiting. Oscar is standing next to it, his arms crossed. I start to eat; it's vegetarian ravioli. Again, I have the impression that he bought it somewhere, from a caterer or a take-away.

My fighting spirit has been rekindled now that I know the world outside is looking for me. It's only a matter of time before they find the shelter, I'm sure.

Out of the corner of my eye, I see a camera. Oscar must have put it up while I was knocked out. It's one of those wireless things hanging from the ceiling in the corner. Oscar has clearly lost all faith in me.

"I know where I am," I say. "In a shelter under the garden shed of your old house."

He doesn't answer. Is he going to stand there until I finish eating? Will he tie me up again?

"Your house burned down. What happened?" I ask.

His shoulders tense briefly, almost imperceptibly. I know I'm treading on thin ice, but I don't care anymore. I've killed my chances of falling into his good graces anyway.

"Is that how you got those scars?"

His jaw tightens. My questions irritate him, but I have to know.

"And your mom... did she survive?"

That was the wrong question. In one move, he stands next to me and snatches the tray from under my nose. For a moment he towers over me and I'm afraid he's going to hurt me, but he thinks again and turns around. As he rushes up the stairs, he hisses through his beard, "Julie Meskens, you're an even more vicious bitch than I thought you were. From now on, I'll put your food on the stairs. Have fun on your own down here." And away he goes.

Defeated, I slump back down on the bed. What have I done to deserve this anger? I understand less and less. Why am I a vicious bitch? There's something about that fire; he blames me. How can I make him understand that I had nothing to do with it? I hold back my tears. Luckily, he hasn't chained me up again, but even though I've had a couple of big mouthfuls of ravioli, my hunger isn't satisfied and I feel empty.

For Hannah, it's so important that I eat well, that I stay healthy. I get up and open the fridge to get a piece of fruit, but it's empty. Could he have forgotten to fill it? No, I'm sure there was an apple left and some jars of yogurt. I feel the color draining from my face as the realization dawns on me that he's taken everything out. To punish me, of course.

Damn it, Julie, what have you done? I look around. Only now do I notice that my books are gone. I swallow; the books were about the only thing that helped me forget how lonely I am. The DVDs are gone, too. I quickly check the TV cabinet and, yes, Dr. House is gone.

I've betrayed Oscar and he punishes me by taking away all my privileges. With a jolt, I lift my mattress up, although I know without looking that my nail clipper with the file is gone. It was just a little thing but it made me feel I had a chance, however minimal, of getting out.

I lower myself onto the bed, defeated. If I thought I was alone before, now I really am.

Pieter

Rutger Stevens has an alibi, and Oscar Plessers has disappeared.

Where is he? He can't have gone up in smoke, can he? If only the police had a clue pointing in his direction, something concrete on which they could build a case to get a search warrant.

Pieter's phone rings. It's Serge. "Yes?"

"We received a tip from a cashier in a supermarket who recognized Oscar Plessers."

Immediately, he jumps up.

"When? Where?"

"In June or July. She couldn't remember exactly. The woman remembered him, especially his hand with the scars, and thought he was behaving oddly. He had a cart full of things for a baby."

"That was before Julie even disappeared?"

"Yes, a few weeks before, and miles from where he lives, as if he deliberately didn't want to be seen in his own neighborhood with that stuff."

"And that woman is absolutely sure it was him?"

"One hundred percent, although he was wearing glasses at the time. Combined with the fact that he didn't tell us he knows Julie and had feelings for her and that he disappeared during the investigation, it's enough, we hope. Van Dijck has asked the investigating judge for a search warrant."

Finally.

Julie

I am broken.

I'm so broken that I can't break any further, like crystal grinding back to sand. The silence and emptiness around me have a crushing effect. Every attempt to get through to Oscar fails. He comes in at the oddest times, sometimes even in the middle of the night. My meals are very sparse. I would do anything to talk to him. Though I despise him, he's all I have.

He keeps me at a distance, which probably makes his task, whatever it is, easier. Once he was mad about me, now he's mad *at* me.

My back hurts more every day. I know it's because my muscles are weakening from lack of exercise and I'm worried about giving birth soon. I'll need my strength.

Since I have no distractions now that my books and DVDs are gone, I prowl around in the basement continuously like a tiger. I know every nook and cranny. I try to do my yoga exercises but my legs have weakened and I fall over. Despondent, I sit on the floor staring at my swollen ankles. I get up to walk again. I sing, very loudly and out of tune. There's no one to hear it anyway, except Oscar, if his camera has sound.

I undress in the dark now because I assume that thing doesn't have night vision. Every now and then I shout at him—things like "I know you're watching" and "coward" and more of that. Just like he was shouting at me a few months ago. The scum. I hope he hears it.

Would Tom still be in prison? Would he and Eloise take care of each other? Tom doesn't know that I know all about his night with Eloise. Eloise and I always tell each other everything. I thought he'd find it embarrassing, so I never quizzed him. It didn't matter to me, but that was then and this is now. When will he give up hope of ever seeing me again? When will he declare me dead and move on with his life? Would he still live in my flat? Not if it were up to my dad, I think.

These and other questions I ask myself, but also Hannah. I talk and she answers. She thinks I'm not trying hard enough to escape, but it's easy for her to talk in there. She doesn't see how hopeless the situation is, and how fat and cumbersome I am.

For the past few days, I've been having more Braxton Hicks contractions. I know it's normal, but I'm worried anyway. What if she comes too early, I wonder again. I think I can handle a normal birth—I'm not afraid, really—but what if it's not a normal delivery? Will Oscar take us to a hospital? I laugh derisively at my own naivety. Of course he won't.

At the moment, she's still breech, I know that can change, but...

There he is again, putting the tray on the stairs.

"Coward!" I shout. "Come down and talk to me if you dare." But he's gone already.

The Last Day

Oscar

He's shivering. It cooled down significantly last night, which isn't surprising considering it's almost September. He pulls an extra blanket over his body and stares at the dark sky. For ten days, he's been living in hiding. He's thrown a mattress in his car and lives there now. During the day, he tries to move as little as possible and not attract attention. He only needs to go out for food, though that will become harder from now on.

His picture appeared in the newspaper two days ago. He hadn't expected that so soon. He's made some stupid mistakes. He shouldn't have disappeared from his flat so suddenly, as that made him suspicious, but he panicked when that stupid journalist was at his door.

In his mind, the plan was perfect: as soon as Julie was unconscious, he'd taken several ampoules of blood and spread them on the living room floor. Then he wiped up the blood with a dishcloth that he then stuffed into the dustbin. He also smeared one of Tom's t-shirts and then hid it in a plastic bag at the back of the wardrobe. Together with his own testimony about the so-called quarrels he'd heard, this was enough to give the guy a good scare and keep him behind bars for several hours. He hadn't expected the police to consider him the prime suspect for so long, but that was a nice bonus.

He'd felt the greatest satisfaction when he'd put the police in Rutger's path. At last, that dirty rapist was put in a cell where he belonged. Oscar had lured him out of his house under the pretext that he would give him a thousand euros if Rutger picked up a parcel at a certain address. Of course, nobody lived at that address. He'd broken into Rutger's hovel and hidden the grey wig and blanket he'd used to kidnap Julie in his garage. The idiot had no password on his computer, which stood like an altar on a table in the middle of the living room, so Oscar also sent an e-mail from a Hotmail address he created on the spot. Everything ran smoothly...if only that fool had gone home after his failed mission. But no, Rutger managed to be spotted by a security camera, thus inadvertently providing him with an alibi.

Oscar needs more time. He can't wait for Julie to give birth, by which time the police will have found his basement. He has to face the fact that his plan to take Julie's baby has failed, just like every other plan he ever had, like the one to become a doctor or the one to start a family with Julie. Or the biggest plan of all: to live rather than to survive.

He won't allow that little bitch to win. Oscar may not get what he wants, but Julie will surely get what she deserves: a lonely death in the dark.

His hatred for Julie has been growing for years like a fungus over everything he does. He never thought it could get any bigger, but it does. It's not the attack with the teapot that makes him so furious now. It's normal for someone in captivity to try to escape. Besides, it was his own fault; he'd allowed her to trick him. Of course, she hadn't really been ill.

No, what pushes him far beyond his limits is that she pretends not to know his house has burned down. It's toppling him over, making him come very close to the verge of that gaping hole before him, into which he mustn't fall because if he does he'll completely lose control. He'll lose the life he's worked so hard for, the life he painstakingly rebuilt after Julie abandoned him.

To think that he did it all for her, that he had held that burning cigar against the curtains next to the sofa on which his mother slept until they caught fire. He had only been a kid, a naive child who thought that his mother's death would release him from pain, that it would bring him closer to Julie.

Of course, he'd known that he'd end up in a foster home again, but given his age he reckoned he would be given more freedom. With a bit of luck, he could even continue to go to the same school.

A bit of luck... It had all turned out very differently. He'd stood mesmerized watching the flames consuming the curtains like hungry snakes, licking the ceiling with their tongues. There was nothing in the house he wanted to save. The few books he wanted to keep were already in the shelter. Nivens was gone and he had nothing else. To make it look like an accident, he had to run outside with only the pajamas he was wearing.

The sofa on which his mother lay caught fire, but she didn't wake up. Empty bottles lay next to her, some still containing a little booze. The alcohol would speed up the process, he realized, but he stood as if glued. For the time being, he was safe in the hallway, but he couldn't stay there for much longer.

The carpet caught fire, then the table. The smoke billowed and his eyes began to sting. This brought him out of his trance. One last look, he thought, and he would run outside.

If he had done exactly that, everything would've been different. But just as he was about to open the front door, he realized that he'd left the only possession he attached any importance to in his room: Julie's handkerchief. Her scent had been on it since New Year's Eve six weeks earlier. He had to have that handkerchief. Without hesitation, he slammed the living room door and ran up the stairs, followed by billowing smoke. He burst into his room and groped around in his bed. Damn, where was that thing? Everything felt the same: sheets, blankets. He took the bedclothes off the bed and shook them.

Where was it? Smoke filled the room and increasingly obscured his view.

There it was: a white cotton square with an embroidered border. He grabbed it and turned around.

Smoke. Suffocating smoke.

It fills the room in black waves.

It's everywhere. In his eyes, in his mouth.

He coughs, his eyes burn. A moment ago, he could see the door to his bedroom, but not anymore.

He shouldn't have gone upstairs again; the fire consumes everything so quickly. Too quickly.

He searches his way by touch.

There.

Quick.

Down the stairs, into the dark hall.

The front door beckons; if he goes out now, he's saved.

But he can't resist the urge, has to see with his own eyes. His lungs are burning, his ears are ringing, his eyes are dry.

Hot, it's so hot.

He has to be quick, pulls open the living room door.

Yells.

His hand!

Flames screeching through the door, roaring past him.

Pain!

That smell, he's nauseous; he wants to bend over but can't stay here. He has to leave. His legs can no longer carry him, but he has to go. Has to.

One last look at her on the sofa. He doesn't see her, only flames and black smoke. She must be there. For sure. He has to leave now.

He has to.

The floor is burning, the ceiling is burning, his pajamas are burning. A few more feet; come on, Oscar, a few more feet.

He throws his body out onto the wet grass, his loot clutched in his hands. Rolls as far as he can.

Pain.

Pain everywhere.

Sirens.

And then nothing.

He gave up everything for Julie. Everything. That she's now acting as if she doesn't have a clue only confirms what a bitch she is and that she's in the basement for good reason. It proves that she's playing with him, mocking him. As if his life is worth less than hers.

Oh, Princess Julie.

He laughs softly. This time it's his turn. He takes the taser and a knife from the glove compartment, gets out of his car, and starts walking through the woods towards the house.

Julie

33 Weeks Pregnant
Day 24 in the Basement

I wake up and, for a second, I don't know where I am. This happens sometimes; it's a wonderful moment of ignorance in which I don't feel alone in the world.

Without artificial light, it's always dark in the basement, so when I open my eyes I stare into black nothingness.

What woke me?

I lift myself up on my elbows and prick up my ears but hear nothing. My head hurts. My mouth is dry, so I roll over on my side and sit up to get a glass of water, but then I hear it again: someone is opening the hatch. Is it Oscar again? He was here just a few hours ago.

My question is answered in the affirmative when the bright light of the fluorescent lamp switches on; I'm temporarily blinded. Immediately, I feel in every cell of my body that things are very wrong. I blink frantically and scream when I see what Oscar has in his hands: the taser he had with him on my first day. And a large knife.

I don't understand what's going on, but I don't have time to think. I have to act, so I don't make a sound and with all my might I rush to the bathroom. Before he realizes what's happening, I've shut the door behind me. Panting, I lean against it. There's no lock on it and I know it's only a matter of time before he comes in, but I've gained a few seconds.

Something must've happened. His plan has somehow failed and, in his panic, he now wants to kill me.

I do *not* want to die.

I suppress the panic that's paralyzing my brain; if ever there were a time when I needed to stay focused, it's now.

His breathing is clearly audible on the other side of the door. It seems as if he's waiting for something. I get a Braxton Hicks contraction again and furiously ball my fists. I can't let my emotions take over. I must remain calm. I can do this.

"Why are you doing this, Oscar? Is there anything I can do to make it up to you?" I shout with my mouth against the door.

To my surprise, he replies. "What you've done, you'll never be able to make up." He says it coldly and calmly.

"Then tell me what it is. At least let me understand before you kill me."

He doesn't answer, but I can hear his breathing. All I can do is crawl through the dust and beg his forgiveness, although I don't know what for.

"I'm sorry your house burned down. I'm sorry your mom died."

Silence.

"I'm sorry I didn't visit you at the hospital."

He hums something on the other side of the door.

"But I didn't know, Oscar. I didn't know about the fire. I never knew!"

I listen anxiously to see if there's any reaction, but all I hear is his breathing quickening slightly.

"Otherwise I would've come to see you. But my mom was dead, Oscar. You knew that, didn't you?"

Silence. I convince myself that he won't hurt me as long as I keep talking, so I can't stop.

"She was hit by a car on Valentine's Day."

Silence.

"We never found out who it was. Probably a drunk driver."

Don't stop talking. Don't stop.

"All I know is that it was a red car."

Is it my imagination or did he really start breathing faster?

"My dad didn't want to return to the village, so after the funeral we moved out. I didn't get to say goodbye to anyone."

I'm not imagining it. I said something that upset him.

"Oscar?"

Oscar

As if paralyzed, Oscar sits slumped on the floor, his back against the door with the knife in his hand.

That fateful Valentine's Eve, he'd decided that enough was enough. He'd seen his mother driving off to stock up on booze and had waited by his bedroom window for her to return. When she'd left, both her car's headlights were on; when she returned, only one was. She'd parked the red Clio in its regular spot next to the house and had staggered inside. He could clearly see the dent in the hood in the light of the façade lamp, but that night he didn't care which animal she'd hit this time, or which lamppost had toppled over. He'd felt so numb.

"Oh no," he groans when he realizes what happened. "Oh no."

Not only was his own mother responsible for the death of Julie's mom, but it was also her fault that Julie left him overnight. All this time, it had been his own mother who had snatched Julie away from him. And now he's done something far worse, because unlike his mother, who was drunk, Oscar knew very well what he was doing. He had hated Julie even though she couldn't have known that he was in the hospital.

He feels the blood rushing in his ears; his fists are clenched. Even now that she's dead, his mother manages to ruin his life. It's all her fault. Trembling, he gets up. He has to get out of here. For years, the hatred for Julie had consumed his insides until there was nothing left but emptiness and darkness. If only it could swallow him up now. If only he could disappear forever. Damn, if only he'd died in the fire.

His chest rises and falls as if he's just finished a sprint. The grey basement walls no longer give him the protection they once did. This is no longer his lair; he's no longer safe here. He needs to think about his next move. He has to stay calm.

He picks up the knife and taser, walks out of the shelter, and closes the hatch behind him. Outside, it's still dark and he walks towards the forest that welcomes him with its gloomy shadows.

Julie

It remains silent on the other side of the door. A while ago I heard something resembling a sob, then nothing. Only silence.

"Oscar?"

I don't dare move; maybe it's a trap? I put my ear carefully against the door. I no longer hear his breathing either.

Is he really gone? Why? Because of what I said about my mom? But how could he not have known that? That can't change anything, can it?

The bathroom floor feels cold against my buttocks and I'm very uncomfortable. Gently I push myself upright, and once again my belly gets hard. I need to get my stress level down somehow, but it seems impossible. I'm in a state of high alert. Slowly, I open the bathroom door.

I'm completely alone.

He's gone. Really gone. I can't believe it.

I walk to the bed on shaky legs, my hands over my mouth. I let myself slump onto the mattress, tears of relief falling on my lap. I don't care why he's gone; at least I'm safe again.

Thank you. Thank you.

Unfortunately, my euphoria is short-lived and I double up due to severe pain in my abdomen and lower back.

Oh no.

I lie down on my back and put my hands on my belly. For minutes, I hardly dare breathe, but nothing happens. False alarm? My mouth is dry. I roll onto my side and get up, walk to the kitchen, and fill a glass with water.

She mustn't be born yet. I'm thirty-three weeks pregnant. What if her lungs haven't matured enough? What if her sucking reflex hasn't developed? My heart is pounding like crazy, and that's not good. I have to stay calm, especially now. If I get agitated, I'll only make things worse.

I drain the glass in one gulp and lie back on the bed. I concentrate on my breathing: breathe in for six counts, breathe out for six counts. Six in, six out. In. Out.

"Imagine the gentle murmur of the sea, see how the sun reflects on the waves. Feel yourself becoming calm," I hear my inner meditation voice say.

Shit.

I feel my belly tighten again, the skin as tight as a drum. My breath quickens. It feels as if I'm on a rollercoaster at the highest point and then thundering down. I can't stop this with just meditation and breathing techniques. My belly is creating strange shapes and then stretches out in a point, like a triangle. It doesn't really hurt, but it's a bit uncomfortable. I can no longer deny it: these are contractions, probably induced by the stress of Oscar coming in with the knife. With a bit of luck, they'll stop soon, but then again, they might not.

When my belly is soft again, I press on it with both hands to feel how the baby is lying.

Breech. Still.

I know I shouldn't panic, but it's damned hard. Then I realize I left the light on and Oscar can see me through his camera. I don't want that. I stagger up, switch off the light, and lie down again.

I try to distract myself in the dark and think of Eloise, of Tom, of my mom. I think about the time when, as a kid, I'd been whining for weeks about new trainers I wanted. Nikes. They were expensive and my parents wouldn't give them to me just like that for no reason, but I think they got so fed up with my whining that they gave in. I can remember to this day how I felt when I tried them on for the first time. I was prouder than Maradona that made a goal.

My parents had made me promise that I would play soccer on the village field in my old shoes, but what's the point of new Nikes if you can't try them out right there where the difference is made? I held out for a few days, but in the end, I smuggled them into my rucksack and played anyway.

The shoes gave me wings. I scored goal after goal and felt invincible. That is, until my foot got stuck behind a branch and tore off my sole. I'll never forget the way Mom looked at me when she found out a few days later. Her disappointment hit me so much harder than the loss of my precious Nikes, but no matter how angry Mom was, Dad never found out.

Here comes another contraction. This time I feel more pain, but it's manageable for now. Hopefully, it doesn't get worse. I can do this. I know I can do this. In my head, I go through the phases of childbirth. The faster the contractions come, the more painful it will be and the more dilated I am. At the moment, there's quite some time between them, but I'll have to time them. I don't have a watch, and I can't see the wall clock in the dark, so I'll have to count. As soon as I feel my belly relax again, my breathing stabilizes and I start: One. Two. Three. Four. Five. I can do this. Six. Seven... Eight... Twenty. Fifty-three. Ninety-four.

I doze off, my eyes falling shut. Mom wanted another baby, but Dad was happy with just me. She must have persuaded him because when I was five or six and I was in kindergarten, Mom became pregnant again. She shared her joy with me: I was going to be a big sister! But I wasn't happy at all; I didn't want to share Mom with some little stranger. Mom was mine and mine alone. Secretly, I wished the baby would never come, so when Mom ended up in the hospital after a miscarriage, I felt guilty for weeks. I thought I had wished the baby dead and cried myself to sleep every night. Mom was beside herself when she found out, holding me so close I could hardly breathe.

"Julie, dear girl. Of course it's not your fault. The baby just wasn't strong enough."

I smelled her scent. "But now I won't get a little brother or sister," I said in my constricted voice.

"You are enough for me," she replied. And that was that.

Ouch. My belly pulls into a point again, even harder this time. I've lost count. That means the contractions are still far apart. I hope they will stop if I just keep calm, so I breathe through them and try to get some sleep, but to no avail.

I'm wide awake and I know why. My body is ready. It keeps me alert because I'm going to bring a child into this world. In disbelief, I shake my head. "No!" I cry silently. I want to scream but I can't alarm Oscar, wherever he is.

Again, panic overwhelms me; I feel it closing my throat. This dark basement is no world to be born in. I need more time; if I can just hold on a bit longer, maybe he'll release me.

"You really can't be born yet, Hannah," I whisper. "Please, can you stay there? Give me a chance to get out of here. I know I can, but you have to give me more time. You don't want this, I promise. It's too soon."

In response, my stomach contracts again, and the pain in my lower back takes my breath away. I try not to shout and concentrate on the breathing technique.

I wish Tom were here. Or Eloise. Someone. But I'll have to do this alone, in the dark and as quietly as I can.

Oscar

Oscar shakes his head in despair as he wanders through the forest. His hands won't stop shaking and his stomach feels as if it's been turned inside out.

Not only are the police looking for him and he can't return to his flat, but it will only be a matter of a few hours, a day or two at most, before they raid the house and the garden shed and find Julie.

He knows he has to get away, run, get out of here before the manhunt begins.

Julie. He thought he'd lost her.

His Julie.

He could call the police with an anonymous tip about her whereabouts and then drive as far away as possible, across the border. To France, maybe, and then via Luxembourg to Spain, into the deserted inland. The cash he has will get him by and he can always make himself useful at the fruit harvest to earn money…but then it will have all been for nothing. Years of planning and preparation. He'll never see her again.

And the baby. *His* baby.

For ten years, he's been living towards this moment, his revenge, and again it's his own mother who throws a wrench in the works. He can't let her win. He won't let her decide on his life from her grave. Yes, he's made a mistake, but he can put it right if he just thinks it through and doesn't allow the panic to set in.

Maybe it's not too late. If he explains to Julie what happened, would she understand? Would she see that it was his love for her that maddened him and made him take her? Would she understand that no one will ever love her as much as he does? That they can be happy together, somewhere far away from here?

He's come to a clearing in the forest, the moon shining down on him and coloring his white hair silver.

He should at least try.

With a jolt, he turns and runs back in the direction of the village.

Julie

Ninety-eight... ninety-nine... No! I can't stand it anymore. The contractions are coming so fast that I don't have time to recover. It's so dark in here. My hair sticks to my scalp. It hurts so much. I wish Mom were here; she would know what to do.

I hear someone scream. My hands grip the edge of the bed and my breath falters. Am I going to die here? Now?

It's me who's screaming. It's all going wrong. The baby is in the wrong position. I've tried to turn her, but I can't do it alone. My body is being torn apart, I'm going to die, I know it. I see a light in the distance. Is this the end? Is this what people see when they have a near-death experience? The outlines of a figure stand out against the bright light. I'm no longer alone.

"Mom? Is that you?" It's Mom!

A new contraction announces itself and my body splits in two. There is a storm in my head, dark clouds gather, flashes of light spark before my eyes. I'm soaked. Where am I?

I'm lying on the bed.

"Mom? Mommy, is that you? I'm sick, Mom."

"Do you have a fever, dear?" A cool hand on my clammy forehead, a thermometer under my arm. A glass of water is put to my lips. "Drink up, dear. The doctor will be here soon."

"Mom, I feel so bad. It's so light in here."

"It will get better, dear. It's just a flu. Hey, and you don't have to go to school now. Isn't that nice?"

"But I like school, Mom. I want to go back to school. I'm so alone here. Mom? Mom!"

I forgot to count between contractions, or maybe there's no time between them. I don't know. My eyes hurt; I keep them closed. "Are you still there, Mommy?"

A hand on my head again, heavy and rough.

Whose hand? Where am I?

I remember now. I'm in the basement trying to give birth on my own. The baby is breech and although I feel a strong urge to push, I know that with breech you can't push until the very last moment. I have to hold on until I'm fully dilated. But how will I know when that time has come?

The next contraction comes. I roar myself through it, but in the background I hear another sound. Or rather, I don't really hear it, but I *feel* that someone is here with me.

Here comes a push contraction.

Can I? May I?

I have to. I can't stop it. I shout and scream; the urge takes over and then ebbs away. I can't do it. I can't. But I have to. Another push contraction. The thunder roars in my head. I'm on all fours on the floor, roaring and pushing until I can't take it anymore.

A voice penetrates my consciousness. A man's.

Oscar?

I can't hear what he's saying because my ears are ringing. I see blood, so much blood. It sticks to my hands and knees. To my nightdress. This is not going to work. I can't get the baby out—not on my own and not in a breech position.

Another push contraction and again I push as hard as I can, but I'm weakened. It doesn't work.

The contractions stop for a moment. I try to catch my breath. So much blood. With my hand, I reach between my legs: I feel two little feet. This is unreal; this isn't happening to me. I try to open my eyes. The light is on in the basement and Oscar is sitting next to me. He too is covered in blood. His pale face looks worried.

"Oscar, the baby is breech," I say. "I can't do this on my own. You have to take us to a hospital."

I feel another push contraction coming on. I push with all my might and feel the baby sliding further down the birth canal. When I feel my body burst from the pressure, I scream out. The urge to push ebbs away, but the baby isn't yet born. This isn't good: her head has yet to go through. If I'm not sufficiently dilated, she won't make it and neither will I.

With the next push, I know I'll have to give everything I have left in me. My life and hers are at stake.

"Oscar, please, help us," I beg.

He starts to say something but I can't hear it because the rollercoaster can't be stopped anymore.

I scream as my primal instincts set every muscle in my body in motion. The thunder in my head increases, the flashes of light dance before my eyes and turn into red and black spots. I can no longer hear or see as I push the baby's head out.

Oscar

The fluorescent lamp hums above his head and starts to flicker. Petrified, Oscar stares at the basement floor where Julie lies on her side in a pool of blood. Her nightdress is suspended above her hips, blood seeping from between her legs. With his eyes, he follows the umbilical cord to the small body lying next to her, smeared with blood and mucus.

It doesn't move. Or does it? He's not sure; it could be an optical illusion because of the flickering light.

He can't get his body to move. He knows that he must cut the umbilical cord and clear the baby's airway, but it feels as if someone is sitting on top of him and has knocked all the air out of his lungs.

Shock. He begins to tremble uncontrollably. His arms and legs shake so hard that he can't stand upright. He knows he has to. He has to save them.

Julie. It's Julie.

He wakes up from his trance and cuts the umbilical cord. In one movement, he takes the limp baby in his arms and clears her airway, gently patting her back. A plaintive moan escapes the tiny body. She's alive. He wraps the child in a towel and walks back to Julie to check her pulse. Her heart is beating, albeit weakly, and she's having difficulty breathing.

He strokes her pale cheek. "I'll be back," he murmurs, though he knows she can't hear it. He also knows that he can only save one of them at a time. His car is parked too far away.

With the child in his arms, he runs the same way back through the forest. He doesn't dare stop, although the baby feels like a rag doll in his arms. Night is turning to dawn and he can see just enough to make his way through the trees without a flashlight. Branches whip around his ears and scratch his arms; here and there a bird wakes up. Oscar keeps running until he can run no more. His left leg sends him sharp pain signals and he limps with every step. For a moment, he doesn't know where he is; everything looks the same in the dark, but then, just before he starts panicking, he sees his car in the distance.

Out of breath, he jerks open the door and lays the wrapped baby on the passenger seat. He flings down and drives off with skidding tires, as fast as he can, holding the baby in place with one hand.

"Julie, my Julie," he says continuously. The sun slowly rises and the city comes to life. With screeching tires, Oscar stops in front of the emergency department of the hospital where he worked until recently. With the baby in his arms, he rushes inside.

"I need help! Premature, weak response, born breech!"

People come at him from all sides. A nurse takes the baby from him and disappears with her, half walking, half running. Another nurse takes hold of his shoulders, leads him to a chair, and says something to him, but Oscar doesn't want to sit down. He has to go back to Julie. He jerks free and runs outside back into his car.

He hits the accelerator hard and drives back the same way he came. He can still save her. He may have to leave the baby behind in the hospital, but he can save Julie and flee with her. It's possible.

He was gone for almost an hour.

"Let her live, please," he mutters, but even before he enters the village, he realizes that running away together is no longer possible. The blue glow of flashing lights is reflected in the church tower.

He's too late.

Pieter

"Goddamn, goddamn, goddamn," roars Pieter De Saegher all the way to the village. "Faster, dammit, faster!"

He's furious with himself. He should have followed his instincts, followed the leads more fiercely, and reacted faster. He slams his steering wheel with both hands and screams in frustration.

Twenty minutes ago, Serge had informed him that the search warrants for Oscar's flat and old home had been approved, but Pieter had barely got into his car when he heard the shocking news on the police radio that Oscar had turned up at the hospital where he worked with a newborn premature baby in bad shape. Immediately afterwards, Pieter heard police sirens screaming through the streets.

All this time, Oscar has been holding Julie. Not Tom, not Rutger. Oscar. Where else but in that house of his?

Pieter presses the accelerator even harder. Having driven the route several times by now, he arrives at the address in record time. Among the many cars parked in front of the house, he recognizes Chief Inspector Van Dijck's. An ambulance comes to a skidding halt.

Pieter jumps out of his car and follows the ambulance staff along the path to the garden shed. He realizes once again that this is the exact same path he had recently taken. How could he have messed this up?

The garden shed is open; a policeman stands next to the door. The man lets the paramedics through and holds up his hand to stop Pieter, but he knocks him aside with one powerful blow. That he's in big trouble for appearing at a crime scene and that Serge will never forgive him doesn't even occur to him. He doesn't think anymore. This is about Julie.

When he sees the open hatch in the floor at the back of the shed, he can kick himself. How could he have missed that? And how is it possible that he didn't try to switch on the light in here that night? There's a bulb, and the switch is to his left, but he doesn't remember seeing it. At least, not consciously. If he'd noticed that switch, or the bulb, he would surely have tried it. Then he would've known that someone was using the shed.

Pieter thunders down the stairs. The smell is the first thing he notices, as if he'd stuck his nose into a bucket full of copper pennies. Only then does he see Julie, lying there on the floor, and he stands frozen. He feels his blood drain from his face and a whistling sound takes over his hearing. As if in slow motion, he sees the paramedics kneeling beside the body lying in a fetal position. Her blond hair is fanned out on the green carpet. There's a bandage around her head. Her face is so pale, almost transparent. A brown bloodstain has drawn an erratic pattern around her body. The officers who were first on the scene stand pale faced with their backs against the wall to give the paramedics some space, but they all know, they all feel, that help comes too late. Death has arrived before them; its presence is tangible in this shelter, as is Julie's. Witness to that is a plastic tray on the table with a tangerine peel and an empty yogurt pot on it, the remains of what must have been Julie's last meal. A towel hangs over a chair to dry. The scene looks absurdly normal and homely except for the lack of any daylight.

Pieter's gaze slides down to the body again. The body he got to know so well two years ago. Only a few hours earlier, she gave birth. All alone. She had done nothing wrong; she didn't deserve to die in this grey basement. He could've been on time, but judging by the amount of blood he can see, something must've gone wrong with the delivery. So much blood.

Pieter tries to hold back tears of helplessness. How much pain did she have to endure? How scared had she been? He wipes his sleeve over his eyes and looks at Van Dijck, who's standing next to him, hands over his mouth.

The weight of his responsibility weighs heavily on his chest. The Julie Meskens case has ended in the worst possible way, and a few miles away, a baby lies fighting for her life.

Why?

Why?

Hannah

Hannah

"What are you saying?" Tom is still in bed, his hair standing on end, trying to decipher through the haze of sleep what Eloise is saying. No, what she is shouting. She's hysterical.

"The baby, Tom! She's in hospital!"

"Julie's baby?"

"Yes, of course! Oh, Tom, everyone's going crazy. Haven't they called you yet?"

He checks the screen of his phone, but sees no missed calls. It's seven o'clock in the morning. His fingers grip the sheets tightly.

"No, they haven't. Where's Julie? Is she okay?" His brain frantically searches for answers and scenarios: Julie has given birth. So she's alive. She gave birth too early. Much too early.

The baby.

Julie.

Clutching the phone under his chin, he puts on trousers and a t-shirt and runs down the stairs.

"I don't know anything about Julie yet," Eloise goes on. "Esther only knew that the baby was admitted."

Esther? Who is Esther? Too much information, too little time.

"Which hospital?" he asks in a hurry while standing in the living room, panicking, as he searches for his keys.

Eloise gives him the address and then says, "I'll see you there; you mustn't be alone now."

He finds his keys in the kitchen. He puts on his trainers without tying the laces and is about to step out of the flat when the doorbell rings.

He quickly checks the intercom: it's Van Dijck.

This is really it. They've finally found her.

With trembling legs, he waits in the doorway for the chief inspector to come up the stairs. He's not alone. In his wake is a woman Tom doesn't recognize.

"G-good morning, c-come in," Tom stutters, his legs trembling harder and harder.

Van Dijck looks tired, with blue circles under his eyes. He introduces the woman to Tom, but he doesn't register her name.

"Julie," he says. "Is she... Have you found her...?"

"Sit down, Tom," says Van Dijck calmly.

His face. Why does he look at Tom like that? Why doesn't he tell him where Julie is? And why does that woman look at him with such pity? Ice-cold fingers clasp his throat.

No. No. No.

"I'm sorry to have to tell you..." Van Dijck begins.

No! He can't breathe. He can't breathe.

"Where's Julie?" he says. The words seem to be pumped out of his mouth, one by one, under pressure.

"We found Julie's body."

He wants to roar, to cry, to knock over the table so it splinters on the floor. He wants to grab Van Dijck by the throat, strangle him with his bare hands until his eyes pop out of their sockets and he takes those words back. They've found Julie's body. Only her *body*. Not Julie.

He wants to say something, but the words remain stuck in his throat. His tongue feels thick and heavy. So do his arms and legs. As if he were moving under water. He closes his eyes and drifts away. Water fills his nose, his mouth, his ears. It fills his lungs. Is this how it feels to drown?

Julie is dead. It's over. Dead. His mouth tries to form the word. Dead. Dead.

The curtain has fallen, the performance is over. Applause. Everyone goes home.

Van Dijck talks to him. Words, and more words. Tom nods.

The woman is talking to him. He nods again and tries to keep his eyes open. She holds his hands.

Julie is dead. Dead. Dead.

***

Eloise holds him in her arms. How long has she been here? Her eyes are red from crying, he needs to comfort her. But he's underwater, still.

His body is so heavy.

***

Is he dead?

No, he's not.

Julie is dead.

Dead.

Dead.

He wants to disappear.

He wants to bury himself deep underground.

Where the worms are.

Where it's dark.

***

Does he want to say something at the funeral?

They gave him pills. Eloise watched him take them. She helped him wash and dress.

No, he's not going to say anything.

His parents are here, and his brother and sister, too. Colleagues from school. Even pupils. So many people. So many faces. Arms around him. Strange smells. Handkerchiefs. Wet cheeks.

That journalist is standing in front of him. He can't remember his name. Peter? No, Pieter. Yes, that was it. He looks tired. His lips are moving.

"Sorry," he says. But Tom has no idea why.

"The funeral home doesn't have enough room for everyone," says Eloise. People are standing outside on the street.

"For Julie," says Eloise.

Because Julie is dead. Dead. Dead.

A man takes his hand and says something. Tom looks into a face that could be his: white skin, red eyes, blue circles. The man talks and Tom wants to answer, but only whisps of air come out of his mouth.

Puffs.

Eloise puts him on a chair in the front and comes and sits next to him. She says he can live in Julie's flat as long as he wants. That Mr. Meskens has said so.

Mr. Meskens.

She says he can cry if he wants to. That it will do him good.

But he can't. Julie smiles at him from the large projection screen at the front of the room. Julie, with her windblown hair, by the sea, barefoot.

He closes his eyes and dives underwater again.

***

You have to go to the baby, Eloise says.

She lives with him now. She cries a lot. He can't comfort her.

He tries, though. Every day he picks up pieces of himself, pieces of his dead heart. But they pulverize in his hands. He's cold inside.

At night, he lies on his back in bed. He lies staring at the ceiling with Julie's clothes around him. He wishes he could go to sleep and never wake up again. Eloise lies next to him. She looks at old photographs. Tells him about memories that were not his, but now are.

You have to go to the baby.

Sometimes Julie visits him in his dreams and he wakes up soaked with sweat. She screams his name, she runs away from him, he sees her drowning while he stands on the shore, unable to do anything, stuck to the ground. When he wakes up, he thinks for a millisecond that it was only a nightmare, until he realizes again and again that he has lost her. Then he screams into his pillow until Eloise holds him tightly.

***

He has lost Julie forever and ever. He will never smell her hair again, never wake up next to her or make coffee for her, play the piano for her, make guacamole for her, lift her soup bowl from the highest shelf where she couldn't reach it. The list of things he will never do again is too long and its weight keeps him in bed.

You have to go to the baby.

If only he could have her with him for one more night to tell her how much he loves her. Tell her that he can't live without her. That he knows they were made for each other, even though she sometimes doubted that. He would kiss those doubts out of her head if only he had the chance, but he'll never have that chance now. Never again.

***

Eloise is back at work. Her job is what keeps her going, she says. She visits him every evening, but doesn't stay the night. His mom brings him food he doesn't eat. She goes around with a duster, asking him things like, "Are you eating enough?" "Will you take a shower, son?" And, "When are you going to see the baby?"

Not yet.

***

Today, for the first time, he sits at his piano. Music is his life. Or was his life. Chords are so much easier than words. What he can't say, he can play. Without thinking, his fingers move over the keys as if by themselves. At first, he hesitates in the low notes, but soon his hands fly back and forth across the keys. His entire body moves with them, his head bobs up and down, his eyes are closed, his hair sweeps in front of his face.

Faster his fingers run, he can hardly follow them anymore and he has to get up. The stool falls over with a bang.

He whacks even harder on the ivory keys, making the piano roar and shout. Louder. Louder!

The sweat runs from his body and the drops make splashes on the keys. His vision is blurred.

At last. At last.

He cries.

***

"We need to talk," says Eloise.

"What is there to say? Julie's dead."

She puts her hand on his arm. "Julie's no longer here, but your daughter is."

He pulls his arm away. No, not yet.

But Eloise continues talking. The baby was born much too early and can't yet breathe or eat on her own. It's not certain that she'll make it; any infection could be fatal.

He can't even care for himself at the moment, let alone a fragile baby.

"She's doing very well, you know," Eloise continues. She visits the baby, she says. So do his parents and Julie's dad.

She pulls her handbag closer and takes out her mobile phone, scrolling across the screen and pointing it at him. A little pinkish baby with a lot of tubes in her head looks at him. His daughter.

He feels nothing.

"I can't, Eloise. I'm sorry."

"She can't help it. It's not her fault that her mom's dead."

The police had a search warrant and would've raided the house that day. If Julie hadn't given birth too early, if the baby hadn't been breech, if the placenta hadn't been torn... A sob escapes from his throat and Eloise quickly puts her mobile away and takes him in her arms.

"Don't worry. I know. It's all right. We don't have to talk about it. You have all the time. She's in good hands."

But he doesn't have all the time and he knows it. Sometimes time runs out faster than you expected.

"What if she dies, too?" he whispers.

"What if that happens before you've had a chance to get to know her?" replies Eloise as she gently strokes his arm.

That would tear him apart; Julie would never forgive him, wherever she is.

"At least give her a name. Do it for Julie."

She's right. He owes that much to her.

Eloise helps him up. "Come on, take a shower and I'll drive you."

***

He has a cap on his head and a face mask on. A midwife leads him to the baby's bed.

"I'm here if you need me," Eloise says, patting him encouragingly on the back.

"Sit here and I'll hand her to you," says the midwife. She carefully reaches into the incubator and holds the tubes aside as she lifts the baby out.

"Support her head with your left arm and her body with the other... Yes, good," she says as he takes the bundle from her.

The baby is wrapped in a striped blanket. Her light hair peeps out from under a white little cap. She has a miniature nose and a pink pout, and she immediately reminds him of Julie when she doesn't get her way. He smiles.

"She looks like Julie," he says from behind his mask, unable to take his eyes off her.

"Yes, she does," Eloise says.

A warm glow spreads from his belly and melts his heart. This is Julie's daughter. His daughter. Their child.

"Hello, Hannah Julie Van de Velde," he says. Welcome, little one.

***

Every day, Tom drives to the hospital. Even though he has no idea how he'll fare in the coming hours, days, weeks, and months, at least he has a clear goal for each day. When he holds the tiny baby against his body, he feels Julie's presence. He can even almost smell her. Her body may be gone, but in his memory, she will live on forever.

"Has anyone told you about your mommy?" he asks the warm bundle in his arms. The baby moves for a moment and lets out a contented sigh.

"No? Well, that's because it's my job to do so, as I'm your daddy. Listen carefully," says Tom. He takes a deep breath and begins: "Once upon a time, there was a beautiful young woman called Julie."

Epilogue

"Higher, higher!" she shouts to Tom. Her blonde hair is blowing in the wind. Her yellow dress fans out over her outstretched chubby legs, which end in bare feet with black soles. Her laughter echoes against the houses surrounding the playground. She just about fits into the children's swing, and soon she'll be allowed to go on the big one.

Tom lifts the girl, swings her over his shoulder, and walks over to the bench where Eloise is sitting. She's wearing big sunglasses and is using a magazine as a fan to keep cool. Next to her is a wicker bag from which she takes a banana and starts peeling it.

A man walking his dog stops to chat with her as the sound of an approaching ice cream truck can be heard in the distance.

***

From behind a tree, Oscar watches the scene. He rolls a cigar between his fingers and smells it. It's exactly a thousand days since he last saw her, when he pushed her into the nurse's arms.

Hannah.

Julie's baby.

His daughter.

He looks at the trio one last time and then turns and walks away. He must prepare.

He has so much to do.

Acknowledgments

Alone is a fictional story and none of the characters exist in reality. Fortunately, Julie Meskens was never really locked up in Oscar's basement.

But not everything in this book is fiction.

The story is based on events that happened in 1998, the year I was pregnant with my son. I had just moved into a new flat and was settling in. My boyfriend at the time, who is now my husband, regularly parked his car in front of the building.

You can probably guess what happened: his car was scratched. Twice.

It didn't have the swear words on it that Julie's boyfriend Tom's car had, but still: they were deep, ugly, deliberately applied, hateful scratches.

Then I heard someone shouting loudly when I was home alone. It came from nearby and it freaked me out completely.

"Whore!" screamed the voice, from the top of his lungs. "Fucking bitch!" and "I hate you!" and so on.

It turned out to be my downstairs neighbor who was yelling, and after this had happened several times, I began to realize that he wasn't shouting at his phone, but at me.

Me.

A girl who had never exchanged a word with him, except for the obligatory good morning or good evening when passing him in the hallway. I was baffled.

My boyfriend and I decided to go to the police with our bizarre story: scratches on his car, insulting roars from my neighbor. Was there a connection?

Yes, there was. Unlike in this book, the real police took immediate action. They questioned the man and it turned out that he was indeed responsible for the scratches.

But why? Why did he target me? Why did he hate me so much? What had I done?

The answer baffled me even more. As it turned out, my neighbor suffered from a severe personality disorder. When I came to live in the apartment above his, he "fell in love" with me, even without really meeting me. In his mind, we were in a relationship, so as soon as my boyfriend came into the picture and my pregnant belly started to grow, this man's 'love' quickly changed into jealousy and anger. I had betrayed him.

***

It was only more than twenty years later, when I was writing and researching this book, that I learned this man suffered from a rare disorder called Erotomania, also known as Clerambault's syndrome. This is a disorder more common in women than in men, but in the latter group, it leads more readily to stalker behavior and aggression. It manifests itself in the belief that someone else is in love with you, or even that you're in a relationship with that person. This can be someone you have never met before, such as a celebrity, an acquaintance, the husband of a colleague, or the girl that lives upstairs from you. There are several possible causes for the development of the disorder. It can serve as a coping mechanism to deal with extreme loneliness or a great loss, or with both, as in the fictional case of Oscar.

Thanks to the swift and decisive action of the police, the real incident never escalated and I moved away immediately. I'm very grateful for the understanding and respect that my boyfriend and I received from the Antwerp police when we reported it.

But there's no book in that. So it all goes down a bit (a lot) differently in *Alone*.

***

Thank you to First Commissioner Freddy Rottiers and Chief Inspector Dasy Wagemans for helping to keep the manuscript as realistic as possible. If you, dear reader, find any mistakes, this is entirely my responsibility and I will shamelessly file them under "creative freedom."

I'm sorry I didn't portray Chief Inspector David Van Dijck in a very positive light. I promise to make up for that in the next book.

I would also like to thank my personal proofreaders/friends Joke Vander Aa, Gisy Van Hove, Vicky Maggelet, Melissa von Wenz: you help me grow as a person and as a writer. Thank you, Elise Aertgeerts, for sharing your disturbingly good knowledge of narcotics with me. Thank you, Jenny Masters, Paula Bosher, Ruth Swallow, and Ashley Long, for proofreading the English translation. And last but not least: Kathleen Ferny, I am eternally grateful for your help in editing and translating this book. You are a gem.

Special thanks to Sandra Vets, Cathy Carlier, and Melissa Vandeputte of Hamley Books Publishers for giving me the opportunity to have the book translated into English.

To my family, who, as always, are the victims of my hunger to write: thank you for your understanding and patience, even if it wasn't given entirely voluntary. Luckily, you like to eat pizza.

My heart goes out to anyone who has ever been a victim of stalking, which has only been recognized as a separate crime in Belgium since 30 October 1998. Do not wait to file a complaint. Do it immediately.

Finally, I would also like to thank the neighbor below who unintentionally inspired me to write this story. I hope that in the meantime he's being treated correctly, if that is even possible.

Barbara

About the Author

Originally from Antwerp (Belgium), Barbara De Smedt moved to Portugal in 2019 after having fallen in love with the country during a road trip around Europe.

As a lifelong learner, she studied languages and Psychology. For the past 20 years she built her own international health and wellness business, together with her husband.

Today Barbara dedicates her time to writing full time, enjoying her family and taking long dog walks.